"Sharon Ewell Foster is a beautiful fresh voice in today's world of fiction. Her compelling stories draw us to a place where we somehow feel we belong, a place we want to visit again and again and again."
 —Karen Kingsbury, author of
  One Tuesday Morning

"Sharon Ewell Foster writes with a fresh understanding of the human heart as well as a delightful sense of humor. Her stories touch me and teach me and never fail to satisfy."
 —Robin Lee Hatcher, author of
  The Victory Club

"Sharon Foster's writing just keeps getting better and better! Ain't No Valley, her characters practically leap off the page—deeper, funnier, more heart, more soul than when we met them before in previous books. I'm breathless!"
 —Neta Jackson, author of
  The Yada Yada Prayer Group

"I undeniably love Sharon Ewell Foster—her words, her characters, her stories. Foster writes with truth, love, humor and grace so powerful, that if you haven't already fallen in love, you will after reading Ain't No Valley! Highly, highly recommended for you and your friends!"
 —Marina L. Woods, Editor-In-Chief and Founder,
  The GOOD GIRL Book Club™

"What a spin! Naomi and her circle of sister-girls had me smiling from the first page to the last. Loved it!"
 —Robin Jones Gunn, author of
  the Sisterchicks™ novels

Acclaim for Sharon Ewell Foster

"Foster is one of the brightest lights in Christian fiction. She takes us to places that our hearts sometimes fear to tread, and she rewards us with wonderfully complex characters who live with us long after the story ends."
—Angela Benson, author of
Telling the Tale: The African-American Writer's Guide

"Sharon Ewell Foster writes with boldness and sensitivity. Her believable characters easily find their way into my heart and stay there as friends."
—Alice Gray, creator of
the STORIES FOR THE HEART series

"Foster introduces a vibrant new voice to inspirational fiction, offering wisdom and insights that are deep, rich, and honest."
—Liz Curtis Higgs, bestselling author of
Bad Girls of the Bible

"Foster's prose is often evocative and eloquent."
—*Publishers Weekly*

"To read a book by Sharon Ewell Foster is to have had an inside look at the heart and mind of God."
—Regina Gail Malloy, Heaven 600 Radio

"Foster is an author who allows God to use her through her novels. . . . With every page, readers are left feeling inspired and hopeful with the knowledge that through God, all things are possible."
—Lisa R. Hammack, Ebony Eyes Book Club

"Foster's characters are unforgettable; full of life and unhesitatingly charming. . . ."
—Kweisi Mfume, President and CEO, NAACP

A Novel

ain't no Valley

SHARON EWELL FOSTER

BETHANY HOUSE PUBLISHERS
Minneapolis Minnesota

Dedication

I dedicate this book to my family—my daughter and son,
Lanea and Chase, my cousin LaJuana,
and my best friend Portia.
Thank you for loving me and encouraging me to grow.
I dedicate it also to my mother,
who taught us to embrace art and
to value new adventures,
and to my father who was always there.

It is also for all the people, like me,
who have dreaded facing the valleys in their lives.

Books by Sharon Ewell Foster

Ain't No Mountain

Ain't No Valley

*Ain't No River**

*Passing by Samaria**

*Riding Through Shadows**

*Passing Into Light**

*Multnomah Publishers

SHARON EWELL FOSTER, a single herself, never shies away from confronting difficult issues with truth, wit, and humor. This double Rita-Award finalist and Daily Guideposts writer has found loyal fans that cross racial, religious, age, and gender boundaries. A former U.S. Defense Department instructor/writer/logistician, Foster is the author of the bestseller and Christy Award-winning *Passing by Samaria*. Born in Texas, raised in Illinois, and living in Baltimore until recently, she has two grown children (her favorite editors) and now makes her home in Chicago.

ACKNOWLEDGMENTS

Thank you to April Milton—and to Phyllis, Jackye, and the other women of Florida's Onyx Book Club—for sharing your ride on Wheel of Fortune.

Thank you to my family, friends, pastors, and teachers. Thank you to my friend Margaret-Ann Howie, Rev. Valerie Wells, Angela Smith, and all my New Psalmist family for your encouragement and prayers.

Thank you to the Bethany family, to my editor Joyce Dinkins, to my publicist Robin Caldwell, to my friend-writers, and to the Writer's Loft Workshop in Chicago.

Thank you to Pastor James Meeks for the "hater-ade" reference.

And, finally, a special thank you to Neta Jackson for constant encouragement and prayer.

Thank you, God, for inviting me.

CAST OF CHARACTERS

The California Dreamers
    Naomi "the hair girl", a dentist and a former Baltimore charmer
    Ruthie "the beach girl"
    Anthony "the guitarist" and financial manager
    Moor "the African prince" and bridegroom

The Baltimore Charmers
    Latrice "the nail girl"
    Thelma "the eye girl"
    Mary "the bride"
    Mary's church protegées
        Cat
        Pamela
        Agnes
    Puddin "the hip-hop Godmamma"
    Joe Puddin's husband
    Moor's best friends
        Blue
        Brighty
        Ali

The North Carolina Contingent

Meemaw "everybody's grandmother"

Garvin Meemaw's granddaughter and attorney

GoGo Garvin's husband

Big Esther Garvin's best friend and beauty shop owner

Inez Zephyr "the town busybody" and Esther's customer

Monique Meemaw's young friend in Jacks Creek and unwed mother

Mr. Green grocer in Jacks Creek and Meemaw's longtime Jewish friend

Jonee Garvin's Thai lawyer friend from D.C.

Ramona Garvin's "fight-for-you" friend from D.C.

Then the angel said to me, "Write: 'Blessed are those who are invited to the wedding supper of the Lamb!'" And he added, "These are the true words of God."

The Revelation of the Apostle John 19:9

PART ONE

The Invitation

The Parable of the Wedding Banquet

"The kingdom of heaven is like a king who prepared a wedding banquet for his son. He sent his servants to those who had been invited to the banquet to tell them to come, but they refused to come.

"Then he sent some more servants and said, 'Tell those who have been invited that I have prepared my dinner: My oxen and fattened cattle have been butchered, and everything is ready. Come to the wedding banquet.'

"But they paid no attention and went off—one to his field, another to his business.

"Then he said to his servants, 'The wedding banquet is ready, but those I invited did not deserve to come. Go to the street corners and invite to the banquet anyone you find.' So the servants went out into the streets and gathered all the people they could find, both good and bad, and the wedding hall was filled with guests."

—THE TEACHINGS OF JESUS THE CHRIST AND SERVANT-KING AS RETOLD BY THE APOSTLE MATTHEW 22:2–6, 8–10

ONE

Los Angeles, California

The lights shining on her were hot. She wanted to wipe her face or at least sit down. Naomi looked down at her yellow suit, fluffed her blonde hair, and reminded herself to be vivacious—her brown skin, her yellow hair, and a big smile—it was good television. Pat Sajak was standing next to her and she had to be ready.

Pat Sajak is standing next to me!

And Vanna White was in front of her, poised by the puzzle board, ready to touch the letters with her small, thin hands.

Vanna White is in front of me!

Naomi closed her eyes and imagined what was true—she was poised, ready to spin the Wheel of Fortune.

I should be getting ready for Mary's wedding. Naomi pushed the thought away. She had to keep her head clear. She had to stay relaxed. She didn't have time for guilt. This was her big chance.

It was something she'd dreamed about for years, that she'd be on national television spinning the wheel. It was on her private list of things she'd always wanted to do—like taking a cruise and seeing Paris. No one knew about it. She didn't even tell her girlfriends Mary, Thelma, and Latrice. She knew what they would say.

"Girl, you crazy!" *"What about your job?"* *"What about my wedding?"*

So, she didn't tell them, when *Wheel of Fortune* came to Annapolis in May, that she had gone to the auditions. Naomi went alone. It was *her* adventure.

She'd lost her husband in a messy divorce that also took her children. There was no joy in her work—combing through X rays looking for enough specks on teeth to fill her HMO quota and pushing sealants and rinses to middle-class parents worried about their children's molars just so she could afford to buy a bauble or another teapot at Saks to make herself happy. The only thing was that the pleasure of buying didn't last long. It was the same as her encounters with men: intense but fleeting.

But *Wheel of Fortune*, this was her moment. Of course, her chances were slim to none, but it was something she'd wanted and Annapolis was probably as close as the television show producers were ever going to come to Baltimore.

The drive up Interstate 495 to Highway 97 that day had been easier than she had imagined. She exited off the highway and pulled into the Westpoint Mall, still known to locals as the Annapolis Mall. It was easy—because of the crowd, the balloons, and the temporary bleachers—to find the audition site. People—all colors, all shapes, all sizes, all types—were gathered early Saturday morning, hoping for an opportunity to spin the wheel.

Naomi had parked her Cadillac CTS far from the crowd and had begun to walk, sometimes running, to make her way to the crowd.

"We can only seat a thousand people," one of the producers had shouted over a megaphone. "So, make sure you get one of these tickets!"

The crowd had surged toward the young woman. Bodies crowded around her, extended hands waving for tickets, until the young producer was almost invisible. Naomi had moved to a steady jog, hoping she would make it while there were still some tickets left on the roll.

Wheel of Fortune big red letters announced on a huge banner. The parking lot in front of Nordstrom, just to the right of the California Pizza Kitchen entrance, had been cordoned off. People filled the area and shouted, laughed, and jumped up and down hysterically each time the young woman tore a ticket from the roll.

Just before she had reached the group, Naomi had seen a distinguished-looking elderly gentleman drop to his knees and raise his hands in the air when a red ticket was pressed into his hand. A young woman wearing jeans became a whirling dervish—twirling and leaping as she ran around the perimeter of the crowd.

When Naomi got her ticket—when the young producer had pressed it into her hand—Naomi froze. It was like a dream, like a dream she thought she remembered of a circus and cotton candy. It was like a pink, yellow, red, and blue dream full of clowns and laughter. She could feel the smile fixed on her face, but could not speak. Then she felt herself screaming. She was jumping up and down, and then she ran for the bleachers.

Naomi was glad that none of her patients or their parents were there to see her, but as she looked around at the other ticket holders and their loved ones, she wished she had brought one of her girlfriends with her.

Mary would have been excited for her and would have

given her good advice. But, right then, Mary's mind was on her August wedding. And the truth was, Mary had every right to be excited about her new life in California with her husband-to-be, Moor. Naomi had imagined her friend, her brown skin enveloped in her eggshell-colored gown. But she couldn't imagine long. She jumped from her seat and squealed as she squeezed the ticket in her hand.

The boy in *Willy Wonka and the Chocolate Factory* must have been feeling this way when he got his golden ticket! Naomi clapped her hands together and thought of Latrice. Her chunky-but-funky friend wouldn't be jumping. She'd be doing the Electric Slide and waving her hands in the air— and hoping someone would see her trademark long, painted fingernails—as she celebrated Naomi's victory.

If Thelma were there, looking at the world through her blue contact lenses, she'd be telling Naomi not to get her hopes up. *"Behave with some dignity; you don't know who's watching,"* Thelma would have said. And, she would have added, there was no point in getting worked up about something that had a snowball's chance of happening. The producers were going to hold a drawing. Out of the one thousand ticket holders, they were going to select only twelve people—calling them out in groups of three—to audition. Not good odds, Thelma would tell her. She loved Thelma, and Thelma was right, but Naomi didn't need anyone putting a damper on her party.

She had jumped to her feet again and shouted at the sky. It had been a long time since something good had happened to her. She needed this. She needed a sign that things were about to break. Naomi closed her eyes and moved her lips. "Thank you, God." It was almost as if He were making things up to her, making up for all of the things that had happened to her.

A young man in a green *Wheel of Fortune* jacket told them to write their names on their tickets. Then he and two other young men collected the red tickets and dropped them into a spinning barrel.

That spring day, Naomi had watched the tickets tumbling over each other like paper cherries. She watched as though she would recognize her ticket among all the other identical tickets. *Don't be disappointed. You're not going to win.* Still her heart felt like it would burst from her chest and she could hardly breathe. The producer, the one who had given out the tickets, stopped cranking and began to pluck tickets from the basket.

It was enough to have gotten to the auditions. How many people ever did anything like that? It was enough to have gotten a ticket.

Naomi watched as the producer called the names. The lucky contestants screamed. One woman slumped, almost fainting until one of the ticket takers caught her. The crowd gasped and then tried to pretend they weren't a little disappointed when she revived: her unfortunate demise would have meant another chance, another ticket for some luckless soul.

It was enough to be in Annapolis on a sunny day. She would take advantage and do a little shopping.

"Naomi Holt!" The producer's eyes scanned the audience. "Naomi Holt!" Her smile was ultra bright. "Naomi Holt?"

It was enough to have been invited to the party. She didn't really expect to win.

The producer took a deep breath and exhaled. "All right,"

she said cheerily. "I'm going to try one more time. Naomi Holt!"

Naomi still could not remember how she had gotten to the stage that Saturday. When she looked back, she tried to convince herself that she had raised her hand and inched her way demurely down her row. More likely, she had jumped to her feet—and over the heads of the people seated in the rows in front of her. It didn't really matter now. Today she was here, in Los Angeles, in the Culver City area, at Sony Studios playing *Wheel of Fortune*. The cohosts were smiling at her.

Vanna was thinner than she would have ever imagined.

Every day, for the four weeks after the Annapolis audition, the highlight of her day was hoping to see a letter from Sony Studios. *"If we've selected you to be a contestant for the Annapolis tapings, you'll receive a letter from us in three weeks. If you don't hear from us in three weeks, this has still been a blast! Right?"* The producer's words had kept her running to the mailbox, excited and breathless. Three weeks was the limit, but she had given them an extra week, just in case.

It was week five and there had been nothing in her mailbox but bills, solicitations, advertisements, and a few magazines. It had been a rough day. Not the kids, or even the parents. But she had put her foot down with the HMO. She wasn't going to let them dictate to her how she should take care of her patients. She probably could have handled it better—if the bridge wasn't burned, there were probably a few planks missing. It was easy talking tough when she was all fired up, but as she cooled, her bank account began to tell her that she shouldn't talk too loudly or make any false moves.

People thought dentists were rich. They thought all doctors were rich. They didn't know about huge insurance payments and student loans. They didn't know about child support.

Naomi had stuck her hand into the mailbox, pulled out the usual suspects, unlocked the door, and entered her home. She dumped her purse, her keys, and her mail on the table. It was feeling like a chamomile day—something naturally artificial to keep her calm.

She had made tea in her favorite peach-colored pot, poured it into her most elegant cup and set, grabbed the mail, and crawled onto her orange couch. She took a sip and then began to sift through her mail. BG&E—her electric bill. C&P—telephone. Sony Studios. Comcast—cable. *Essence* magazine subscription renewal.

Naomi dropped the mail on the couch and sighed. She took another sip from her cup.

Thoughts of her children tried to push to the surface. She flipped through a magazine to distract herself. She sighed again and drank more tea. It would be nice to have some good fortune in her life.

She had lost her husband and her children—one day they were in her life. Then she walked into a courtroom and a stranger had taken them away. She had known her husband was leaving, but not her children. Sometimes when she tried to sleep, she could hear their voices in the house, she could hear their footfalls on the stairs. It wasn't fair. She wasn't a murderer, or even a drunk. Her babies were stolen from her for no reason. And it was no comfort to her that it was happening to more and more women—it felt like revenge for Women's Lib.

July 4th had come and gone. Without the children it

seemed garish. There had been too much hoopla and fanfare. Everything she did was artificial. She had gone through the motions of barbecuing, of pretending to enjoy the fireworks. She had smiled like a mannequin at her date and was only relieved when he had gone home.

Sometimes it felt like God had abandoned her. Or, even worse, like maybe there was no God.

Naomi looked at the pile of mail, again. BG&E. Sony Studios. *Sony Studios?* Her hands shook as she ripped the letter open.

Sony Studios
Los Angeles, CA

Congratulations, Naomi Holt!
You have been selected to be a contestant on *Wheel of Fortune*. Taping will be July 17th. If, for some reason, you are no longer interested. . . .

It had cost her a small fortune to get to L.A. There were no cheap fares available on less than a week's notice. The motel was way too pricey and the food was too high. Still, here she was in front of the wheel. Naomi fluffed her hair. While she was waiting all that time for her letter, she had imagined that the producers hadn't chosen her because of her long blonde hair. Maybe it was too over the top for them—a brown-skinned Black woman with blonde hair.

Yet here she was in all of her blonde-haired glory, the studio lights shining on her, waiting to spin the wheel.

"We cannot allow you to take off on such short notice,

Dr. Holt. It's irresponsible." The droning voice on the phone had been one of the last hurdles to her trip to L.A.

"I already have someone to cover, and things are slow now." Naomi had felt like a teenager begging her mother for the keys to the family car.

"It's irresponsible." The voice on the other end was flat, except for a little bit of *gotcha!* in the woman's tone. It was the same HMO representative she had had a falling-out with in May. Only this time, no matter how Naomi played her hand, the woman would win. "It's certainly your decision. But I don't think the company would look favorably on a dentist, a professional, abandoning her practice to be on a *game* show."

The woman was right, but that only made it worse. It wasn't a sound business decision. It wasn't a sound professional decision. But she needed it. She needed to go somewhere else. She needed a change, a break. She needed something to make her feel alive. Maybe going to Los Angeles wasn't the smartest business decision—if she told her friends, she knew they would try to talk her out of it. But it was the only emotional decision that made sense. If she didn't go, she felt like she would break apart.

"I'm sorry. I have to go."

"You don't have to go anywhere, Dr. Holt. This is not a medical emergency. This is not an emergency of any sort."

Chamomile, barbecue, and men weren't doing it anymore. Church on Sunday helped, but something was missing. She needed something. "I have to go. I'm sorry about the short notice, but I have to go."

The woman snorted and laughed. "You make it sound so critical. It's just a game show."

"I'm sorry. I have to go." It *was* critical.

"All right. It's your party," the woman said.

The woman was right, it was a party. Here she was in Los Angeles! Naomi stared at the puzzle board and waited her turn. The female contestant to her left was doing well. She had filled in most of the board. The lady contestant pushed the wheel again and landed on Bankrupt.

Naomi looked at the woman and then back at the board. No one knew she was here. She'd left alone. If she failed, if something went wrong, she didn't want shame to ruin the experience for her. If she lost alone, she still would win. If she lost with her friends watching, she disappointed them too. Not to mention that she was playing with that whole *"representative of your race"* thing hanging around her neck. If she lost, she lost for Black people everywhere. It was pressure that most of the contestants didn't have to manage.

When Pat Sajak nodded, Naomi grabbed the wheel—it was heavier than she would have imagined—and gave it a spin.

She had received a call at her hotel, before she boarded the van that brought her to the studio, that she had been fired. And the bad news hitched itself to the wheel's Bankrupt slots and stuck out its hands and its tongue at her each time one of the black cards went by. *I'm gonna git you!* The wheel landed on seven hundred dollars and she asked for the consonant *c*. She already knew the answer; she had just hoped to avoid going bankrupt. Naomi smiled at Pat and Vanna, who smiled back at her. Victory was sweet! She could hear herself screaming the answer. "Secretary of the Treasury John Show!"

The answer would put her ahead. She was on the way to changing her life! It was proof that she had made the right decision.

Pat's smile faded. "Oh, Naomi! I'm terribly sorry." He turned his head and smiled at the next contestant. "Jerry, why don't you give the wheel a spin?"

Naomi realized she was still smiling. The bad news sitting on Bankrupt laughed out loud at her. She was surprised that Vanna and Pat did not hear.

The contestant to her left, Jerry, was beaming when he gave the wheel a spin. It landed on two hundred dollars. "Secretary of the Treasury John *Snow!*"

"That's right, Jerry!" Pat looked ecstatic.

How could Pat look happy? She'd lost her job. And it was pretty certain that she was about to lose the game. How could he be smiling? She'd missed the puzzle by one letter—it was a name she should have known, she should have known the Treasury Secretary—and in the process she had embarrassed Black people everywhere. This experience was *supposed* to change her life.

There was a break in the taping. A makeup artist came and stood in front of her. As the studio audience watched, the woman called Dotty quickly threw a cape over Naomi's chest and shoulders. "Don't you give up, honey!" Dotty's hair was platinum blonde and she had an Elizabeth Taylor-like mole on one pale, wrinkled cheek. "Don't you frown. You perk up. Listen to Dotty." The ancient toad-like woman whispered to Naomi as though she were a co-conspirator. "The show ain't over until it's over, you know what I mean?" Her lips were painted an obscene shiny, moist hot pink. "This ain't the end. I seen much worse. This is just the opportunity for a comeback." Dotty whipped the cape off of Naomi. "In situations like this, you got to pick your chin up, get tough, and say a little prayer to the man upstairs." Dotty nodded her head. "Now, you smile, you hear me? You didn't come all this way for nothing. You win this thing, honey!" Dotty winked. "Us blondes got to stick together!" Despite her shape, Dotty flounced away, dragging the cape behind her.

TWO

Pat was standing next to her. "It looked close there for a while, Naomi from Baltimore. But you pulled it out at the last minute. You're tonight's big winner on *Wheel of Fortune* by just fifty bucks!" He began to walk away and waved at Naomi to follow.

Everything seemed brighter, more colorful, and more concentrated than real life could ever be. The studio was much smaller than it appeared on television. The Wheel, with its spinning, blinking, dizzying colors and prizes, and the puzzle board for the bonus round were very close together.

"Okay, Naomi. Go ahead and spin. Let's see what prize you're playing for!"

She stood before the much smaller bonus prize wheel. The lights were bright. She felt dizzy. She couldn't breathe. It was like a dream, a good dream, but she was reacting as though it was a nightmare. "Are you really sure? I can't believe this is happening!"

Pat laughed and played to the audience. "Well, it won't be happening if you don't spin the Wheel." He chuckled and looked at his watch. "And Vanna's got to go catch a car pool."

The small in-studio audience, the audience that seemed so huge at home, hooted.

Naomi closed her eyes and gave the Wheel a spin.

"Wow!" Pat said. "Open your eyes, Naomi from Baltimore! You're playing for one hundred thou-ou-ou-sand dollars!"

Naomi picked her consonants and her vowel. When Vanna turned the letters, Naomi knew she had won before the time was up. *God Bless America*! It was such a simple puzzle.

"You've won one hundred thou-ou-ou-sand dollars! And with the rest of your cash winnings, you've won over one hundred-thirty thou-ou-ou-sand dollars!" Pat was all smiles.

Naomi didn't remember leaping on Pat. She just remembered the assistant floor director wrestling her off of the game show host.

"Thelma? Thelma? I'm calling from Los Angeles!" She couldn't get reception on her cell phone. Naomi looked into her garbled reflection on the silver face of the pay phone. She fluffed her blonde hair with her free hand. People walked back and forth all around her. She glanced at the departure board for her Baltimore flight.

Thelma's matter-of-fact voice sounded like it was coming from a deep hole. Her cell phone connection was full of static and kept breaking up. "You're where?"

It wasn't until Thelma said it that Baltimore seemed so far away. "I said I'm calling from Los Angeles. I was on *Wheel of Fortune*!" She wasn't sure why she had called Thelma, the mother-rep of the group. Maybe she needed to talk to someone who would ground her.

"You what? You're where?"

She was three hours behind Thelma. That meant that what had happened to her this afternoon at Sony Studios, what was happening to her now was already Thelma's past. "California! I'm in Los Angeles. I just taped *Wheel of Fortune*. You know, with Pat Sajak and Vanna White? And I won, Thelma!"

Thelma was sounding like she didn't want her past rewritten. What seemed like joy to Naomi was sounding like nuisance and foolishness coming from Thelma's mouth. "Stop playing, Naomi. You are beginning to act too much like Latrice. Now, where are you? The connection is horrible. You keep breaking up."

"I told you. I'm in Los Angeles. I'm at LAX, at the airport. I just got through taping *Wheel of Fortune* and I won. I thought you'd be happy."

"No kidding!" It was about as excited as Thelma would get. She paused like she was trying to get herself together, like she was trying to force herself to say something positive. "So, how much did you win?" Leave it to Thelma to head straight for the bottom line.

"Over one hundred-thirty thou-ou-ou-sand dollars!" Naomi mimicked Pat Sajak.

"How long were you on?"

"The taping took about twenty minutes."

Thelma chuckled. "Well, I'd say that was a pretty good hourly rate."

Naomi cleared her throat. She might as well get it over with. It would give Thelma some time, before she saw her, to let off some steam. "It's a good thing, too, because I lost my job."

It was obvious Thelma didn't hear her. She must still be

thinking about the money. "You lost what? You've got your ticket, don't you?"

Naomi looked at people passing by—carrying shoulder bags, dragging suitcases, holding onto children and each other—while she spoke. "Yeah. Sure. I've got my ticket. It's my *job* I lost."

Thelma was quiet. Naomi knew it would only be for a moment, Thelma had understood her this time. "You lost your job?" Naomi could hear it. Thelma was trying to control herself. "Why? How?"

"It's nothing. I'll get another one. I hated my job anyway."

Thelma couldn't hold back any longer. "Are you crazy? You're a dentist. It's not like cooking fries at a grill. Dentists don't just lose jobs. They don't just quit their jobs." Thelma exhaled and her voice was shaking. "What happened?" Thelma's tone said it all. Professional people didn't lose their jobs. Professional women certainly didn't lose their jobs— especially professional Black women—it was like an insult to the ancestors.

"The HMO didn't want me to come to Los Angeles. I found out about the show taping at the last minute. I got someone to cover for me but they said it was irresponsible."

Thelma growled. "And I think they were right! It was totally unprofessional!"

Naomi got that teen-aged feeling again—that my-parents-just-don't-understand feeling. "I had to come."

It was no surprise to Naomi that Thelma was angry. The four of them—Thelma, Mary, Latrice, and Naomi—were more fortunate than many of those they lived and worked with. They had gone to college together—and they had graduated. After graduation, they had escaped from the reality of most women like them to successful jobs. She was a dentist, Thelma a teacher, Mary worked at the post office, and Latrice—as hard as it sometimes was to believe—was a moderately successful art dealer.

Naomi knew, as Thelma spoke on the other end of the line, that her job success did not belong only to her. It belonged to all the mothers and grandmothers who had scrubbed floors and washed clothes by hand until their knuckles were swollen and raw. *"Baby, we so proud of you!"*

Her career belonged to Thurgood Marshall, Dr. Martin Luther King, Medgar Evers, and Malcolm X. Her success belonged to all the freedom riders, all the civil rights workers, all the preachers, and all the teachers of her community. *"You made it, baby—and you didn't get pregnant, neither!"*

Naomi's job title belonged to all the people that had hoped, prayed, sweated, and bled to make a way for her.

Thelma spoke for all of them, and Naomi could feel and hear the disapproval and disappointment weighting her friend's voice. "Girl, are you crazy? Have you lost your mind? You are a dentist! People would kill to be where you are, and you are throwing it all away!" Anger caused Thelma to slide out of the slang that the four of them slid into naturally, maybe to remind themselves that they were still a part of the community that birthed them and loved them.

Sometimes success felt like a noose around Naomi's neck, or a stone that kept her weighted and tangled, never able to push her way up through deep waters to the surface above. She was drowning in an ocean that other people thought beautiful, while above her was the promise of light and air that would allow her to live, to breathe again.

She knew it made no sense to Thelma. Even if she tried,

Thelma wouldn't get it—her world and everything in it was rational.

"I had to come."

"And what about the wedding? What about Mary's wedding? I guess you don't care. You don't care if you ruin it. She expects you to be a bridesmaid."

"I'll be there." She didn't think she was going to be there.

"What about the shoes and the dress?"

She couldn't worry about it now. Her thread was too thin. "Whatever you all choose will be fine for me."

Thelma huffed. "In all the years I've known you—"

Naomi took the phone away from her ear and spoke into the mouthpiece. "I've got to go, Thelma. I'll call you later." She was grown enough to end the conversation.

The wedding would have to go on without her.

Naomi didn't think she was ever going home.

THREE

Meemaw should never have volunteered to sew beads on Mary's wedding dress. Garvin imagined her grandmother sitting in her favorite chair drowning in a valley of eggshell white fabric surrounded on all sides by mountains of tiny, tiny beads. And as she imagined her, she had to revamp the image the way she always did. Instead of a frumpy grandma, Meemaw was transformed into a silver-haired fox in the middle of the fabric valley. Garvin never quite got used to the trim, sophisticated Meemaw.

GoGo's my personal trainer, baby. Didn't I tell you? And he calls me Miss Evangelina.

Garvin still shuddered at the thought, and what might have happened if the rumors in town had been true-rumors that the much younger former pro football player was after her grandmother; rumors that her trainer, GoGo, was getting a little *too* personal. She still never quite got over the image of shapely, silver-haired Meemaw in leg warmers. But at least she had gotten used to GoGo's name—Garvin had thought she would never get used to that.

In Garvin's dream, Monique—the young unwed mother that Meemaw had befriended and taken into her home years ago—and her small daughter Destiny sat at Meemaw's feet, wide-eyed and overwhelmed by all the cloth and beads.

The wedding was coming so quickly.

Meemaw already had sewn too many beads on the gown to turn back. They couldn't mail the dress back to Mary like it was—beads sewn here and there in no apparent pattern—but it also didn't look like Meemaw was going to get the dress done in time. Meemaw's intentions were good, but good intentions just weren't good enough. Garvin sighed. While she was checking on a thousand other things for her cousin's California wedding, she probably needed to start trying to find a replacement gown now too.

Bringgg! Bringgg!

When she picked up the phone, Garvin knew right away that it was Esther. Even midweek the background noises at Big Esther's Beauty Shop were a dead giveaway.

"Girl, help me so I don't kill somebody!" Esther stage whispered.

Garvin laughed while she imagined Esther strapped into her new handless telephone set that made her look somewhere between a McDonald's order clerk and Lieutenant Uhuru from *Star Trek*—which was also a good description of life in the beauty shop.

Esther was still in the same storefront building set on a busy—if there was such a thing—Jacks Creek street. Paneling dating from the sixties still covered the walls. Though it was clean, most of the chairs and hair dryers were hand-me-downs and had known the bottoms and heads of women, both Esther and her seniors. But though the shop was old, Esther kept abreast of every space-age advance in straightening and coloring hair. Though the truth was, having straight hair was still about caustic, creamy goo applied to the hair.

Garvin leaned her elbows on her desk, twisting in her chair. "What's up, Esther?"

"Oh, girl, you know you own the world. I'm just trying to find a little corner and stay out of your way."

As Esther spoke, Garvin imagined her draped in her usual black top that hung loosely over ankle-length spandex running pants. Not that Esther ever ran—Garvin supposed her friend wore them for comfort. "So what's going on, Esther?"

"I was calling to tell you—"

"Now you make sure you don't get distracted talking to your friend and burn me!"

Garvin could hear what must have been the client in Esther's chair speaking in the background.

That was the problem with the convenience of the handless phone. People—especially people in the forty-years-behind-the-time southern town of Jacks Creek—felt they could interrupt whenever their sweet hearts desired.

"I have been doing hair all my life!" Garvin could hear Esther getting wound up. "I do your mama's hair, your auntie's hair, and I ain't never burnt them." Esther, most likely, by now had a hand on one of her hips. "I have owned this shop since I graduated from high school. Twenty years ago!"

Twenty years? Twenty years? Had it been twenty years since they graduated from high school?

"Yes, I've been right here in this shop for twenty years. And I didn't get all this—" Esther's hand was probably off her hip and waving around the shop, probably a black application brush with a blob of white goo on the tip was in the other—"burning people's heads." By now, people in the shop were scooting down in their seats and looking for places to hide.

The client sounded contrite. *"I know. I know, Esther. You do a good job. You know I know you do a good job. I'm just tender-headed, that's all."*

"We all tender-headed!" Esther was still laying down the law.

"But you know my head can't take a perm long." Why didn't the client just give up? Didn't she know silence was the best policy? Instead, she kept talking. *"It's probably the Indian in my family."* The client's voice was full of familial pride dampened by her desire to coax Esther back from Alert Status red to a calmer yellow.

Esther wasn't backing down. "We *all* got Indian in our family."

Garvin laughed. It was like listening to a radio soap opera.

The client's voice sweetened. *"Esther, I been meaning to tell you. You sure do look good."* She was using the honey ruse. *"You just fallin' off, girl!"* Obviously, she was hoping the way to Esther's heart, the way to most any woman's heart, was to compliment her on weight loss. *"You been drinking Dick Gregory?"*

Garvin laughed out loud.

"No! I am *not* drinking Dick Gregory's weight-loss formula."

The client was pouring the honey thicker now. *"You sure? 'Cause you lookin' good, girl. You doing Richard Simmons?"*

Suddenly, there was a groaning noise and then the sound of rushing water. "Here. Lean back."

The client made a startled sound. Garvin was sure the groaning was the metal chair as Esther swung it around and released the back so that the client's head tilted toward the sink. The chair and sink ensemble was Esther's one space-age equipment investment. The rush and splash of water made it clear that Esther was rinsing the relaxer cream out of the client's hair.

"Are you sure you're not rinsing me too soon?" The client's voice sounded panicked. The fear of nappy roots was a dreadful thing. *"I'm not even tingling yet!"*

Esther's voice dripped sarcasm. "We don't want you to burn, do we?"

Garvin chuckled patiently while the audio drama continued to unfold. She flipped through some paper work as she listened. When the water stopped running, Garvin heard the chair creak. Though the client was quiet, Garvin had been through the process enough to know that Esther was applying creamy conditioner to the client's hair. The snap of a plastic cap going on the woman's head confirmed her imaginations. She could hear Esther moving about, the rustle of the client's plastic protective cape, and then a click. "Here, you sit here." Garvin knew she was seating the woman under one of the antiquated hair dryers. They were so old, the clear plastic hoods had yellowed. The warm dryer heat would intensify the conditioning effect of the cream. "I'll be back."

She could hear Esther slumping onto a chair. She sighed. "Garvin, wanna switch jobs?" she huffed.

Garvin looked at the piles of paper in front of her. "Right, Esther. You know you love your job, and fussing about it is one of the best parts."

Esther caught her breath, and then laughed. "Okay, Dr. Freud, you analyzed me today, okay?"

"No problem. No charge."

Esther laughed again. "What I really called for was to tell you about how excited I am about going to this wedding. Me and Smitty both are!"

Smitty had been part of the summertime charm of Big Esther's Beauty Shop a few years back. Then, Smitty was his name and snow cones were his game. When women in the shop, hot from summer heat and hair dryers, heard the tinkle of his bell, they piled out to the street. They gathered around Smitty's white truck, jumping like five-year-olds waving their coins. Smitty was thin and diminutive and, though he was obviously happy for the business, his eyes looked worried that he might drown in the sea of giggling women in capes, clear plastic caps, and pink and metallic-colored rollers. Then Esther batted her eyes and jostled her way to the front of the pack, now Smitty was her husband.

"Maybe I'm excited because me and Smitty didn't have much of a wedding."

Garvin giggled thinking about her Amazon-like friend and her tiny husband standing side-by-side taking their vows. "Well, whatever wedding you didn't have, you all got the market cornered on love."

"Yeah, we do!" A blush tickled through Esther's voice. "But you and GoGo ain't doing too bad either."

"Yeah." Garvin's face warmed. It still made her blush to hear her husband's name.

"You sure we're not crowding in, going to the wedding? We don't even know Mary and Moor."

"No, girl. Meemaw is pulling people out of the hedges and the highways. It's becoming more like a family reunion, or one of those family-and-friends days at church. The groom is from Africa and he doesn't have many people coming. And for some reason, he and Mary both have people that can't come for one reason or another. So, it's like the old people say, 'Whosoever will—'"

"'Let 'em come!'" They laughed as they finished the saying together.

Garvin nodded her head. "So, we're just inviting people. We're going to make it a celebration come heck or high water! The people that come just get to get in on the party!"

"I know that's right! Well, I'm excited. I'm looking for a dress. And me and Smitty and the kids are talking about it all the time." Esther sounded like she was talking about the senior prom or homecoming. "I'm even excited to see who's going to show up. I'm happy to see anybody . . . just no Inez!"

Garvin chuckled. Actually, it would be a treat to get away from the town busybody. There's one in every town, and in Jacks Creek it was impossible to avoid Inez Zephyr. If she wasn't in Esther's shop, looking out the front plate-glass window for gossip tidbits, then she couldn't be avoided at the grocery store or standing in line at the post office. And as easy as Inez was to spot—she was the one person in America still ordering shiny, flowered polyester dresses from the catalog stores—it was hard to dodge her in a small town. Inez was a *professional.*

But California was a long way away. Just a vacation from Inez, let alone the joy of a marriage, was reason to celebrate. Garvin laughed with satisfaction. "Yeah, no Inez."

As she hung up, Garvin looked out the window of her office. Green leaves trailed down in front of it. Where she worked now was a long way from the law offices where she'd worked in Washington, D.C. Her clients were different; instead of helping corporations get more money, now she served kids, helping them get their lives together. She looked at the peach-colored roses in the vase on the side table near her desk. They were from her garden. *Her* garden. When she worked for Winkel and Straub law firm, she had never imagined she would be back in Jacks Creek. She certainly had never seen herself married, or with a baby—and there was no time for gardening. None of this had been part of the plan.

When she'd been put on administrative leave because of the trouble with Gooden, and when she'd come back to Jacks Creek to rescue Meemaw. . . . Rescuing Meemaw? Garvin laughed and looked at the picture of her grandmother on her desk. She should have known better. But it had never occurred to her that her life would turn out this way. At the worst of it, she'd thought someone was out to get her.

Garvin looked back out the window. It was hard to know what God was up to when He was messing up your plan. She smiled as she looked at her husband and daughter's pictures on her desk. *Thank you, God.*

Now all she had to worry about were little things . . . like beads on wedding gowns. The dress was pretty enough without them. Meemaw's modification was just one more thing—in addition to trying to help Mary get the food and the location together—to be anxious about.

She had to admit that what there was of the detailing was beautiful, but there was still so much more beadwork to be done. Garvin sighed. Meemaw was so stubborn. It was a good idea, but what if she didn't get Mary's dress done in time?

But then again, what were beads on a dress compared to what she had promised to do? Why had she opened her big mouth? A lot of good she was going to be able to do with wedding preparations in California when she was in Jacks Creek.

Garvin dialed her friend Jonee's number by heart. Her friend was still an attorney at Winkel and Straub. They didn't talk everyday, but distance and time had not weakened their friendship.

"Winkel and Straub. Agnes speaking. May I help you?"

It was all so familiar. Being an attorney at Winkel and Straub meant heavy large glass doors, plush carpeting, and layers of receptionists to screen your calls. "Garvin Daniels-Walker. May I speak with Jonee Rainat, please?"

Being a juvenile advocate at the courthouse in Jacks Creek meant worn wooden benches in the hallways, crying babies, and doing your own photocopying. She looked out the window at the grassy lawn, then back at the flowers and pictures. It also meant a different kind of success and even greater peace of mind.

"Hey, Garvin. What's up?"

Garvin thought she could hear her friend trying to switch gears—from cool corporate lawyer to best girlfriend. "All is well, Jonee. It's good to hear you. I know you're busy, so I'll try to be brief."

"No, I needed this. Something to calm me down."

She imagined her diminutive friend as she spoke. Garvin always saw Jonee's eyes—large, brown, and almond-shaped. "I'm calling about my cousin Mary's wedding. I hope you'll be able to come."

"Be able to come? Girl, I wouldn't miss it! I won't know anyone but you, but I thought, 'What the heck!' I'll be able to see you, and that cute baby. How is Princess anyway?"

"Oh, she's fine. Two going on forty. You know the deal."

Garvin imagined Jonee's smile as she spoke. "No kidding. Children aren't like they were when we were kids." She laughed. "We're beginning to sound like our mothers, aren't we?"

Garvin laughed with her. "Yeah. I guess that's how it

goes." Hearing Jonee's voice made her aware of how much she missed her. "It's going to be great to see you." She leaned back and swiveled in her chair. "Guess who else is coming?"

"Who?"

"Ramona. You remember her?"

"I know you all were friends. She's the one who got knocked down at the Metro station, right?"

Garvin chuckled. "Ramona was down, but not out."

Knocked down at the station. Flat on her back, her skirt flying up like Sophia—the character Oprah played in *The Color Purple*—right in the middle of the D.C. morning rush hour. It had been a turning point in Ramona's life. She had gone from huge hoop earrings and being the queen of time-off to cycling cross-country and reigning as first lady of the small storefront church her husband pastored. "She is so happy. And just think, I tried to talk her out of dating the guy."

"That's what we attorneys get paid to do: we give advice."

"Um hum. Well, it seems like folks are doing pretty good without me." The admission surprised her. It was one of those flashes of self-awareness that confuses less than it clarifies. "Ramona and her husband are both coming from D.C. Maybe the three of you can make your way to California together."

Garvin went on to tell Jonee about the wedding, about the dress that Meemaw was trimming with beads. "She's obviously not listening to me, either." And she told Jonee about their travel plans. "And Meemaw has this crazy idea in her mind about all of us—all the people from Jacks Creek—traveling to California together! Who do you think is going to get stuck making all those flight arrangements? I'm hoping GoGo or somebody will talk her out of it." Garvin's husband would most likely have to be the one to dissuade her grand-mother; poor Monique—now a college student and over-whelmed by her own studies and caring for her daughter Destiny, in addition to Meemaw's tenacity—had already given up the fight.

She briefly shared the other details she knew. "Of course, I can't say much about the dress and beads. I volunteered to help find the perfect location for the wedding and to help Mary make food arrangements." Garvin shook her head as though Jonee could see her. "What was on my mind? Who do *I* know in San Francisco?"

Jonee snickered. "Maybe it's genetic." She giggled again. "But I think I can help you out, though. Do you think Mary would like Thai food?"

"Sure. Sure." Garvin could hear Jonee flipping pages, probably going through her day-planner or her address book.

"I have family in San Francisco. They own a restaurant. They regularly cater weddings. I think they would give you a good price. Should I call?"

"Should you call? Jonee, girl, you need to hang up and be dialing right now!" All these years she had known Jonee and never known . . . but no time to think about that. She was going to get off the phone and do a little praise dance around her desk.

That was another good thing about Jacks Creek. No one was going to burst into her office and interrupt her dance. And if they did, it was likely that they would pick up their feet and join her!

She said her good-bye to Jonee. In the middle of her praise—*Thank you, God, for Thai food in California*—she thought about Meemaw and wondered if her foxy, gray-haired grandmother was ever going to get finished with the beadwork.

The funny thing was, in spite of all her worries, Garvin was beginning to feel excitement building inside of her.

FOUR

Baltimore, Maryland

S omething old, something new, something borrowed. . . . Latrice went over the words in her mind while she looked out the side window of her car at her girlfriend Mary. They were there to borrow the veil Mary was going to wear. Latrice tapped her long shiny nails on the steering wheel. She was trying to be patient, trying to be a good bridesmaid, but she hoped a sister wouldn't take too long. Baltimore was hot in the summer and her skirt, sticky with sweat, was plastered to the back of her thighs. The flowers and the well-manicured lawns in front of the row houses on Old Frederick Road were about the only things keeping her calm, that and seeing Mary so happy.

Sister Puddin and Brother Joe—now Deacon Joe—stood smiling brighter than the June sun, grinning down at Mary, who stood one step beneath them at the end of the sidewalk that led to their house.

"Oh, baby!" Sister Puddin was gushing all over herself like it was her wedding that was going to jump off in August. "I am so happy for you and Africa!" She closed her eyes and tossed her head like she was a young girl. "It's so exciting. It was like it was never going to happen—" she looked at Joe— "at least that's how it felt to me." Her eyes popped open wider, she giggled and blushed. "Did I say Africa? I mean, Moor, of course." She looked bashfully at her husband, Joe, who responded by pinching her side and winking at her. "Stop it, now, Joe," she said none too convincingly. "The girls are watching."

From where she sat in her car by the curb—close enough not only to see Mary, Puddin, and Joe, but also close enough to hear—Latrice smiled to herself. She didn't get called *girl* very much these days, at least not in a way that made her think good things. Usually, it was someone less than a loser trying to make a pass, or a wisecracker using the derivative *gal.* What would make anyone think someone wanted to be called gal? *Come on over here, gal, and get this slop jar.* It just didn't set the tone for pleasant conversation. In response to which she always had to use every sweet piece of spiritual fruit she had not to yell back in reply, "Your Mama!"

But from Sister Puddin, she could take the *girl* with a smile. In fact, it just proved—contrary to what people said— that eavesdropping does indeed pay off. She and Mary and Naomi and Thelma were girls as far as Sister Puddin and Deacon Joe were concerned. It always amused her how people from other cultures reacted to seeing a woman in her thirties saying, "Yes ma'am" or "No sir" to another more senior adult. It was all about respect, even though there were moments when it got old. But then there were moments like this when she was called girl, and she could pretend that her biological clock wasn't alarming to wake the whole city.

Not that it mattered. She wasn't looking for babies—she *was* the baby. If a man was meeting *her* needs, he wasn't going to have time to share with children. People could think whatever they wanted to; they could call her what they pleased— as long as they were ready for her to call them something back. Besides, it was nobody's business. She liked kids—*other* people's—she just didn't want to give up the attention.

Latrice fanned herself with her hand and looked back at Sister Puddin. She was as sweet and plump and every bit as chocolate as her name implied. Puddin was middle-aged, but she still was giving fat girls a good name. And her red husband looked at her like she was Lola Falana.

"Just think, an August wedding! Mary, I know it's gone be so beautiful!" Sister Puddin stood close to her husband. "And I hope the veil—" she held it out to Mary—"is the beginning of as many memories for your marriage as it was for ours."

Deacon Joe leaned over and kissed Sister Puddin, whispered something to her, and began to tickle her until she swatted away his hand. "Stop it, now, Joe. I ain't playin' with you, boy."

Deacon Joe pulled Sister Puddin to him like he had heard all these protests before. "Sister Mary don't mind. She's about to be married herself. She probably takin' notes."

Sister Puddin blushed and pretended to ignore him. "I sure do wish we could be with you all, at the wedding and all. You know I wouldn't miss it for the world. I feel about you and Moor like you are my own two children. I've got a lot of love invested in you all."

Latrice snickered to herself in the car. No kidding, Sister Puddin had a lot invested. She had done everything she could to get Mary and Moor together through her computer dating service. And when that hadn't worked out, the sister had proved she was willing to put her chicken where her mouth was, if she had to. It had all come out after the brouhaha last year. Their whole church, the neighborhood, even the whole city had been caught up in it. Sister Puddin had a lot invested all right.

"You know we would be in California with you for the wedding if we could. Wouldn't we, Joe?"

"That's right," Joe said while still looking at Sister Puddin like he couldn't wait for dessert.

"But Joe made anniversary plans for us and we just can't back out. You know, his book sold so well, he was able to pay for a cruise for us. I'm so excited!" she twittered.

Mary gently rubbed her hand over the veil she held in her hand. "Don't you worry about a thing. We know you'll be with us in the spirit, and it means so much for you to allow me to borrow your veil."

"Well, I just thought, when I saw the gown, that my veil would be perfect."

Latrice waved her hand, hoping a touch of cool air would tease her. It still took some getting used to: to think of Mary being married. It seemed like she went from dowdy to diva-licious in one afternoon. Latrice giggled. Actually, it *was* one afternoon—the makeover of a lifetime. She looked at her own long, carefully painted nails. She had made sure Mary's nails were done fit for a queen, their good friend Naomi had supervised the blonde weave—and all that was good until Thelma had insisted on the green contacts. Still though, Mary had left the salon a new woman.

Latrice knew Sister Puddin thought she had gotten Moor and Mary together. And she wouldn't have hurt Sister Puddin's feelings for the world. But the truth was, *she* and Naomi and Thelma deserved credit for *their* part. Moor, the man Puddin called *Africa*, probably never would have noticed Mary without the makeover. That was the honest truth.

Still, it seemed so sudden—it had been about a year—

Mary getting married. What was even harder to imagine was Mary being gone, moving to California. Moor's training program had carried him to San Francisco, and soon Mary would be going away. But the smile on her friend's face was worth it.

Mary in California . . . well, at least *her* going made sense. But Naomi . . . that was a whole other story. It was like the girl had lost her mind, left her job, and gone ahead to California like she was that crazy girl in that movie, *Member of the Wedding*. Who could figure that one out?

Mary, still standing on the steps, nodded. "Thank you—thank you both, again."

Deacon Joe squeezed Puddin around her ample waist. "Well . . ." Puddin bent over, Joe's arm still about her, and waved into the car at Latrice. "Don't let me keep you girls, now. I know you got a lot to do."

Latrice waved back. Sister Puddin and Deacon Joe were like teenagers with each other. What they had was what the old-school soul group, the Spinners, sang about: a mighty love. They gave her hope. Not for herself . . . she was okay where she was, doing her own thing . . . but hope for love in general.

Mary, obviously taking Sister Puddin and Deacon Joe's hint, turned and started for the car, waving over her shoulder.

"You be sure to take lots of pictures, and send me and Joe copies!"

"Yes ma'am!" Mary walked to the car door and grabbed the handle.

Sister Puddin's giggles and protests floated on the air as they drove away.

Just as Latrice was about to slip out of her robe and into

a hot bath, "Mr. Bubble, I'm comin', baby!" the phone rang.

"I don't think there ought to be a wedding, and if there is one, I'm not going to be in it!" It was Thelma. "You may be able to go along with this and act like everything is okay. But I'm not going to participate in this madness!" Thelma yelled into the phone the way people do when they've been carrying on a six-hour argument in their heads that they're determined to win. "There's a thousand reasons why she shouldn't get married. But for one, Mary doesn't even know this man. What if it doesn't work out? What about that?" Thelma said, like she was slapping a poker hand down on the table.

"Thelma, girl, what is the matter with you?"

"I'm her friend, and I'm not going to let Mary make a fool of herself. I love her too much to let her do that."

"Maybe you have to love her enough, Thelma, to let her try." Latrice shook herself. She had to be dreaming—she never sounded so sensible when she was awake.

"What? What did you say, Latrice?"

Latrice could imagine Thelma's eyes all bugged out—her blue contacts rimmed by the reddened whites of her eyes. "What I said was, calm down, girl. It's not a matter of national security."

"I don't know how you can be calm. Our best friend is about to go off and ruin her life with some man we don't even know. We don't even know his people!"

"Oh, Thelma." Thelma had always played the mother/ teacher role in their group. But right now she was bucking for an Academy Award. "What we have to hope is that it works. And you know what? If it doesn't, she won't be the first."

"See, you're taking this as a joke, Latrice."

No, it wasn't funny at all. She looked from her bedroom into the bathroom. The mountain of fragrant bubbles that had been calling her name—it was her special mixture of Mr. Bubble and JLo perfume—was slowly dissolving into a mound. A tub full of hot water going to waste was no joke. "I'm not laughing, Thelma. I'm just not freaking out. I can't control Mary. She's a grown woman." Latrice giggled. "Besides, it's hard to wait when you're being good."

"Ha ha!" Thelma laughed like a maniacal member of a debate team, as though one of the debate points she had gone over in her mind had come up at last. "It's true. Mary's grown. But she doesn't have the *experience* that you and I have. You know that." Thelma cleared her throat. "You and I have been around the block. See, she's been running around like 'The Flying Nun' and now she's acting crazy over the first man to pay her any attention. See? She *can't* wait. You know what I mean?"

Latrice looked at the tub again. The mound was barely a bubbly hump now. She sighed and flopped onto her bed . . . might as well get comfortable.

"Truth be told, Thelma, Moor wasn't Mary's first date. Remember? You know, remember Reggie?" Latrice paused to let her words sink in.

She could tell by the way Thelma stammered that she remembered. "Well. Well. It almost worked out. I mean he made her a nice dinner—"

Latrice laughed. "Girl, that man was one step away from being Jeffrey Dahmer. Poor Mary almost *was* dinner! Ain't no telling what he would have done if he had gotten ahold of her. Didn't he chase her down the hill to the bus stop? You know he had a cleaver in his hand!"

"Oh, Latrice, you're exaggerating!" Thelma sputtered.

"Okay, so the date with Reggie didn't work out. But don't forget about Floyd and his all-you-can-eat ribs and sauce. What about that date? The one *you* set up?"

Latrice quickly changed the subject. "What I'm trying to say, Thelma, is that Mary is a grown woman. We have to trust her. We have to be her friends and let her live her life."

"The way I see it, we have to be her friends and try to *save* her life." Thelma wasn't letting up. "Girl, we don't know *who* this man is, or where he's from. Lesotho? Who do you know from Lesotho? What kind of country is that? If he's from Africa, why couldn't he be from Nigeria or Senegal, or somewhere somebody has heard of before?" Thelma was on a roll. "No, he comes up with the name of someplace we've never heard of. Girl, the Negro could be from around the block and putting on an accent! Don't laugh, Latrice. I've heard of it before. Has anybody done an investigation? No! No, that would make too much sense!" Thelma was huffing, and Latrice could imagine her blue contacts about to pop out of her eyes. "We don't know a thing about this man!"

"Well, Thelma, why do you think he wants to marry her?"

"Girl, you heard him say he was from a poor country! The O'Jays sang it and it still is the truth, 'for the love of money!' That Negro's from a foreign land, all right. From a city called No Job in the heart of a land called South Baltimore! I don't trust him at all!"

"Oh, Thelma, girl. Take a pill and call me in the morning."

"Go ahead and laugh! And you can do whatever *you* want to, Latrice. Make fun. But I'm not going to make this easy for Mary. I'm not going to go along with helping her ruin her life. I'm not going to let Mary down!" Thelma was working herself up to fever pitch. "And I'm certainly not going to fly off to California like I don't have good sense, for some wedding that probably won't even jump off. Not to mention that Naomi's already there and has lost her mind—I think that weave finally pulled the brains out of her head."

Latrice laughed. "Oh, Thelma." She had thought the same thing about the weave herself.

"No, really. I'm serious. I think my friends are losing their m-i-n-d minds, and I have to do whatever I can to stop it. I've got to take care of us. I can't drag Naomi home from California and shake some sense back into her head, but I can tell Mary what I think and try to keep her from going."

"Oh, Thelma. Don't ruin it for her."

"I'm not playing, Latrice. Laugh all you want. I'm going to tell her the truth so she won't ruin her life. I'd rather hurt her now than have her hurt later. And if that doesn't work—" Thelma paused dramatically—"I'm going to boycott the wedding!"

FIVE

It was pretty clear that Mary was in love. It was summertime in Baltimore. It was hot, and they were walking past all kinds of snow cone trucks and stands and Mary—who normally couldn't bring herself to pass a one—didn't seem to be noticing.

"You're going to *love* flying into San Francisco. The Golden Gate Bridge is beautiful, the bay is beautiful, but the thing that always gets me is the houses. They are painted all these unusual rainbow colors. Just wait and see."

Latrice nodded. She was too busy trying to keep her breath, walking in the heat, to waste time talking. Daydreaming about walking was one thing—actually putting your feet to concrete was something else. Mary was doing enough bubbling for both of them.

"And it's going to be so much fun—the three of us flying first-class. We are going to do it up!"

Latrice grinned. That was all she *could* do. All of her energy was going toward convincing herself that she was not hot, toward telling her thighs not to even think about chafing, and toward telling the sweat that was trying to roll down her forehead not even to try it.

Mary pulled an envelope out of her pocket. "I got this

letter yesterday from Moor's grandmother." She held it up. "Look at the stamps."

What stamps? Latrice barely could see. Sweat had come down her forehead and was in her eyes. She tried to make herself smile and look interested.

"Do you want me to read it to you?"

She nodded. Whatever Mary wanted her to do was fine, as long as they hurried up and got to wherever they were going. She still could not figure out why they had to walk down Baltimore Turnpike. Why couldn't they just take the car?

Mary began to read. Latrice thought she could hear traces of an accent; Mary read as though she was the old woman from Lesotho, the tiny southern kingdom in Africa.

> My dearest granddaughter,
>   I hope you do not mind my calling you that. I have heard so much about you. Moor's letters are full of talk about you. Every word makes this old woman's heart smile. The whole village is talking about you and coming to my home to see your picture.
>   "She is a beautiful, fat woman," they say. "The kind of woman that the men in your family like. Brown, pretty, a very natural girl."
>   It pleases me that you have made Moor happy. Now in the mornings when I pray for him, when I thank God for a grandson so handsome the sun rushes through the night so it can

get back in the sky to see his face, when I thank God for a grandson so clever the fox comes to him for answers, when I thank God for a grandson so loving that he makes spring blush, I also thank God for you, my child. Thank you for a granddaughter worthy of this man.

When we look at your picture, and hear the stories Moor tells, we all agree that we know why it took so long for Moor to find you. It took every second up to now to make such a wonderful mate, to prepare such a wonderful bride as you.

Moor tells me that you are alone, that you have no family. That is true no more. Soon I will fly to America. You will have to pray for me because I will have to travel a long way from my village in the mountains, and I have never flown before. But I know that at the end of my journey I will hold in my arms the beautiful granddaughter that I already hold in my heart.

Until we meet,
Wazzala, your Lesotho grandmother.

Mary looked up from reading the letter and sighed. Abruptly, she pointed. "Here."

"Where? What?" Latrice wiped her brow. There was so much sweat in her eyes she could hardly see.

"This is where Moor told me to turn to find his friends."

"What friends?" Latrice looked around as they crossed the street and started down the alleyway. "Girl, where are you taking me?"

"You've heard me talk about them. You know, Brighty, Blue, and Ali—the one the old men call the White Black Muslim."

There was a table in the alley ahead of Latrice and Mary. At the table sat two old men, both of them in sleeveless white T-shirts. One of them, a brown-skinned man, wore a white mesh Ravens football cap. Gray hair peeked beneath the edges. The other old man—much fairer in complexion—wore a broad-brimmed straw hat. Sitting near them, on what looked to be an upside-down paint can, was a young White man—probably in his early twenties—with long blond dreadlocks.

The old man in the baseball cap spotted them first. He sat forward as though he was straining to see. His face broke into a smile. He pointed at Mary. "I know you. You the prince's bride!"

He looked at the other two men. "Stand up, fellas. Here comes the prince's bride!"

"Well, sure enough." The other old man grinned. "And he got just what he asked for, didn't he?" He gave Mary a sly look from underneath his hat. "You a *pretty*, fat thing. And your friend with you, she's a stout thing too!"

"Hush, Brighty!" The first old man hit the other on his shoulder with his cap. "Don't embarrass us in front of the ladies!"

The second old man looked offended. "Well, Blue, that's

what he said. 'I want a fat wife.' That's what the prince said. I ain't making it up. Am I, Ali?"

The young man smiled bashfully and shrugged his shoulders. "Nice to meet you, ladies."

Blue held his baseball cap in hand. "You ladies have a seat."

"No, I'll stand, if you don't mind." Latrice spoke up quickly. The rickety chairs the two old men were sitting on looked like they could give way at any moment.

It was funny. She called herself fat all the time, but she wasn't used to hearing it from anybody else. But the two old men reminded her of old men she'd been seeing all her life. They were the comic wise men that could be found in every community. While they made you laugh, they had the first word on everything from the weather to the mayor.

"You sure, now?" Blue asked as he began to ease onto his seat.

"I apologize. No offense meant, now. I don't want you going away from here mad at me. Telling the prince and all." Brighty squatted until he reached the seat bottom. "'Cause he's a righteous man, but around here, folks know *he* don't play."

"That's right," Blue nodded. "Did he ever tell you how he met me?"

Brighty yanked his hat off and started fanning. "Now, Blue, don't get started with one of your stories, now. You know these young ladies don't want to hear that. It's too hot!"

Blue looked wounded. "I was gone make it short, Brighty. Don't nobody interrupt you when you on one of your long diatribes." He waved his hand. "I was just gone tell them how the prince swooped down like a big Black angel and rescued me." He slapped his knee and laughed. "That thug he clobbered didn't know what hit him! That's for sure!"

Brighty shook his head. "Blue, these fat girls—I mean, these women don't want to hear none of your old tales, now!"

Blue shook his finger at Brighty. "Why you got to keep doing that? Why you got to call them fat?"

"'Cause you know it's the truth. If she wasn't fat, we wouldn't have been looking for her all over kingdom come. But that's what the man said he wanted." He looked at them.

Latrice looked at Mary. She was smiling as though they were calling her exquisite.

Blue nodded reluctantly. "It's true. We were going to grocery stores, waiting at bus stops. . . ." He raised an eyebrow, looking in Brighty's direction. "Though some of us looked harder than others." He pointed to Ali. "And this boy here was on the computer day and night."

Ali shrugged. "Not day and night. But—"

"He was on the computer looking for you on that computer dating service." Blue kept talking. "I was on the bus one time, looking, and I saw a woman—" he squinted—"she looked a lot like you. Except—" he wiggled his fingers over his head—"she had funny-colored hair." He pointed. "And funny colored eyes." He looked Mary up and down. "But she sure looked a lot like you."

Brighty nodded. "That boy—that man about worried us to death looking for you." He mocked Moor's voice and accent. "'I do not need a woman, my wise fathers.'" He shook his head. "That boy was about pinin' to death. So, whatever you do, don't diet!"

Mary laughed out loud. Latrice tried not to—the last thing Blue and Brighty needed was encouragement—but soon she was laughing too.

Mary smiled at each one of them. "I'm here because

Moor asked me to come. You're invited—we want you to come to our wedding."

Blue laughed. "Do tell?"

"Yes, it's going to be in San Francisco."

Brighty was smiling. "Well, ain't that nice? It sure would be nice to go. Where's it gone be?"

Blue shook his head. "I don't know why you'd ask, Brighty. You know it's gone be in a church, seeing how the prince is almost like a preacher. But you know you ain't gone set foot in no church. The roof might collapse." Blue chuckled at his own joke.

"You funny, ain't you?" Brighty waved his hand at Blue. "You don't know *where* I been."

"I know you ain't been to church."

"Well, I might start. How 'bout that?"

"Lay you five to one, you won't."

Brighty adjusted his hat. "I never been to California—"

Blue grinned. "And they never asked you to come—"

Brighty cocked his hat to the side. "But once I get there, the young ladies ain't gone want me to leave!"

As the two old men bantered, Latrice recalled stories Moor and Mary had told her: stories about the three men, of them eating together, talking, and in winter, of them huddled by the fire.

Ali interrupted. "Come on, you guys. We got company."

Blue and Brighty seemed to have forgotten that Mary and Latrice were there.

Mary smiled. "It's okay." Then she nodded at Blue. "And, Mr. Blue, I *was* that woman you saw on the bus. Looking at you now, I remember you."

"But you had funny-colored hair . . . and green eyes!"

Mary laughed. "And you had on a black suit."

"Well. Well, it sure was you. Ain't that nothin'!" Blue took off his hat. "We old men, and this boy here is in college. We don't have no money. But I sure did make a promise. That day on the bus. . . ." He looked at the two other men. "We kind of promised about going to the wedding." He looked back at Mary. "We'll have to see what we can do."

Brighty leaned back in his seat. "We sure do miss the prince."

Blue nodded. "Sometime, you pray for somebody to get something good. It's sweet," he smiled, "but I can't say I ain't got a little bit of regret." He looked at the younger man. "But we still got Ali."

Ali smiled as though he were a son looking at his fathers. "I'm not going anywhere."

Brighty leaned forward, looking Ali in the eye. "That's what you saying, boy. But someday, some woman—"

Ali waved his hands in the air. "I keep telling you guys, I already got a girlfriend."

Brighty continued. "I ain't talking about a girlfriend. But someday, some woman is gone want you, too—though you might have to cut that crazy hair off your head for her to be able to see you! Ain't that mess hot?"

Ali blushed. "Come on, you guys."

Mary smiled at each one of them. "I hope you'll think about it . . . about coming to the wedding."

"You sure, now?" Blue looked at Brighty. "'Cause we wouldn't want to come up in the church and mess up the wedding. You know, a bolt of lightning might come crashing through the roof."

Brighty turned his head. "Very funny." He looked at Ali. "I don't see you picking on this boy, and he's a White Black Muslim."

"You guys—" Ali protested.

"Ain't no point in picking on Ali—he's confused."

Brighty tapped his finger on the table. "I just don't know how I feel about going to church. I ain't shamed to say it."

"You live in a church. You are the church. God's presence is always with you." It surprised Latrice that she had said it. In her heart she felt it was true, and it was also true that she felt love and joy in the old men's presence. "God's seeing you all the time."

The two old men looked at each other.

"Think about it, all right?" Mary pressed again.

"Well. . . ." Blue looked at Latrice and then back at Mary. "Yessir, we promised." Blue nodded. "We'll have to see what we can do."

Latrice and Mary giggled during the walk back to Mary's house. They stopped halfway at a snow-cone stand.

Mary crunched her spoon into the ice and cherry syrup in her cup. "Moor will be so pleased if they come. If I can make this happen for him, it will be perfect. He's taking care of everything in California. It's all moving smoothly—like running water. It will be a happy ending if I can just make this happen."

Latrice laughed and sipped chilled orange syrup from her own cup. "Yeah, like Naomi said. 'It's all groovy, baby! California dreamin'.'"

6

SIX

San Francisco, California

I *want 2 thank u 4 lettin me be mice elf again.* Sly Stone's
lyrics ran through Anthony's mind.

People probably thought rain didn't fall so high up.
That's probably what they thought unless they lived or
worked that high above the ground. The truth was, it seemed
to fall harder, and if there was lightning or thunder, it was
even more threatening high up. There was nowhere to run,
and there was further to fall.

Anthony looked through his office window out over the
city of San Francisco. It was a beautiful day, and six huge
panels of glass gave him an unencumbered view. The people
on the streets below looked like moving confetti, and the cars
moved quickly and erratically like insects, the trolley cars like
caterpillars. What he liked most about the view was the pyr-
amid-shaped Transamerica building in front of him, and that
some days, when the fog was light, he could actually see the
water of the bay.

He stared out the window and breathed deeply. In one
direction was the orange and elegant brightness of the
Golden Gate Bridge, in the other was the hulking isolation
of Alcatraz Island. He tried to relax and not feel like a fail-
ure. Anthony tried to pretend—tried to fool his mind into

believing—that things were as they had been before. So that when he remembered looking out the window, it would be a good thing. He would remember the clear blue sky. He would remember the sun and the bay. He wouldn't remember, he didn't want to remember feeling low on the inside. *I want 2 thank u 4 lettin me be mice elf again.*

Anthony was yellow.

Not that it mattered much to him. He didn't see himself that way. He didn't know what it meant not to be yellow. It meant more to other people. They were more or less afraid, more or less comfortable, or more or less distrusting depending on where they stood in relation to his yellow, but it didn't matter to him. Though it was true it had gotten him into some doors and some beds, it didn't have anything to do with him or how he saw himself, or what he thought.

It was part of his hand and he played the card. What he really thought of himself was that he was Ant-nee. That's what his family called him. *Hey, Ant-nee!* That's what his old neighborhood friends had called him, and he always held his breath waiting for the day when other people would find out his real name.

Anthony looked at his hands, then turned to look at the empty drawer and the half-filled brown cardboard box on the desk in front of him. A lot of good yellow was doing him right now.

The square box sat in the middle of the overly large mahogany desk. He looked down at it and felt ashamed. He wasn't sure why. Whether it was because the desk meant so much to him that he was already missing it, longing for it, and was ready to pay Luther Vandross to sing to it so it wouldn't leave him—or at least so it would follow him. Or it might be he was ashamed because now he could see just how big and ridiculous the monstrosity looked sitting in his huge office.

When people walked in, they genuflected to it, and it set the tone—established how important he was.

Maybe he was simply ashamed because he had been fired.

Anthony picked up his pearl-handled letter opener. The blade was sharp. He stopped short of dropping it in his box. It was company-issued to him. But would they let him keep it? Probably not. He set it next to the stapler he never used.

And what about his hand-held computer? He slid the sleek, silver metallic personal computer from the pocket of his tailored gray suit. His numbers. His appointments. His schedule. His thoughts and ideas. They were all in the little machine. He set it next to the letter opener. *Definitely not.*

He wasn't sure what had happened. One minute he was yellow and fair-haired.

"Hey, Tony! Had your joe this morning?"

He had stopped in the hall to chew the morning gristle with Steve. Boss wasn't the word for Steve. They played handball together. They strategized together. They talked about family together.

"You know it, man." He had nodded at Steve. *"But this is definitely a two-cup morning. I'm about to have another one."*

"That's one of the things I love about you, Tony. You're a man who knows how to hold his liquids!"

They had cocked finger guns at each other and nodded and smiled as though they had the world on a string and played paddleball with it just to stay in shape.

Then, nonchalantly, *"Hey, Tony, can you drop by my office for a quick second? I've got something I need to discuss with you?"*

"Sure thing." No telling what it was. Maybe the big boss

was leaning on Steve, and he needed to let off some steam. It could have been the wife wanting a new play pretty, or maybe trouble with the kids. It could have just been wishful thinking about a nice-looking woman he had seen on the commuter train.

Anthony got a cup of coffee, signed a couple of letters—to use up some time. He was past the rush-to-your-boss's-office stage at this level. They were comrades, partners. It was crude and tasteless to think of it any other way.

On his way to Steve's office, he had nodded to his receptionist and had congratulated his secretary on her new baby and told her it was good to have her back. He politely had laid two folders in his administrative assistant's in-box and thanked her for the last work she'd done for him. He had patted the mail clerk on the back and told him to keep up the good work—he had his eye on him.

On his way back from Steve's office, he wondered if all of them had known before he did. It had been a short meeting. *"As you know, we're reorganizing. Sorry to say this to you, buddy. . . ."*

Anthony wondered whether the mail clerk knew his eye on him meant nothing; he was impotent and blind. Had the receptionist and the secretary discussed it already, and was the appreciation and workplace affection in their eyes actually pity?

He looked at his hands like they weren't attached to his body, dropping things into the small box. At least Steve had spared him the indignity of being escorted from the building, of having them pack his things and mail them to him.

There was a quick knock at the door, and it opened before Anthony could answer.

The dark, smiling face that poked inside was a sharp contrast to the white shirt and red tie, but it was almost the same color as his black suit. "I hope I am not interrupting. I wanted to give you this!" Moor was beaming as he held a cream-colored envelope in one hand above his head. "It is final! We are getting married!" He walked through the door and quickly toward Anthony's desk. "It is sudden, but not too soon!"

Moor had not been at the firm long. He had transferred from Baltimore and was in San Francisco for the firm's eighteen-month banking and economics apprenticeship program.

"I wanted to make certain you got this right away!" Moor's South African accent made *this* sound like *thees*. He talked about his woman nonstop and told the story of how he had found her—and almost missed her—in Baltimore. He folded his arms and chuckled when he told the story of the two old men and the graduate student who had helped him to find her. *"A hidden treasure in a most unlikely place,"* he had said.

Anthony was pretty sure Moor didn't know; the news hadn't made it to the water cooler yet. Moor extended the envelope and Anthony took it. For a moment, he stared at Moor's hand on the envelope. *Maybe if I were darker . . . or maybe if I were Hispanic, I wouldn't be packing.*

When Moor's broad smile narrowed and one of his eyebrows lifted, Anthony knew the man in front of him was beginning to get it. He nodded his affirmation and then continued to study Moor's face.

No, it wasn't race that had gotten him the boot. He looked at Moor's smooth skin. Maybe it was age. Forty-two wasn't old unless you were out of a job. When you had a paycheck, relaxed facial muscles and graying at the temples were handsome. It was older-man mystique and power. Now it only felt old.

Moor looked at the box and then back at him. "Why are you packing?"

An American never would have asked. He would have been embarrassed, pretended he didn't see, and backed out of the door. Moor didn't have those occidental sensibilities—he stared and appeared honestly confused.

Anthony tried to think of an excuse. *I've decided to strike out on my own. I've decided to resign for personal reasons.* Something he could say, any excuse so he wouldn't have to tell the younger man that he had been fired. *I'm taking a sabbatical, a leave of absence. Seeking broader horizons. We're parting because of a difference in philosophy.*

Then he thought he should warn Moor, let him know the grim hatchet man was coming for him too. *You just wait; they'll give you the sack, the boot, the pink slip.* But it wasn't true. They weren't going to get rid of Moor—in fact, they wanted him to stay. They were going to try to convince him to join the firm.

It wasn't because of age or race. That would have made it easier. They were simply letting him go. "I just got fired." Then he said what he always said, without thinking, when bad things happened beyond his control. "It's okay. I'll be okay. I've got my 401k. I'm going to take a little time and enjoy myself before I get back to the grind. I'm okay."

Moor shifted from foot to foot and kept clearing his throat. He lifted the envelope. "You are my only friend here."

He didn't know that Moor thought of him as his *friend.* They had eaten lunch together a few times, they'd talked, but the admission surprised him a little. Anthony prayed that Moor would not get emotional, that he would respect Western sensibilities and not break down. "It's no problem."

Moor stepped closer to the desk. "You will be all right? I will see you? You will come to the wedding? It is very soon—in August."

Anthony took the invitation from Moor's hand. "Yeah, sure. I'll be there." He slid the envelope into the pocket that once held his hand-held.

"And I don't know many people here. I have friends in Baltimore, but it is a long way and they are poor. You will be my best man?"

Was the guy kidding? What was he supposed to say? "Yeah, sure." He would call the guy later and beg off. What a goofball.

"I will pray to God for you."

"Yeah. Thanks. Right."

When he stepped from the elevator, the light from outside poured through the glass wall. He nodded at the uniformed security guard, who sat at the front desk, and walked over to shake the old man's hand. He knew his name was on the security guard's list and that the guard had been alerted that he was leaving—that he had been fired.

The hunched-over man with fuzzy gray hair winked at him. "You take care of yourself, young fella. Keep your head up." His gray mustache puffed up and down as if it were alive. He looked at the list that Anthony was certain had his name on it. The old man tapped the paper with his finger, and then looked sympathetically at Anthony. "One monkey don't stop no show, now. This ain't the end. This is the first day of the rest of your life. Make it the best day."

Anthony nodded and headed for the tall, heavy glass doors. It was like leaving the Emerald City. And everybody in it still needed brains and hearts—they all had plenty of nerve.

Before he got to the train, he dumped the box and stuffed it in the trash. It was bad enough that *he* knew that he'd been fired. He didn't need to share his good fortune with everyone else on the train.

When he settled into his seat, staring at the ads on the wall, he began to feel as though he were the lead character in the movie *Shaft*. What he really needed was to see his woman.

PART TWO

The Preparation

The Parable of the Wedding Banquet

"Then he said to his servants, 'The wedding banquet is ready, but those I invited did not deserve to come. Go to the street corners and invite to the banquet anyone you find.' So the servants went out into the streets and gathered all the people they could find, both good and bad, and the wedding hall was filled with guests.

"But when the king came in to see the guests, he noticed a man there who was not wearing wedding clothes. 'Friend,' he asked, 'how did you get in here without wedding clothes?' The man was speechless."

—THE TEACHINGS OF JESUS THE CHRIST AND SERVANT-KING AS RETOLD BY THE APOSTLE MATTHEW 22:8–12

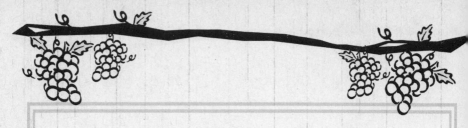

The Parable of the Ten Virgins

"At that time the kingdom of heaven will be like ten virgins who took their lamps and went out to meet the bridegroom. Five of them were foolish and five were wise. The foolish ones took their lamps but did not take any oil with them. The wise, however, took oil in jars along with their lamps. The bridegroom was a long time in coming, and they all became drowsy and fell asleep.

"At midnight the cry rang out: 'Here's the bridegroom! Come out to meet him!'

"Then all the virgins woke up and trimmed their lamps. The foolish ones said to the wise, 'Give us some of your oil; our lamps are going out.'

"'No,' they replied, 'there may not be enough for both us and you. Instead, go to those who sell oil and buy some for yourselves.'

"But while they were on their way to buy the oil, the bridegroom arrived. The virgins who were ready went in with him to the wedding banquet. And the door was shut.

"Later the others also came. 'Sir! Sir!' they said. 'Open the door for us!'

"But he replied, 'I tell you the truth, I don't know you.'

"Therefore keep watch, because you do not know the day or the hour."

—THE TEACHINGS OF JESUS THE CHRIST AND SERVANT-KING AS RETOLD BY THE APOSTLE MATTHEW 25:1–13

SEVEN

Los Angeles, California

I f she was going to go crazy, she might as well go all the way. Naomi laughed to herself as she laid the map she had purchased out on the table top of the booth in front of her. The waitress walked up to take her order. "Wait a minute." Naomi closed her eyes, wiggled her index finger in a circle, and then touched it to the map of California. "Sonoma County Valley."

The waitress nodded nonchalantly. "That's a nice place."

Naomi picked up the map and looked more closely. "Bodega Bay?"

"Yeah. That's where they shot that Alfred Hitchcock movie. You know, *The Birds.*" She tapped her pen on her pad. "Man, I love that movie! Especially that part where that little kid gets pecked in the head by that blackbird." The waitress shuddered and laughed at the same time.

Naomi folded the map and sat back in her seat.

The waitress continued talking. "And Tippi Hedren. Man, she looked great in that role. I would kill for a part like that. There aren't many parts like that for actresses nowadays."

Naomi didn't know what, if anything, she was supposed to say in response.

The waitress sighed. "So what are you gonna have? The baked chicken's on special and it's pretty good. You can get a baked potato, and a salad comes with it, and dessert."

"That sounds good. I was looking at the map instead of at my menu. Thanks for the suggestion."

"No problem, sweetie. How about apple pie for dessert and iced tea to drink?"

Naomi nodded. She looked at the folded map and then back at the waitress. "I guess it must look pretty crazy, picking out a place to live that way?"

The waitress smiled and waved her hand. "Sweetie, you wouldn't believe how many times I've seen people do that. This is L.A. Nobody's judgin' ya—not about that, anyway. You take it like it comes out here, know what I mean? Lots of people come here to start over. Go west, young man. You know what I mean? You can't get no *westier* than this. You do what you gotta do. Pointing a finger at a map is better than most folks do. They just take what they've been handed and hate it all their lives—that's crazy, if you ask me. You're choosing, even if it is with your finger on a map." The waitress walked away as though she had finished a successful State of the Union address.

As the waitress walked away, Naomi unfolded the map again. She had a destination; now she needed a plan. It couldn't be that hard to get there. She dialed 4-1-1 on her cell phone. "Yes, operator, I need the number of a travel agent in Bodega Bay, California."

EIGHT

Bodega Bay, California

Naomi stepped off the bus and dragged her suitcase from the gaping belly underneath. This was not the California of fast cars, movie stars, and Beverly Hills. The Sonoma County Valley was quiet. Verdant hills and lowlands, some planted with rows of grapevines that looked to her like small trees, sloped gently into the bay. Instead of highways and stoplights, what she had noticed, once she had left the L.A. and San Francisco airports behind, were farms and fences surrounding grazing herds of black and white cows and flocks of cottony sheep. There were hardly any cars on the road. No one seemed to be in a hurry. There were even deer, which picked their way, nibbling at plants, seemingly unafraid of people they moved near. She smelled the salty bay water, her lungs opened, and she breathed.

Her suitcase wheels bumped over the pebbly blacktop as she headed for the boardinghouse the bus driver had pointed out to her. She stopped to look out over the bay. It was nothing like the Baltimore Inner Harbor. Whether they were tourists or locals, the people, like the bay waters, were peaceful.

Gently bouncing, the water was sometimes green but mostly gray with sparkling flecks of light like she had seen in magazines. Naomi set her suitcase upright and moved closer to the water. Fat, beautiful seals rolled in the water, swimming and diving. When they leapt from the water, the sun arched over their sleek backs. In what looked to be a family, they barked and played as if they were free, as though no one had told them they should be performing with beach balls in aquatic centers or that someone might want to bash them over the head. They were casual.

Birds—ducks, sandpipers, and others she did not recognize—dived in the water and danced on marshy land peeking through the bay waters. People with sun-bleached hair and sun-baked skin walked barefoot on the beach, carrying fishing rods and pails. None of them looked as though they were worried about time, or meetings, or HMOs. She wasn't going to have much use for her suits; everything here was casual.

Seagulls flew overhead, calling in high-pitched squawks and plopping cigarette-sized droppings wherever they chose. Naomi looked up and the sun hit the tip of her nose, washed warmly over her face, and slid down her shoulders.

She didn't think she was ever going home.

The houses along the way that could, backed to the water; decks jutted out from their rears, over the bay. From a distance, they looked like stones planted in the green hillsides. The houses on the other side of the street faced the water, their window eyes wide open to the sun. Their exteriors were wind-washed shades of blue, brown, or white with white trim, and near most of the houses were small boats with paddles, or kayaks. Dog tails, ferns, and purple, yellow, and white wildflowers grew near the houses and on the beach, stretching their heads and arms toward the water.

When she stepped up on painted concrete blocks that formed the steps, she saw a girl sitting on the porch of the house on Lanyard Street. Seashells and starfish hung from the screen that wrapped around the porch.

The young woman's hair was the lightest brown and stringy; it may have been blonde when it was clean. One bare foot was on the bottom of the chair, while the other dangled over the rail of the metal fan-back chair. She wore two T-shirts: one yellow underneath, and one longer, blue, tie-dyed shirt on top. The girl, who looked to be in her early twenties, looked at Naomi as though she was sizing her up. In her lap was a bowl of cooked shrimp. As she peeled them, she dropped the shells into a bucket next to her and popped the shrimp into her mouth.

Normally the shrimp would have smelled, but here their aroma blended with the smells of the bay.

"Hey." She nodded her head toward the door behind her. "You movin' in?"

Naomi nodded and gave a noncommittal smile. "Yes." She didn't know if the girl was a burnout or a beach bum.

"Good." The girl popped a shrimp in her mouth. "This place will be good for you."

Naomi wasn't sure if she should be insulted. "Really?"

She smiled. "Yeah, it's cool." She pointed with her thumb. "I live upstairs."

Naomi looked at the note she held to check the address.

"You know what apartment?"

Naomi looked back at the girl. "First floor."

"That's what I thought," the girl said. Holding a shrimp in her hand, she pointed toward the front door. It was white with four rectangular panes of glass—two on top and two on the bottom. "Just push the door open. Look to your left and you'll see the mailboxes. Then you'll see a little table there with a metal box shaped like a treasure chest. When you lift the lid, inside you'll find keys for your place. You'll be able to tell from the little tag that hangs from the ring."

Naomi looked at her piece of paper again. "Is Mrs. Dovecheck here?"

The girl shook her head. "She's never here, man."

"Well, what do I do about my lease? About signing and doing an inspection?"

The girl tossed her hair out of her face and laughed. "I told you this place would be good for you. Just hang loose." She smiled. "Did you talk to Mrs. D?"

Naomi looked at the girl, at the door, at the piece of paper, and then back at the girl. The place had been one of the few that she could afford when she had looked in the paper. Maybe she was being too hasty.

She had called her realtor already in Baltimore and asked him to check into renting out her place. In the meantime, she'd tried to find someplace quickly so she wouldn't use up the money she had in hotel charges.

The girl was still peeling and popping shrimp, patiently waiting for her response.

"Yes. Yes, I spoke to Mrs. Dovecheck."

"Then everything's copacetic. Mrs. D wouldn't have let you have the place if she didn't get a good vibe from you. A good vibe will beat a piece of paper any day."

Copacetic? A good vibe? It might be smarter to back out of this before she got in too deep.

"It's gonna be okay," the girl said. "Just relax. Float, okay?" The girl wiped her shrimpy hand on her blue tank top. She stuck it out. "I'm Ruthie."

Naomi switched the note to the hand that held the handle of her suitcase, stepped closer, and shook Ruthie's hand. "Naomi." She would have to wash her hand right away.

"Well." She stepped back and then shifted from foot to foot. "I guess I should go inside."

"Yeah," Ruthie said. "Take a load off."

Naomi pushed open the door. The smell of cedar and pine oil rushed out to her. The air inside was as fresh as the air outside.

"Hey, Naomi?"

Naomi leaned her head back out of the door.

"Do you know Jesus?"

Naomi felt nervous and wondered why she always felt that way when people asked her. Maybe it was that she worried they would be fanatics, harass her with Bible tracts, or play the *I know Him better than you do* game. She avoided those people and even ran from them. It felt funny not to trust people who believed the same thing she did, but that's how it was. She spoke softly. "Yes, I do."

"Good," Ruthie said and nodded firmly. "'Cause He's a friend of mine."

Naomi's bedroom was nice enough. Actually, it was pleasant. She looked around. The walls were the palest peach color. The ceiling slanted to meet the wall behind her. There were two small bookcases stuffed with books, and on top of each bookcase there was an ivy plant that grew out of a ceramic pot. The leaves trailed almost to the floor. On the walls were framed pictures of the bay, sailboats, and fishermen. It felt like some place that could be home.

With her shoes off, she sat on the bed, her checkbook, cash, and credit cards spread in front of her. She wasn't broke, but she wasn't going to be dining at the Ritz either. Naomi poked at her checkbook as though touching it was going to change the balance.

She couldn't believe she was out of a job. Uncertainty was drifting in to replace the waves of relief she'd felt earlier.

Naomi sighed and looked out of the window. She was glad. She really was. Well, she was kind of glad. She loved dentistry, but she hated her job. No, she *had* hated her job. What she needed was time to rest and think about what she wanted to do. She needed time to dream.

Being fired was a blessing in disguise.

Maybe.

Naomi looked at the cash in front of her. On the other hand, people rarely got fed or paid for their dreams. And she had to eat.

She would have to pray that her place in Baltimore got rented soon. She had enough money in her checking account to pay her rent for four months in advance. If she was careful, there was also enough money to cover her utilities. Naomi pushed at the small pile of bills. She had blown a good portion of the cash she had just getting to Bodega Bay. There was no direct route—a plane, then a shuttle, then a cab, then a bus—it all had been money she hadn't planned to spend. Eating was another matter. The money from *Wheel of Fortune* was going to be a blessing—what was left after taxes—but that would be months from now. She wouldn't see the money until long after the show aired. In the meantime, she was going to have to learn to love soup and crackers and peanut butter. She frowned. And to drink more water—tap water—at least until she found a job.

Naomi walked to the window, unlocked it, and slid the wood frame up and open. The water-cleaned air rushed in the room. *I hope I'm not being stupid. I hope I haven't ruined my life. God, help me.*

She breathed deeply again. How could something that smelled so good be wrong?

When she stepped out onto the porch hours later, Ruthie was still there.

The girl was sitting out on the concrete steps, her face tilted into the sun. "I thought you might be coming down. I was gonna come up and get ya." She kept her eyes closed as she spoke. "You hungry?"

Naomi heard her stomach growl, but thought about the three dollars she had in her pocket. She'd put the rest away. She would budget herself and pinch off of her stash to make it last. "Sort of, but I'm just going to get something small. Maybe some crackers."

Ruthie tossed her stringy hair. Naomi noticed a tattoo on the girl's arm. It was a cross ringed with a crown.

The girl jumped to her feet and stretched. "There's no such thing as a little hungry when you breathe this air. That's for sure." She scooted her feet into a pair of orange flip-flops and pulled out a wedgie. "Come on, let's go. I'll show you around."

Naomi shifted from foot to foot. If she was going to be hungry, she wanted to do it alone. She didn't need someone else along to feel sorry for her or to ask a lot of questions. She didn't want to have to explain to anyone else why she was just getting crackers, especially some Jesus freak.

Jesus freak. Naomi hadn't heard the expression in a long time—not since the seventies. She looked at the girl—her hair, her clothes. It was the wrong decade and the wrong century, but that's what the girl looked like—an outdated hippie sporting a Jesus tattoo.

"I'm not that hungry and I really wouldn't be good company."

Ruthie turned to look at her. "It's cool, man." She smiled. "I won't bite ya. You don't know your way around. Be cool. We'll hang. It'll be all right." Ruthie nodded several times. "Hang loose, mama. It's California. Breathe deep."

It wasn't until Ruthie said it that Naomi realized she had stopped breathing. She looked at the girl again. What would Thelma, Latrice, and Mary say if they saw Ruthie? She looked like she could be stoned or homeless. She wasn't the kind of person they would be caught dead with—she looked more like someone they would talk about as they walked past her down the city streets.

"My goodness, Naomi, did you see that child? She looks like she's been thrown away."

"Grab your purse, girl! She's probably hopped up on something and looking for her next fix at your expense!"

"I know that's right. And look at her hair. She's probably got lice, or fleas, or something!"

But her girlfriends weren't here.

What was it going to hurt? Getting something to eat together didn't mean she and Ruthie were going to be friends. Besides, the girl obviously wasn't going to leave her alone. And the truth was, Ruthie was right—she didn't know where she was going. If she was going to eat, she probably needed some help. "Okay."

Ruthie climbed the rocky slope from their house to the main road as though she had on hiking boots. A navy blue backpack she had grabbed from a nail near the porch doorway bounced up and down as she walked.

Naomi looked at the bobbing knapsack. Why did the girl need to take such a big, empty bag with her? When they were in the store, she was going to keep her distance from Ruthie. The last thing she needed was to be in a strange town and have people think she was a shoplifter.

Ruthie stopped and looked back and stuck out her hand. Naomi grabbed it and let the girl help her the next few feet up the gravely slope.

"Man, am I glad you ditched those high heels." Ruthie waved her hand for Naomi to follow her down the road. "Come on."

It was a short walk, maybe half a mile, the way Ruthie cut between houses, around corners, and over worn footpaths. The people they encountered waved. *"How's it going, Ruthie?"* They smiled and nodded at Naomi. When they emerged from the last clump of trees, they stood before four whitewashed wooden buildings. The largest had a sign hanging over the large open doorway: The Wharf at the Tides. Next to it was a smaller grocery store with a glass window. Ruthie walked inside and Naomi followed.

There was a glass counter with pastries and loaves of bread. It called to Naomi—*fresh bread! fresh bread!* She knew she didn't have enough money to buy; she turned her head so she wouldn't be tempted. She walked toward a rack with individually wrapped snacks.

"Ruthie! How are you, honey? I was wondering when I might see you."

Naomi positioned herself so that she could see around the rack. There was a heavyset woman with gray hair speaking to Ruthie. She wore a white apron tied over a green flowered dress. She smiled and her eyes twinkled behind her glasses.

Ruthie tiptoed and reached over the counter to grasp the woman's hands. "Oh, you know me, Mona. Groovin' on Jesus!"

Groovin' on Jesus? Naomi shuddered. She pretended to study a package of cheese crackers. The Lord was probably shaking His head right now!

It's going to be okay. Naomi settled herself on the inside. She knew the way to the store, now. She could come by herself from now on. And here was a rack of cheap snacks. She could make it until times got better. The girl was not her friend or her problem. There was no point in getting worked up about her.

Mona giggled, and Naomi peeked around the tiny bags of potato chips to watch. Mona put a hand to her mouth, and then began to snort and heave as though laughter was forcing its way in spurts from inside her shaking belly out through her mouth and nose. "Well, I expect if you're going to groove on something, Jesus is the one to groove on!" Mona spurted some more. "Groovin' on Jesus. You're a stitch, Ruthie!" After a few more snorts, Mona wiped her eyes. "Well, I see you got your backpack. I got a few things for you, if you like?"

Ruthie waved her hands in the air like *hallelujah!* and then lowered them and unzipped her sack. "You know me, Mona. I never turn down a blessing!"

Mona disappeared into a back room and then returned with several loaves of bread and what looked like a pound cake. "These were left over from yesterday. I had some the day before, and a nice pie, which I had to throw out. But these were so nice, I hoped you'd be coming by today."

Ruthie accepted the baked goods and tucked them into her backpack as though they were fragile, precious treasure. "We are going to feast tonight!" She touched the wrappers. "We'll probably have to freeze some of it." She smiled love and appreciation to Mona, who smiled it back at her. Then

Ruthie looked toward the rack where Naomi was still trying to hide. "I haven't even introduced you to my new friend."

The introduction happened too quickly and unexpectedly for Naomi to react.

Mona's smile included her. "I was wondering if she was with you." She walked from behind the counter. "Mona Springarden." She held her arms open wide.

My new friend? Naomi looked at Ruthie who was smiling at her as though she was her newborn baby, and then she looked at the other woman. Naomi replaced the package of crackers she held and walked toward Mona. Her smile seemed to shine from inside and she smelled like cinnamon, vanilla, and warm bread. Naomi wanted to stick out her hand to shake instead of hugging. But how did you refuse a hug from a woman who had just given you bread and saved you from a night of crumbled crackers?

"Her name's Naomi," Ruthie inserted.

Mona squeezed Naomi with one circling arm and tilted her chin up with the other. "Welcome to Bodega Bay, Naomi. Welcome."

Trying to look interested, but not overwhelmed or hungry—trying to look like a professional on vacation—Naomi looked briefly in the bag. The sweet vanilla smell of the pound cake made her mouth water. "Very nice," she said, not knowing what else to say.

"Groovin' with Jesus," Mona repeated, shaking her head and laughing as they walked out the door.

Naomi walked behind, not sure how she felt about the bread and the cake. Her stomach growled—her belly seemed pretty certain—maybe it was just her head and heart that were having the problem. She followed as Ruthie walked over the planked walkway to The Marina and inside the large open doorway.

Groovin' with Jesus? If she wasn't careful, people were going to think she was a Jesus freak by association.

Men inside the wharf—a fish and seafood warehouse— packed ice around fish and assisted customers. The smell of the bay mingled with the brine in the air. Through large windows, she could see out to the water and boats tied to the dock.

"Hey, Ruthie!" one of the men yelled. "So how'd you like the shrimp?" He wore a flowered, well-worn, short-sleeved shirt with a nametag that said Bob. His arms were hairy, deeply tanned, and heavily muscled. His belly was slightly rounded, he was balding on top, and there was gray at his temples.

Ruthie grinned. "Primo, Bob!" She tossed her hair. "Those shrimp were righteous, dude!"

Bob nodded and smiled. "That's what I thought." Nodding at Naomi, he waved for them to follow. He pointed into some ice bins. "You in the mood for some lobster?" He looked over his glasses at Ruthie.

"Sure," she said. She tapped the backpack. "We already got some nice bread. A little lobster would set it off. We'll be munchin' like royalty." Ruthie dropped the bag off her shoulder. "By the way, Bob, I want you to meet my new friend Naomi."

Bob shifted his clipboard to his left hand and reached out to shake. "So, you're visiting us here in Bodega Bay?"

My new friend. Again? Naomi squared her shoulders and extended her hand. She made certain that she spoke each word clearly and looked Bob in the eye. "I just moved here." Naomi waited for Bob to ask her the three-million-dollar question—why? She didn't know why people asked, as though they expected that she would pour out her deep dark secrets to them, tell them why she had left her job and Baltimore to move to Bodega Bay—just because they asked.

Instead, Bob stuck out his neck like a turtle and grinned. "Cool," he said, as though it were the most natural thing in the world, as though people quit—or got fired from—their jobs everyday and moved to Bodega Bay. "It's a righteously sweet place."

He looked back at Ruthie. "You got time?" He walked over to a side of the cavernous room where young men wearing rubber gloves dug through metal bins full of ice.

Naomi followed behind Ruthie, who had picked up the backpack and walked to join Bob.

He dug in a nearby wooden crate and pulled out a pair of bright green, thick rubber gloves, which he tossed to Ruthie. "If you do, I got some choice claws you can have. You'll have to work to dig them out, but whatever you find is yours." He smiled. "And there might be two or three big lobsters in there. You know folks won't buy 'em if they're missing a claw or if one claw's bigger than the other." Bob, mimicking the younger men who worked near them, bent over and with his bare hand began to dig through the nearest bin of ice. He snatched out a large lobster, waving one large banded claw, its tail moving back and forth. "See? Like this one." He pointed with the hand that held the clipboard. "Lots of choice meat, but missing one claw." He dropped the lobster back on top of the ice. "If you can find 'em, you can have 'em."

Naomi looked at the lobster and thought back on many candlelit seafood dinners she and her girlfriends had eaten at Phillips Restaurant in Baltimore. *Expensive* candlelit dinners.

She could imagine the four of them sitting at a table, laughing, and drowning a steamed, seasoned tail in drawn butter. She touched a finger to the side of her mouth to make sure she wasn't drooling.

The sound of Ruthie snapping on the large rubber gloves that swallowed her small hands reminded Naomi that she wasn't in Baltimore, but in Bodega Bay in an open warehouse surrounded by fishermen. Bob had walked away and now stood with a group of them near the open front doorway.

Hunching her shoulders, Ruthie motioned for Naomi to take the backpack. "Oh, man!" She lifted the first lobster and dropped it into a large, red plastic pail. Holding her green-gloved hands in the air, the girl bent over and stared at the ice as though she was deciding where to make the first incision.

Ruthie plunged both hands into the ice and hooted as she pulled out a large loose claw and another lobster with mismatched claws. She scraped through the ice as if she were digging for gold, and each time she found a piece of treasure she hooted, "Thank you, Jesus!" After she had dug out several handfuls of seafood booty and the pail began to fill, she called over her shoulder. "Hey, Bob?"

As he approached, Ruthie held up a lobster and two loose claws. "Some of these—quite a few of these—look like matches. Like the claws just fell off or somethin'."

Bob winked. "Well, who could tell something like that, Sherlock Holmes?" He rested the clipboard on his hip. "Nothin' I can do about it now. You just go ahead and take what you want."

He smiled at Naomi as he walked past her to rejoin the group of fishermen standing by the door.

When the pail was full and Ruthie had covered the lobsters with ice and put the bucket lid in place, she peeled off the gloves. "We got more than enough for tonight—probably enough for tomorrow and the next day."

Naomi wanted to say, "No, thank you. A little bread will be enough for me." But the rumbling from her stomach and her watering mouth quieted her tongue.

Ruthie took the backpack from Naomi and slung it over her shoulder, lifted the bucket of lobster, waved to the grinning Bob, and headed out the door. Naomi followed, feeling the dollar bills that were still in her pocket.

They went back the way they had come, Ruthie's now full backpack and the bucket bouncing and swinging as she walked. When they reached the porch, Ruthie continued up the steps, through the front door, then up the stairs to her apartment.

Naomi hesitated and then followed. She watched as Ruthie unpacked the shoulder pack, gently patting each loaf of bread as she removed it. "Thank you, Jesus!" she whispered each time, and Naomi felt the same discomfort she had felt earlier. *"Jesus is a friend of mine!"*

Of course Ruthie was grateful, but she didn't have to go out of her way about it. Naomi looked at her digging in the bag and thought about the young men digging in the bins at The Marina. She was sure they had been embarrassed by the young woman's behavior. *"Thank you, Jesus!"* Ruthie didn't have to make other people uncomfortable or be crazy about it. It wasn't right. And the truth was, even in private it was still embarrassing.

Ruthie reached in a cabinet and produced a large silver-colored stockpot. She filled it with water and placed it on the stove to heat.

Naomi watched and listened as Ruthie whooped and

danced as though she were Rumplestiltskin. She felt the money in her pocket. Maybe she should find her way back to the store and buy the crackers. She cleared her throat to get Ruthie's attention and then pointed. "Don't you feel funny about all this?"

"About what?" Ruthie opened the bucket and began to remove the lobsters and claws from the pail, rinsing them under running water.

Naomi pointed at the bread, the cake, and the seafood. "All this. We didn't work for it. Don't you feel funny? It's like begging."

Ruthie laughed. "Man! You got to loosen up! It's gleanin'. Like in the Bible." She nodded. "God's righteous, man. He's always givin' us stuff we don't deserve. Be cool. We're just acceptin' the gifts the Big Man puts on the table."

Naomi squeezed the money in her hand. "I don't know. . . ." *The Big Man?*

" 'Sides, I gotta trust God, man—I got no choice." Ruthie shook her head and kept working, adding seasoning to the pot. "You got a job?"

It was none of the girl's business. She didn't have to explain to her what had happened. It was private. Naomi shook her head. She didn't have a job now, but she would have one soon. She wasn't a burnout.

Ruthie shrugged. "Me neither, man. I was a hop-head until Jesus stepped up to me, man. I'm clean now."

Naomi tried not to react. She had hoped that what she believed wasn't true.

"But, so far, no job. People around here still remember and some of 'em—mostly the ones with jobs—" she laughed—"they don't want me to forget." She looked in the pot to check for boiling. "I work at a community volunteer center, but it don't pay. So, He keeps takin' care of me. Now, you got no job and He's takin' care of you. I'm lettin' God take care of me. It's gleanin', man."

When the water began to boil, Ruthie dropped several claws into the steaming pot. Ruthie smiled and tilted her head. "You sure you know Jesus? It seems like you got a lot to learn."

Naomi wasn't sure what to say to the strange-looking girl. Should she be offended? She had been in church all her life. Of course, she knew Jesus. It didn't make any sense to listen to the girl anyway. Ruthie was an admitted drug addict, for goodness' sakes. Should she just put off the comment to the girl's weirdness? What she really should be doing was getting her unemployed self out of the crazy girl's apartment and downstairs to her own.

"No offense meant, man." Ruthie dropped a lobster into the steaming water. "I'm just thinkin' you're like most people. You say you believe but you don't trust Him to do nothin' or show up in your life, man. You don't expect Him to do any-thing." She pointed at the pot and at the bread. "All this is is me expectin' and lettin' God show up."

"We're supposed to take care of ourselves. We're supposed to be independent and not rely on anyone else."

"Look, you don't have to eat it if you don't want it. All I know is, if I get hungry, God feeds me. If I get sick, He makes me well." Ruthie stopped stirring and smiled. "You know the coolest thing? It's actually kind of weird and kind of deep, man." She nodded her head full of stringy hair. "When things get bad, I'm kinda learnin' to start sayin' hal-lelujah! You know, to kind of see it as a blessing?"

Naomi stared. How could not having enough money to buy food or pay rent be a blessing? What it was, she thought, was trouble, trouble that made for knots in the stomach and sleepless nights. It was all like walking on a tightrope. How could you celebrate being without?

Ruthie kept on talking, not seeming to mind that Naomi wasn't answering. "'Cause only people in trouble get to know that God really will come to your rescue." She turned completely to face Naomi. "I was thinking that people who have always been rich never get to know the feelin' of trustin' that God will provide." Ruthie hunched her shoulders. "Anyway, it's way too deep. It may just be a flashback from an old trip." The girl laughed and turned away, and using a long-handled fork, went back to stirring the pot.

When she finished poking in the pot, Ruthie laid the fork on the counter and went to the window. The afternoon sun played across the bridge of her nose. "Man, it's so cool to smell the air and feel the sun. And just think, it's all free! God don't charge nothin' for it. I missed it all before . . . I was so stoned."

She used her hand to brush her hair out of her face. "I was trying to check out of life. I almost succeeded, man. Then Jesus got right up in my face." Ruthie closed her eyes. She held her hand up to demonstrate. "He got right up in my face. That's the only way to change things—you got to let the Lord get right up in your face."

Naomi looked at the girl, then out the window to the beach, and wondered how she'd come to such a strange situation in such a short time.

NINE

San Francisco, California

Desiree was a beautiful woman. Her skin was like dark copper, and Anthony loved to play with her soft, short, black curls. He couldn't wait for her to get home. He wanted to hold her and let her know it would be okay.

Anthony had ripped off his jacket, his suit pants, his tie, and his shirt as soon as he walked through the door. He still hadn't told her. He had hoped to have another job first.

Now as he sliced onions and tossed the pieces into the thin coat of extra virgin olive oil sizzling in the copper-bottomed skillet, he nodded. Maybe this wasn't such a bad thing after all. He never had time, before, to cook for her. Now, instead of grabbing something or ordering in, he could take the time and make her the kind of meal she deserved. He picked up the stainless steel bowl and began to lift pieces of raw chicken from it and to dust each piece in the seasoned flour he had prepared. Then he dropped them one by one into the skillet with the onions.

He breathed deeply and looked around him. The island at which he cooked was covered with marble, pots and pans hung from a rack in the ceiling, and the dishwasher swooshed comfortingly in the background. He was going to have to tell her tonight, but it was no big deal. He was okay. Everything was going to be all right. They weren't hurting. Not by a long shot. He had money. Not to mention that he'd be getting something from unemployment—if he bothered to sign up for it. It wasn't like he'd be out of a job that much longer. He had lots of prospects. Lots of people had tried to hire him away from the firm over the years.

Besides, Desiree had a great job. And she was a supportive woman. She had hung in there with him over the years. She was smart. She was beautiful. She was sexy. This was just one more little bump in the road. They'd get over this one and wouldn't even feel it.

He wiped his hands on the dish towel, picked up the remote, and changed the CD to Kenny G. Desiree always liked that. It would put her in the mood. Music, good food—she'd be purring.

Using a two-pronged fork, he turned the chicken to brown on the other side. Then he sliced celery and carrots and sprinkled the pieces over the frying meat. Anthony reached for the opened bottle of burgundy and waved it under his nose. He lifted it to his lips, then laughed. He hadn't sunk that far; he wasn't drinking out of the bottle yet. He poured some of the deep red wine into a glass, and then poured it over the chicken. He poured a half glass, took a sip, and nodded again. He looked over at the rice steaming in the automatic cooker on the counter. Chicken with wine sauce; Desiree would love it. It was all going to be okay.

He watched from the window until he saw her park the Mercedes, then he opened the door and leaned against the jam. When she was close enough to see, he gave her the look. She stopped on the sidewalk, lightweight trench coat over her arm—you could never be certain what the weather was going to do in San Francisco—and briefcase in her hand. Desiree shifted her weight to one hip and laughed the laugh that still made him want to buy her things. "Will you give me a chance to get in the house, man? Can you at least do that much for me? Please? I know you're the king, but could you let the queen sit down for a second before you start making your needs known?"

Anthony knew she would make him laugh. He turned sideways and swept his arm in an arc to usher her inside. "Welcome home, milady."

She gave him a peck as she brushed past him. Her perfume was light but spicy, and he realized he had not prepared dessert. Maybe it was Freudian.

"I am so hungry!" Desiree headed straight for the kitchen. "What's going on?" She whirled around and her smile was like diamonds. Her eyes sparkled. "What are you up to, Anthony? What are you doing home so early?" She dropped her coat and briefcase, stepped to him, and began to tickle him. "What are you up to, boy?"

Anthony laughed. He probably laughed too hard, but he needed it, so he gave in and doubled over. He didn't answer, he only laughed.

She had changed and showered before they sat down to dinner. Now in the emerald green gown that he loved, Desiree looked like everything he wanted. The candlelight warmed the tones in her skin and danced in her eyes.

"So, Mr. Anthony Carillon, what is this all about? Why did you take off early?" She pulled at his hand. "What have you got up your sleeve, mister? I know something is up."

Maybe he shouldn't tell her now. Maybe morning would be better. He didn't want her to worry. He didn't want her to be concerned about him. It might be wiser to wait until morning, or until he had another job—it would only be a few more days.

How would he explain things? He'd managed to keep it from her, so far—rising early, coming home at his usual time. When he didn't get up in the morning, it would cause confusion. Of course, he could continue getting up in the morning. He could shower and put on his suit as if he were going to work. Looking for a job was going to work, wasn't it?

It was better to tell her. He would tell her. She would be hurt if he didn't tell her, if he didn't give her a chance to support him, to let him lean on her. He would tell her now. "You look really beautiful tonight, Desiree. You always do. . . ." He reached to touch the curve of her ear with his finger. "But especially tonight."

She giggled and did a little impatient dance in her chair. "Boy, if you don't stop playing with me and tell me, I'm going to hurt you."

He smiled. If he gave it to her in a light way, she would know it was okay. He broadened his smile. "I'm going to be around home more for the next few days. I'm going to do some things I've wanted to do for you. Like cooking for you, drawing your bath water."

"I like that, Anthony. That sounds real good."

"I thought you'd like that."

She giggled again and tilted her head. "So, how are you going to have all this extra time? What are you planning? You have some special project going on?" Desiree sipped her wine. She held out her left hand, staring at her fingers as she wiggled them.

Anthony leaned forward. "You're my special project."

She looked deeply into his eyes. "Will you just spit it out,

Anthony?" She smiled and blushed. "You know I'm impatient. Tell me! I'm tired of you making me wait." Desiree wiggled her fingers, especially her ring finger, again.

He nodded and smiled. "They let me go. So, I'll be around here to do more until I find something else."

Desiree sat back and pursed her lips. "Right, Anthony. Right. Will you stop playing around? I have to go to bed." She lifted his hand. "*We* have to go to bed. Will you just tell me?"

"That was it, Desiree. They let me go. I cleaned out my desk. You know, they gave the usual excuse—reorganization, but here I am. That's it." He shrugged and made himself smile. He reached and squeezed her hand. "We'll be okay."

Desiree sat perfectly still. She stared at him as though she were waiting for the punch line of a joke that she, so far, wasn't finding funny. "That's it? You're for real?"

"I know you're shocked. I was too. But I've been thinking that maybe it wasn't such a bad thing—"

She pulled her hand from his, rose, and carried her plate to the sink. She raked what was left on the plate down the garbage disposal. There was a muffled clack and clink when she set her plate on the counter. She clenched and unclenched her left hand. "So that was it? That was really what all this was about?"

He hated when she did that. His stomach always knotted when she asked him a question that didn't have a good answer, when no answer would win. "I wanted to fix you dinner. I just . . ."

She rinsed her hands under the faucet and wiped them on the towel. "Well, I think I need to go to bed. I need to get started early in the morning."

He began to clear the table. "Yeah, I guess you're right.

We probably should go to bed now and get an early start." She would feel better after he held her. Of course she was shocked; he was still shocked. "I'll just put these things away and be on."

Desiree headed toward the bedroom. She didn't look at him. "Don't rush. I'll fall asleep more quickly by myself."

When he'd put everything away and watched all the late night television he could stand, Anthony turned out the lights and walked quietly to the bedroom. It was not what he had expected. He had imagined her arms around him, not her being withdrawn. But, really, he should have. Desiree needed time to process what was happening. It happened to him and he had had a while now to take it in, to think about it. It wouldn't take long before she actually was seeing what had happened as good news, before she was encouraging him. In the meantime, he needed to respect her feelings. If she needed space, even physical space, he would give it to her.

He tossed his clothes into the closet, careful not to kick his guitar case tucked to the side. He slid quietly into bed. The sheets were cool and smooth. The bed was large enough that he could avoid touching her, and if he was careful, he wouldn't wake her. As soon as he was under the covers, Desiree rolled until her arm was around him.

"Desiree, I—"

"Don't talk, Anthony."

She was everything he wanted. Soon, the memory of the afternoon he was fired surrendered to Desiree's arms around him, the smell of her, the warmth of her. Like he had known, everything was going to be okay.

They were a team. They had been together a long time. She stuck with him before he could afford the house, the marble, and the Mercedes.

He looked at her face. Her eyes were closed and her breathing said that she would soon be asleep. He had made her wait too long. *"Let's get married, Anthony!" "Are you ever going to marry me, Anthony?"*

He thought of Moor's wedding invitation still in his coat pocket. If he was ever going to marry anyone, shouldn't it be the woman that held him when he had lost everything? Shouldn't it be Desiree? Why shouldn't it be now?

"Desiree, let's do it. Let's get married now."

She was quiet.

"We can go to the courthouse, or we can throw something together. We could get married here with just a few of our friends."

"This is not the time to talk about that now. We have to go—I have to go to sleep. I have to go to work in the morning." Desiree pushed away from him, turned on her side, and soon began to snore.

Anthony looked out the front window. He had been looking for work for four weeks now. *"Don't get discouraged, sir. It takes time. Employment is pretty sluggish now."* That's what the man at the unemployment office had told him. Of course, he *had* a job—it might be a crappy job, but it was still a job. It was easy to be casual when you were the one with the job.

And everything was different now. Everyone wanted résumés sent over the Internet. Not that he was surprised; that's how the firm where he'd worked wanted them. But he never thought *he* would be the person sending one. He thought all that was over.

But it would work out. He was okay. Mostly he was okay.

There were other days when it all seemed like a strange dream.

The phone rang. Anthony checked the caller I.D. It was Desiree calling from her office. "Hello, baby. Man, I wish you were here with—"

"Anthony, I don't think this is going to work out."

"Sure it will, Desiree. I feel like that sometimes—like a job's never going to come. But it's going to be okay. I'm going to be okay. Long as I got you.

"Something will break for us. I've got some feelers out. The job market's sluggish right now."

Her voice sounded strange. The giggle was missing. "I don't believe in a man not working. If I'm working, everybody in the house has to work. If you don't work, you don't eat."

He didn't know what to say. He wasn't even sure he was actually hearing her correctly. "Right. Right. We both believe in that."

She paused. "That's what I know. So, I know you'll understand. This is really hard for me, but you're going to have to go. It's not personal."

Anthony rubbed his eyes and looked out the window. Their street was really quiet in the daytime. He hadn't realized that when he was working all day long. There was so much you missed if you didn't take time, make time.

"Did you hear me, Anthony? I don't want to be nasty about this. I don't want to make a scene." There was no honey in her tone, just salt.

He picked up the newspaper lying on the table next to him. He probably should go through the listings again. It was easy to miss things; usually the best nuggets were hidden away and easy to miss. He would pay for a lead. He would go to a headhunter. He would list himself on résumé search sites.

"Don't make this hard, Anthony. Don't try to play hardball. I already talked to a lawyer. You might have made the down payment and the townhouse might be in your name, but we've been living together for a while now and I've paid my share. It's community property, and I have the right to ask you to leave."

"I'm not trying to make it hard, Desiree. I—"

"I've been patient with you, Anthony. But you're in some really weird place, and I have to get on with my life."

This was not real. It was some reality show; it had to be. Anthony looked around the room. There must be cameras planted everywhere—in his old office, in the living room. This was all a joke. There must be microphones so people could listen in on his telephone calls. This couldn't be happening. He couldn't have lost his job, and he couldn't have now lost his girl.

He laughed. "Stop playing, Desiree."

She wasn't laughing. "I'm not playing, Anthony . . ." She paused. "Not at all. I want you out by the time I get home. I don't mean to be mean about this. I hoped it wouldn't come to this. But I've got to think about myself. I can't go down with you. I've got to think about myself."

"Desiree, we can talk about this. Tonight. When you get home. I can make a nice dinner—"

"No, we can't talk about it."

He imagined how pretty she was as she was speaking—her curly hair, her copper skin.

"I want you gone when I get home, Anthony."

"I thought we were getting married, Desiree. How can you do this?" He sounded like he was begging. "You've wanted me to ask you to marry me. Is that what this is about? If it is, marry me, Desiree. I love you." He *was* begging, trying to hold on to the last thing in his life that made any sense.

"Look, we had some good times. But I didn't sign up for a house husband. Don't make this difficult for me, Anthony. I tried to be patient. I've given you enough time. You know I've been patient. I have to think about myself. Don't make this difficult for me. I want you out before I get home. I don't want this to be messy. I don't want to have to get the police involved."

Of course she didn't want to get the police involved. She just wanted to use them to hang over his head, to threaten him.

It wasn't a reality show; it was real life in all its whacked-out splendor. Desiree was putting him out.

TEN

I 'm okay. I'll be okay.

Anthony sat in the Dew Drop In Diner just off of U.S. Highway 101. Turning a few corners, and up a few side streets, he had left behind the rushing Pacific waters, sandy beaches, and rocky cliffs. Now he was seated by the window and could look out at his 1992 Malibu. The old car, which he only kept to run errands too messy for the Mercedes, looked as if it had been neglected. There was an inch of dust and dirt coating it—it was hard to tell for sure that it was blue. But it was too old and dented to drive with any dignity through a car wash.

The car was stuffed with his clothes, a small TV that had been stored in the garage, and lots of other things they never thought they'd use . . . or, well, things he never thought he'd use again.

His guitar case was in the booth seat across from him. He'd placed it in the front seat of the car with him before he pulled away from the townhouse. Anthony couldn't remember the last time he'd played it, but now the old Fender was his traveling companion. As long as he didn't start talking to it, he guessed he was okay. But he hadn't been able to resist bringing it into the restaurant.

Now here he was hiding out. He had to eat. He felt hungry, and it was the one step he knew how to take. The rest of his life was upside down. So, he found a place, but it was a place that would provide him some cover—a place where no one from his old life, the life that ended that morning, would see him.

"Man, Anthony is just finished, man."

"I know. What do you think he did wrong? He had the world on a string. He must have done something wrong."

He would be okay; he just didn't need to see any of those people. He didn't need anyone feeling sorry for him.

"He lost his job and his woman?"

"His whole life just fell apart!"

He was just down on his luck. The truth was, this actually might be the best thing that had ever happened to him.

Anthony stared at the menu. All the words ran together. Breakfastlunchdinnerhambaconsausagesteaksandwichesfriessaladsoupsicrecreamcakepiepudding. He looked away. The real truth was, it felt like his life was over and like he had been betrayed. He had been a good person. He hadn't hurt anybody. He wasn't greedy. He didn't cheat. He'd done everything right that he knew to do.

He laid his head in his hand, then dropped his hand and sat upright when he thought about how he looked—like some kind of hopeless loser. Anthony pulled his cell phone from the pocket of his jeans. He would call Desiree, just to let her know he was cleared out and that he was okay. She would want to know *that*—that he was okay. He didn't want her to worry. He began to press her numbers into the tiny phone. He stopped.

Desiree wouldn't want to hear from him. She'd made that clear. He couldn't pretend that he hadn't heard the coolness in her voice over the phone that morning. Maybe they could talk later, after he'd gotten himself together. But, right now . . .

The waitress cleared her throat, and Anthony lifted his head. He wasn't sure how long she had been standing there. She looked really young, as though she should be in school copying homework assignments instead of taking orders. Neither did she seem to be enjoying her job. She stood with her weight on one hip, her feet pointing in almost opposite directions, and there was a cynical smirk on her face.

"Are you gonna be eatin' anything today? Or you just takin' a breather?"

Of course he was going to be eating. Who would take a breather in a dive like this? He wasn't going to be taking up booth space. Without looking at the menu or even asking his taste buds, Anthony ordered. "I'll have bacon, eggs, and wheat toast with butter."

"We don't have wheat toast." The girl's smirk deepened as though she'd gotten a personal point for stumping the dummy. As though he should have known that this wasn't the kind of place that had wheat toast, for pete's sake.

"Okay, white toast, then." He tried not to feel like he'd missed an easy question on an exam. He should have known.

"Right. It'll be a few." The waitress took his menu, looked as though she was not impressed with his order, and spoke as she turned to walk away. "You havin' coffee?"

Anthony opened his mouth to say, *no, thank you.* He stopped. He deserved it. He didn't have to eat right, to follow the rules today. He deserved some strong coffee—not designer coffee—and some white buttered toast, something to make him feel better. "Sure, make it black. It's strong, right?"

"Yeah, it's strong. The army comes in here regular to buy barrels of it to pour out on our enemies. Whatever's left over, we make sure we dump at a chemical waste site out back." A couple of old guys at the counter, who looked like plaid shirt-wearing regulars, laughed at the girl's wisecrack. Her face stayed the same as she moved around behind the counter.

She wasn't polite. Anthony looked around the room. She didn't have to be. The floor wasn't clean. It was hot and the air quality was poor. No one was complaining. No one was going to complain. This was their lot in life. This was what they deserved. No one was going to make a stink about it.

It was the same with bus stations and airports; it was something he had noticed traveling when he was in college.

Most times, people flying and riding buses paid pretty much the same fares, but bathrooms in airports never stank. Flying customers would complain; they wouldn't tolerate a foul smell. Kids in bus stations climbed all over the seats, leaving trails of Cheerios and crumbs. But in airports, the waiting areas were cleaned regularly; airport passengers wouldn't accept filth. The air in airports was always cool, airline customers would groan about being too hot or the air being too stuffy.

Bus station patrons accepted whatever they found, whatever discomfort they encountered, as though it was their lot in life. No matter how dirty, no matter how funky, bus riders wore whatever the situation presented, almost as though the poor service was what they deserved. Gashed and ripped seats, floors so filthy the crud looked like linoleum patterns, cafeteria food that looked like roaches practiced gymnastics in it—it was their filthy payment due for not having done better in life. *Look, Mac, take it like it comes!*

Squalor was what the bus riders deserved, and poor service was what he and his fellow diners deserved for coming to the Dew Drop In Diner. Who was he to buck the system?

Anthony looked across the booth at his guitar case. He hadn't opened it in years. His Fender was red and, when he had been younger, what he had intended for his life was that he would play his guitar for a living.

His hair, in his fantasies, was long—sometimes in dreads, sometimes braids. He wore bright colors. When he stepped to the microphone—because he also sang backup in his fantasies—the lights that backlit him were red, blue, yellow, and green. The music was loud and he was sweating. But when the moment was right, he sang and shouted, "Higher!" In his dreams, he always played rhythm guitar for Sly and the Family Stone. Sly, his brother and sister, Cynthia the trumpet player, and Larry the bass player all had Afros and wore bell-bottom pants. But Anthony's hair was always hanging down.

None of that ever happened. It was just a childish fantasy, and like all childish fantasies, he had buried it in a dark corner of his closet. Yet, he couldn't bear to give it away, and sometimes he pushed the clothes back to look at it and make sure it was still there.

Instead, he had gone to college. A corporation had recruited him after graduation. Then, after working there for a while, the firm had offered him greater opportunities and more money. Long hair was something he'd never experienced. Instead, he wore the corporate hair cut, the corporate suit, the corporate shoes.

But, not any more. At least not until he got another job; until then, he could wear jeans and sit or hide out in some place like the Dew Drop In Diner. Until things got better, he would have to take life and his food as it came. Until things got better. But before he got a job, he needed to think about where he was going to live, and before that, where he was going to go.

Anthony looked at his hands and realized he didn't have any friends. There was no one to tell, besides Desiree, that he was leaving.

"You are my only friend here." Moor's words came back to him. Anthony began to press Moor's number into his cell phone. He should at least check on the guy, make sure everything was all right with him at work—and he needed to beg off from the wedding. The last thing in the world he wanted to be now was somebody's best man.

Anthony listened to the phone ringing. Without him there, Moor might be feeling a little lost—San Francisco and the firm were definitely not Africa. The phone continued ringing. It would only be right to let Moor know where to reach him.

Moor's deep voice, heavy with his Lesotho accent, first announced the name of the firm, then, "Hello. May I help you?" The *help*, lost its *l* and sounded like *hep*, but his voice sounded trustworthy and sincere.

Despite the T-shirt he wore and the fact that he was sitting in the Dew Drop In Diner, Anthony made his voice sound like he was wearing a three-piece suit and sitting in a plush office. "It's Anthony Carillon. How are you, Moor?"

"It is good to hear from you, my friend. How are you?" Moor sounded honestly pleased to hear from him. "Are you working already?"

The waitress appeared at the table, holding the plate, silverware rolled in a napkin, and a thick white ceramic cup with coffee spilling over the rim. "Here's your stuff."

Anthony looked at her and nodded to her, but kept talking to Moor. "No, I decided not to rush into anything. You know, to give myself some time to explore my options." He cleared his throat. "Just taking some time to be myself, again." He could still crack himself up, even if he was depressed.

The waitress smirked harder and raised an eyebrow. "You want some jelly?"

Anthony shook his head, hoping she would go away, and that Moor wouldn't hear her.

"Suit yourself," she said. "Just yell or give a nod if you need somethin' else." She pulled out her tablet of checks, ripped his off, and put it on the table. "Pay at the register when you're done."

Anthony nodded again, met her eyes, then quickly looked back at his plate. "And I thought I would take a little time to rest, to do something I've wanted to do."

"I've been praying to God for you."

What was he supposed to say to that? If Moor was praying, from the looks of things, the guy's prayers weren't working. "Thanks. But you don't have to worry about me. I'm okay."

"You are my friend and my best man. I'm praying for you."

Anthony laughed. It was the first time he'd laughed in a few weeks. "Well, okay then. I won't try to stop you. But, thanks anyway." He picked up his fork with his free hand. "I wasn't calling about me. I'm leaving the area—thought I'd take a little ride up the Pacific Coast Highway and let my hair down." He wasn't sure why he'd said that. "I didn't want to leave without checking on you and giving you a number where you can reach me in case you need help."

"You are going away?" Moor sounded surprised.

"Just for a while. I might as well take advantage of the

time off, right? No point in just hanging around the house."
He laughed as though he believed the story he was telling.
"No big deal, though. I'm fine."

Moor was quiet on the other end.

"Just taking some time." Anthony forked his eggs. "Hey,
and don't worry about the wedding. I'll be there." He didn't
know why he said that either. He would call back later to beg
off.

"What will you do? Where will you go?"

"I don't really know. All of this has taken me by surprise.
You know? I keep feeling like I've dropped something along
the way in my life, and that I need to go back and pick it
up." His words surprised him. Why was he saying these
things to Moor? He was supposed to be reassuring the
younger man. "I've been looking for jobs. I really don't know
what to do with myself."

"God's hand and His eyes are on you."

"Yeah."

"Are you certain that you are okay?"

"Yeah. Sure. I've got money." He did have plenty of
money. If he were careful, it would last a long while. "Everything's fine. Just need to find myself."

"Then you are right, my brother, my friend, to go back
to the road you have traveled. Maybe you will find what
you've lost. Don't worry. God has more for you."

Anthony set down his fork, lifted his coffee to drink, and
then set it back on the table. "Hey! Don't worry about me."
He gave Moor his cell phone number. "Call anytime. If you
need to talk or need some help with something at work, feel
free to call." He looked across the table at his guitar case.
"Who knows? Maybe I will head up the road and see if I can
find Sly Stone."

"Eh?" Anthony could imagine the puzzled look on Moor's face and could imagine the younger man scratching his head. "*Si fahamu*—I don't understand."

"Sly Stone. He was the leader of a band in the sixties and seventies and. . . ." It was too much to try to explain over the phone.

ELEVEN

Jacks Creek, North Carolina

Meemaw sat in her favorite padded wooden chair, her lap covered with a cloud of cream-colored taffeta. She pushed her glasses up on her nose to peer intermittently through them at the needle and string of beads she held and then over the spectacles at Monique, Destiny's mother, all grown up. The young woman's wild, curly auburn—sometimes copper—hair flowed around her, even covering part of the book she read. It was the same beautiful hair, but Monique was no longer the young girl who drifted sadly and quietly down the streets of Jacks Creek. She was no longer the subject of gossip. Instead, as a young mother, college student, and friend, Monique and her daughter brightened Meemaw's home.

She looked from Monique back to the dress in her lap. The beads she was attaching were tiny, round, and pearl-like, except that each one had the faintest pastel tint. Some had a turquoise tint, while others were golden, or the palest pink. Meemaw sighed and then chuckled at herself. No one had forced her to do this. Mary, the bride, was satisfied with the wedding gown as it was. Mary was right, it was beautiful as it was, but in her mind, Meemaw kept seeing it with a little something extra. Just a little touch of beadwork would make the gown more than beautiful; it would be breathtaking. But at this rate, the only workout she was going to have for a while was bending her sewing arm. She chuckled again.

Applying the beads was tough for anybody, especially someone who had seen the better side of seventy. But that wasn't good enough. No, she had to take it to the extremes. She had to get *tiny* beads, beads of different tints, so she had to carefully place each bead, so she had to be careful to place each color just so.

When she was in the Sew Shop, her granddaughter Garvin had tried to warn her.

"Meemaw, do you really want to do this?"

"I think it will look nice, Garvina." Her granddaughter, even after all the settling and growing she had done—after coming home to Jacks Creek with a chip on her shoulder as big as Mount Everest, after getting the chip knocked off by her handsome ex-football-player-turned-personal-trainer hus-band, and having a baby of her own—still ruffled a bit when she heard *Garvina.* It was her real name, the name she had changed to Garvin years ago after finishing law school. And Meemaw knew she was wrong to do it, but she couldn't help teasing her. It was too much temptation to resist plucking her practical adult granddaughter's last nerve. "It's a gift I want to give her. And, besides, nobody will have to sit up sewing but me."

And she was right. There wasn't a soul attaching beads but her. Though her eyes, fingers, and back could tell the tale for her. Meemaw chuckled again. It was moments like this that let her know exactly where Garvin got her feisty ways, and her mouth that often wrote checks she ended up having to pay a big price to cash.

Still, she was glad to be doing it for Mary. She was a good

girl—a good woman—and she had come a long way. She had been through a lot—losing her grandmother, locking herself away from the world, and then finally taking back her life and reawakening her spirit. Meemaw had been in Baltimore visiting when Mary went to pick out the gown. It was a thrill that the young woman had invited her to go shopping. Soon as she saw the dress, she knew the beads would be the perfect touch. A beautiful dress for a beautiful young woman.

And that man Mary was marrying, Moor, goodness gracious! Meemaw patted her foot a few times up under the fabric surrounding her. Now that was a good man . . . and pretty easy on the eyes too! The accent just made him all the more exotic. She shook her head to corral her thoughts and then looked at Destiny's mother sprawled out on the floor a few feet away.

Lying on her stomach, Monique was surrounded by open books, notebooks, and pens. Who would have thought, when she was going through so much trouble, when it looked as though she would lose her Destiny, that Monique would now be in college studying to be a teacher. Ugly rumors had almost drowned her. Now Monique lay on her stomach kicking her feet back and forth just like Garvin had years ago when she studied. Her cloud of hair fell over her face until she looked up, as though she felt Meemaw watching.

She smiled. It was so good to see her smiling.

"You need some help, Meemaw?"

"No, I got it, baby."

Monique supported herself with one arm, stretched the other overhead, and turned to look out the window. "It sure is a beautiful, clear day."

"Mm hmm." Meemaw nodded. "And just as certain, it's raining somewhere else."

Monique tilted her head. "You sure you don't need some help?"

"No, I got it, baby." Monique was still as sweet now as she'd ever been.

At that moment, Monique's daughter Destiny exploded into the room giggling, dove, and fell on her mother's back. "And it looks to me like you got your hands full."

Monique smiled at Meemaw and then, looking at her daughter, she changed her expression and the sound of her voice, as if to convince her daughter that she was serious. "Destiny! I told you not to dive on me like that. I ain't playing with you, little girl."

Destiny ignored her and kissed her face. "I love you, Mommy. I just needed a little hug."

Monique seemed to give up trying to be stern. "I needed a hug too."

Destiny kissed her mother again. Meemaw smiled. It was hard to believe how much the little girl had grown.

She tilted her head and put her hand on her little hip. "You need a little hug, too, Meemaw?" Destiny gave out hugs freely, but always as though she was conveying great favor.

Who could resist Destiny? "Well, you know Meemaw always wants a hug from you, baby." Meemaw nodded toward the dress on her lap. "But will you hold it for me for a little while until I put this away?"

"Yes ma'am." Destiny galloped from the room as quickly as she had come. Meemaw yelled after her. "Don't forget about my hug, now, you hear? Don't give it away, now."

Destiny's voice floated to her from down the hall, "I won't."

Meemaw turned back to Monique and smiled. "That's not a baby anymore; that's a woman. You might as well get her a social security card and let her go to work."

Monique nodded. "She's a piece of work all right."

Meemaw lifted the dress and began to sew again. "No point in putting it off; what's got to be done has got to be done."

Monique shook her head at her books. "I know. I know."

It was quiet again. Meemaw picked up a pink bead and slid it over the needle and onto the thread. She kept trying different ways—putting the bead on the fabric and sewing through it—but there was no good way. It was just tedious work, and she was going to have to keep her shoulder to the plow.

"Meemaw?" Monique was sitting up now, her knees folded in front of her almost lotus-fashion. "Is everybody coming to the wedding? Everybody?"

"I sure hope so. Of course, there's going to be Mary and her friends from Baltimore—Naomi, Latrice, and Thelma." Meemaw and Garvin had laughed themselves silly telling Monique and their friends in Jacks Creek, North Carolina, stories about Mary and her friends Naomi, Latrice, and Thelma. Calling them the hair girl, the nail girl, and the blue-eyed girl—the Baltimore charmers—they had told their friends of how the three women gave Mary a ghetto-ized, glam-o-rama makeover, in order to find a man. And of how they did such a good job, he almost didn't recognize her.

"I hear Naomi the hair girl might already be in California by the time of the wedding. And I'm sure Moor's friends will come." Moor's friends were also good story fodder. The two old men Brighty and Blue and the young graduate student Ali, were sure to make things lively at the wedding. Garvin had shared stories, told by Mary, about the three men. "Garvin said she thinks this wedding is turning into a reunion."

Meemaw laughed. "Jonee and Ramona and her husband will try to make their way from Washington, D.C." Meemaw had never met either of them. She only knew that Jonee was a lawyer in the firm where Garvin once had worked—she thought she remembered Garvin saying Jonee was Thai—and Ramona was a close friend that Garvin seemed to think had done the impossible. *She changed her whole life*, Garvin often said.

"I hate it that Cousin Joe and Cousin Puddin won't be there." She smiled. "But at least we won't have to worry about keeping them away from the chicken!" Meemaw laughed to herself thinking of the chicken wars that had gone on between the Baltimore couple. For a while, fried chicken had been much more than an entree. It had almost decided the fate of their marriage.

"Of course, we'll be going. And Esther and Smitty say they're going." Esther and Garvin had grown up together. Esther and Smitty, who was a good deal smaller than she was, were married now and raising a family. "If they go, they'll bring their kids." Meemaw dropped her head and began to sew again.

Monique laughed. "At least Inez Zephyr won't be going. It will be a vacation just to not hear her gossip."

It was understandable why Monique might not want Inez on the trip. She had spread rumors about Monique, who was only a teenager then. The child's problems had been good material for Inez. "No, I guess Inez won't be coming. Though, you know Inez Zephyr: it will kill her not to be invited."

Monique shook her head. "Something might go on, some news might happen that she wouldn't be able to tell."

Meemaw laughed to herself about the town busybody.

"Well, Mr. Green might go." Meemaw used her nail and picked for a pink bead.

Monique raised an eyebrow. "Mr. Green *might* go?"

Meemaw didn't respond. There was no point in stirring up bees. People in Jacks Creek had gotten over whispering about Meemaw and GoGo—his marriage to her granddaughter Garvin had put an end to all that foolishness. But people in town were still wondering about Mr. Green, longtime friend of Meemaw. He was Jacks Creek's grocer—and he was Jewish. *You sure you and him ain't dating, Meemaw? Both of you all been widowed a long time, and ain't nobody seen neither one of you making no other moves—except toward each other! He's always coming around!* Even her family and friends were always questioning and insinuating. Usually, she took sinful pleasure in stirring the pot of doubt swirling around the two of them. Meemaw pushed at one of the beads on the dress. Right now, she had too much on her hands . . . and in her lap.

Monique pushed her hair out of her face. "Do all these people even know the bride and groom?"

Meemaw looked up from her sewing. "Well, no. But that's the good thing about a wedding—it just brings all kinds of folks together. Kind of like the wedding story in the Bible; everybody's invited."

Monique nodded as though she was thinking it all over. "So, how is it you think all of us are going to get from North Carolina to California for the wedding? Me, Destiny, GoGo, Garvin, you . . . and if Big Esther and Smitty come . . . and *maybe* Mr. Green . . . that's a lot of people."

Meemaw stopped sewing and tilted her head. She ignored the question or little remark she thought she heard in the way Monique had said, *maybe Mr. Green*, and shared what she had been considering for weeks now. "I was thinking we should rent or charter a bus."

Saved! The screen door creaked. The front door swung open. Garvin spilled into the room, her arms full of grocery bags. Meemaw smiled at her granddaughter. Her personality was way bigger than her frame. "A bus? Who's talking about a bus? For what?"

Before Meemaw could answer, Garvin's husband, GoGo, stepped through the door carrying their daughter Princess. *Saved again!* Whatever room was left after Garvin's personality entered was taken up by GoGo's frame. "What are you all cooking up, now?"

This was what she loved. Meemaw looked around the room. All of her family coming together—the old and the new. A lot had changed and a wedding would be just the right touch. "Monique and I were just talking about how we were all going to get to Mary's California wedding, and I said I thought a bus might be just the thing." Meemaw tried to look nonchalant.

Monique's face looked dreamy. "Now that sounds good, Meemaw. One of those luxury buses with the televisions and—"

GoGo shook his head. "Here we go, again!"

Garvin frowned. "A bus?"

Monique nodded at Meemaw. "I can see it, now. A luxury bus with—"

Meemaw couldn't help but giggle. She shifted in the chair—it still surprised her sometimes since her weight loss how much room there was in the chair—and each time, she said a silent thank-you to the Lord and GoGo for restoring her body. "No, Monique, I was thinking more of one of those yellow busses. You know, like the children ride." She continued sewing. It was no big deal.

Monique seemed to be holding her breath. "A school bus? A big old yellow school bus?"

Meemaw could see it now: all of them on the road together. Meemaw got new enthusiasm for the beads she was stringing. "No, not a big one. One of those little yellow ones."

Garvin's expression was pleading. "But, Meemaw, those things are uncomfortable." She shook her head. "I can see us all now, bouncing up and down on hard, green leather seats!" Her expression turned to panic. "Looking out those hard to open windows, no air, the loud voices, all of us cooped up together!"

Monique nodded her agreement to Garvin and then looked back at Meemaw. "And they make you look crazy! For hours and hours! For days and days! And all the way to California? All of us?" Monique shook her head, looking at her books. "The last thing I want to be on is a school bus!"

"Oh, I know, baby. But Meemaw can just see it in her mind." She resumed sewing. "And we've got to get it together, make some plans, 'cause I know everything is going like clockwork in Baltimore."

TWELVE

Baltimore, Maryland

There was nothing more tortuous than too tight shoes ... Latrice groaned as she stepped onto her front porch. Oh, it was awful—toes bunched together, heels rubbed raw. If someone wanted to know all her secrets, all they had to do was squeeze her size-ten-wides into eight-and-a-half shoes.

As soon as her front door was closed, and no one could see her, Latrice kicked off the electric blue spike heels she wore, booting them across the floor like a Raven's football placekicker. She'd done her part keeping up the image of womanhood while she was in public, but now her sacrifice was over.

She walked from the front door, dropped her coat on the couch, and—not even bothering to admire the eighteenth-century Joshua Johnson portrait temporarily hanging on her wall—made for her brightly lit kitchen. She looked at the LED display on the clock on the microwave oven perched above her stove—three o'clock in the morning? What she needed was to be in bed. There was shopping to do tomorrow for the wedding—not to mention that Thelma was talking crazy, threatening to boycott.

The stockings Latrice wore made a *shush shush* sound as

she walked, announcing the kissing together of her thighs with each step she took. If modern technology could produce a Stealth bomber, why not a pair of silent pantyhose? When she grabbed the handle of her refrigerator door, it opened wide like old friends were inside welcoming her to a party.

She touched one hand to her well-corseted stomach. There were enough sequins on the dress she wore to make Liberace want to stand up and holler—most of it was blue, like her shoes and her long, hooked nails. It was time to give both of her girls a rest. She wrestled to reach around herself, under her slip, to undo the zipper. Twisting and turning, by the time she reached it there was a cool blast from the refrigerator blowing up her south side. The corset, which unhooked in the front, was easier to reach—but all the hooks and eyes were a lesson in feminine patience. She tossed the items of torture onto a kitchen chair, and then turned back to the fridge, happy to be in only a slip. It felt good to be home.

Latrice looked inside for something that might be calling to her. The truth was, there was no food exciting her. What she needed to do was go to bed.

Brinnnggg.

It was the telephone. And without looking at the caller I.D., Latrice knew who it was.

"Come on, girl. Why you playin'?"

Why couldn't he accept that the night was over? "Tyrone, hang up the phone and go home." No one could beg better than Tyrone.

"Why you actin' this way? We been cool for years."

It was true. She didn't say anything, which actually said a lot.

"For *years!*" he reiterated. Tyrone's voice sounded like he could feel himself gaining ground. "Why don't I stop by the Dog House and get us a little something to eat, and then I'll swing on by." He laughed his *heh-heh* laugh that meant he figured he wasn't going to be begging long.

Latrice was grateful that Tyrone couldn't see her agonizing, dancing from foot-to-foot in her slip, trying to convince herself she didn't want a Dog House dog or an old player. She wasn't a schoolgirl. Latrice made her hand into a fist and then spread her hand open. She looked at the long shiny nails as though they gave her strength. "No, boy. I don't want no dog—old or new. You just keep your car headed for home, hear me?"

"Awww, baby. Don't be that way. I'm gone swing on by the Dog House, like I said. And then I'm gone be back." Tyrone laughed. "And you don't even have to tell me what you want. I know what you like." *Heh-heh.*

Latrice took a deep, silent breath. If that's all he thought it was gone take—a hot dog—to make her change her mind . . .

Of course, those dogs were good. They put just the right amount of chili and slaw on the hot dogs and just the slightest bit of mustard to add tanginess. Her stomach growled and her mouth watered. She hadn't had a Dog House dog in a long time. . . . There weren't many places to get them outside of Baltimore in Columbia.

But, no, she had already told Tyrone no. That was why she was *in her house* and he was calling her from his cell phone *in his car.* "Heh-heh, nothing, Tyrone. You take yourself on home. And I tell you what, if you bring a hot dog up here on my porch, it will just be two old dogs standing out in the cold."

"Don't be that way, Latrice. You know I love you, girl."

Oh, the dog was playing dirty, pulling out the *l*-word.

"You know I love you, Latrice."

He had said it twice. He was really playing dirty.

"Why you doing this to us? Let me just come talk to you. I'll get the dogs and we can just sit and talk about it. We don't have to do nothing. Come on, now. Don't act this way." Tyrone went from pleading to pitiful. "How you think you making me feel?"

He sounded really sad. He was good. As long as he kept his fish on the line, he knew he had a chance.

"Don't do me this way, baby. We got history, girl. You know it ain't no woman I love more in the whole Baltimore area, with your fat, sweet self."

Tyrone knew he was wrong! Now he was using the *f* word.

"You know I got a thing for you, with your baby-fat self. Girl, you breaking my heart."

Like the Temptations, Tyrone wasn't too proud to beg. "Tyrone, boy, go home."

"How I'm gone go home, girl? Like a bee to honey, I'm stuck on you, girl. I'm gone be driving around here all night thinking about you, girl, with your sweet self." He sighed. "Don't do me this way. Didn't we have fun at the cabaret? Didn't we dance? Didn't I treat you right?"

"Tyrone, go home. I'm not letting you in."

Heh-heh. "Oh, I get it. You playin' a game." *Heh-heh.* "You tryin' to play hard to get." *Heh-heh.* "Well, I'm gone swing on by the Dog House while we playin'."

She was not playing hard to get. But of course, Tyrone always believed the woman that didn't want him was the woman that hadn't met him. Tyrone definitely thought when they came up with the saying, "the blacker the berry the sweeter the juice," they could only have been talking about him.

"Tyrone, you know when I say no, I mean no."

Heh-heh. "What you talkin' 'bout, girl? *No* ain't in your vocabulary. At least not with me. You and me got a *understanding.* You just playin'."

"Tyrone, go home!"

"Look, baby, I know you got lots of men. I respect that about you. You always handle your business. But that ain't got nothing to do with me and you—we always had something special. You can't say no to me." *Heh-heh.* His voice had that and-you-know-you-getting-older-and-you-ain't-got-a-lot-of-choices-so-you-better-not-turn-this-down-who-knows-when-you'll-have-the-chance-again sound.

Latrice put her hand firmly on one plump hip. That was the thing about begging. It was an art form. One false move, one push too much, and the game could be over. "Good night, Tyrone. If you call again, I'm gone unhook the phone." She firmly put the phone back in its cradle and walked away.

She didn't have time to be bothered with Tyrone—hot dogs or no hot dogs. Latrice looked at her hands. She had to get her nails done, and she had lots of shopping to do tomorrow. There was wedding music in the air.

The phone rang as she stepped through her bedroom door. She yanked the receiver from the cradle. "Look, Negro, I told you, don't call—"

"I-I'm sorry. I just thought you might be getting in from a date." It was Thelma.

"Oh, girl!" Latrice was glad she'd held back on the other piece of her mind she'd thought to give Tyrone. "What's the matter? Is something wrong?" Something better be wrong. It was after three in the morning.

Thelma sounded distraught. "I thought I just needed to call and tell you I won't be at the shoe store tomorrow."

Latrice flopped down on the edge of her bed. "What happened?"

"Nothing really. I just can't go through with it. I can't pretend everything's okay about this wedding. And I am not going to have my humanity and sanity assaulted one more time by buying another tragic, ruffled dress and another pair of even more pitiful, hand-dyed shoes that I will never, ever wear."

Latrice shook one hand in the air, as though Thelma could see her. "Girl, it is three o'clock in the morning!"

"I know." Thelma ignored her and kept talking. "But if being single is so hot—the be-all and end-all—then why are all my happy-to-be-single friends running to get married—running to get married like it's a going-out-of-business sale at Saks?"

"Girl, what are you talking about, Thelma? Have you been drinking Ripple, girl? What friends running to get married?"

"Well, Mary and Naomi . . . they're both leaving . . . Naomi's already gone."

"Thelma, it is three in the morning! And Naomi is not getting married, remember? Now I agree, it looks like Naomi has lost her mind and run off to California like that child from the *Member of the Wedding*—"

"Member of the Wedding?"

"Yes, girl. It's this old black-and-white movie about this child who loses her mind at a turning point in her life. It's a good movie and the book is even better—" What was she doing? This was not Oprah's book club. She had to go to sleep. "Thelma, I don't have time to fool with you."

"This is not about me, Latrice. This is about Mary and Naomi losing their minds."

"Well, Naomi may have lost it, but she's not getting married. Mary's getting married . . . and like I said, it's hard to hold out when you're being good. And besides that, I have to go to bed."

"I know it's early . . . or late, but this is serious. And I just wanted the two of you to know . . . I'm not going to do it. In Jesus' name, I am not going to be wearing some crazy dress and some stupid shoes. What kind of fool am I going to look like going down the aisle in a fluffy dress holding a too-bright bouquet? I'm almost forty years old. I've had to give up a lot of things, but I don't have to give up my dignity. Mary may want to make a fool of herself, but I don't have to fly to California to walk down an aisle and look like a clown with her!"

"Thelma?"

"I'm not going to participate." Thelma sounded somewhere between teacher and little schoolgirl.

"You're going to participate."

"No, I'm not."

"Yes, you are."

"Why? Tell me why I should?"

"Thelma, I don't have a lot of time, 'cause I've got a lot to do tomorrow. So here it is without any sugar-coating. This wedding is not about you, it's about Mary's happiness. You are going to participate because you are one of her very best friends, and that's what best friends do. You're gone stand up and wish her well. You are not going to sit around drinking hater-ade."

"What did you say? Hater what?"

"Hater-ade, girlfriend! That's right! You are not going to sit around getting drunk on bitterness and being jealous 'cause Mary's getting married."

Thelma sucked her teeth, and Latrice was sure she was rolling her blue eyes.

"You're a good friend, and you're gone be happy if you have to fall on your knees at the altar while the wedding's going on. You're gone be happy because you're gone remember how unhappy Mary was, how sad she was. Shoot, girl. Remember how the child was looking?"

Finally, Thelma laughed. "She was looking bad, wasn't she?"

"Not to mention the perfume, remember? She wore enough perfume to choke a horse—a herd of horses!"

Thelma laughed again. "She sure did, girl. You know I had forgotten about the perfume thing. But after she got with Moor, it did tone down. A lot!"

"That's right, sister girl. And if she's getting married, it's because you helped her get there. You helped pray, remember? And we are going to be there to thank Jesus for helping out Mary and the rest of Baltimore by putting a smile back on her face. And getting her to wash off that funk!"

Thelma sighed and then laughed again. "Well, it's true, she did stink."

"And you gone be happy because we both know if God makes a delivery on Mary's street, we ought to be happy because that means our Daddy is in the 'hood, and we know sooner or later He's gone come down our street."

Thelma snickered. She coughed. "Look, Latrice, I don't have time to fool around with you—you know I'm not looking for a husband. Besides, it's late."

"You called me!"

"I've got to go, but you need to know your neighbors would have a fit if they heard you calling Columbia the 'hood!"

She had to get Thelma off the phone. "It's all relative, baby-girl. Even here in Columbia—the 'hood is where the heart is!"

"Yeah, well, I'll see you tomorrow, Latrice. But I mean it. I'm not wearing a crazy dress, or any funny-colored shoes. Ain't no way in the world!" Thelma always had to have the last word.

Latrice looked through the glass partition separating her from the white-shirted, black-vested, bow-tied ticket concessionaire. The sun was sparkling in the lobby. "One ticket for Gerald Levert, please." No one could wind up an audience like the R&B crooner. If women were going to be throwing underwear up on the stage, she was going to be right there with them, getting hers in the mix. She'd have to remember to buy an extra-frilly pair.

The clerk tilted her head. "*One* ticket?"

"Yes, just one." Latrice proudly held up a single, freshly manicured fingernail. With all the wedding craziness going on, she was going to do something nice for herself.

While the clerk worked, Latrice looked around the opulent lobby of the Meyerhoff Symphony Hall. The lights were brighter, the crystal chandeliers were brighter, and the carpet was redder than she had ever noticed. She turned back to the clerk and then leaned in to speak conspiratorially to the young woman in the booth. "And, girlfriend, I want you to get my seat as close to him as you can get. For these prices, when he sweats, I want to sweat with him. When he breathes out, I want to suck in his air. You know what I mean?"

They laughed together. "I know that's right," the clerk said as she slid a ticket and a white envelope under the glass. "You enjoy it, now. And don't hurt yourself!"

Latrice laughed as she pushed open the glass doors on her way out. She wasn't making any promises!

And why should she? This was a new thing: it was an adventure going to the concert by herself. She hadn't asked anyone to go with her—she hadn't even *told* anyone she was going.

She was enjoying the rush, the feeling people had the first time they sneaked to do something, like the feeling she had the first time she stayed out until five in the morning when she was in college. There was nothing going on except the sun coming up —the party was over—but it was the thrill of the unknown, the undone.

No one would have ever expected her to go to a concert alone. They certainly wouldn't have expected her to enjoy it.

She walked east up Biddle Street to Charles Street. It still seemed funny how bright everything was. Maybe it was just that now that her mind wasn't on men, she was taking the time to smell the roses . . . or breathe in the city air. She walked past Chase Street and thought she glimpsed a recognizable face. But she didn't stop or think about it too much; she was enjoying the city alone.

"Latrice! Hey, girl! Where you going?"

She turned to look over her shoulder just as she reached the corner of Charles and Read Streets. It was Eddy. She hadn't seen him in years.

"Hey, girl, why you trying to act like you don't know a brother? Wait up!"

She recognized his smile right away . . . and his jacket.

Eddy was wearing the same tan jacket he'd worn years ago. But his fashion sense, or lack thereof, really didn't matter. She was enjoying the day alone. She used her thumb and baby finger to make the universal telephone sign. The light turned green and she began to walk again, as she yelled over her shoulder, "Call me, later, okay? I'm in a hurry."

"Girl, you can't get rid of me that easy. I ain't seen you in years!"

She didn't look back—she didn't want to encourage him—but she thought she heard his footsteps behind her.

"Wait up, girl!"

Latrice picked up her pace as she headed south toward Madison Street. Baltimore's colonial influence was apparent in the faces of the tightly packed row houses. The brick buildings were painted colors from white to pink, though some still bore the original brick color. Others had turned into businesses with neon letters advertising their services and wares. Still, there was enough of the original flavor that, if she squinted and looked through the leaves of the trees that overhung the sidewalk, she could imagine a time when there were no cars on Charles Street. Latrice imagined men in knickers and tights with tri-pointed hats and buckled shoes climbing stairs up to the wooden doorways. She imagined that she saw young Frederick Douglass peeking at her around one of the stair railings.

When she passed the stair rail, it wasn't Frederick Douglass who spoke to her.

"Hey, girl!" Tyrone stepped from behind the rail.

"Why you doing me like this, girl? You know I love you."

She walked faster. "I'll talk to you later, Tyrone!" She made the telephone sign again. "Call me later, man!" What was the deal? She was just trying to enjoy the walk toward the harbor. *Men! Sometimes they come out like roaches!*

"Why you walking so fast, girl? Come on, now. We can get us some hot dogs from the Dog House. Wait up, Latrice-girl!"

Latrice was afraid to look back. She could still hear Eddy calling too. "Latrice, wait a minute!"

If she walked fast enough, maybe they would get the message, or maybe they would just run out of breath. She held up her hand telephone again. "Call me!"

By the time she reached the corner of Cathedral and Charles, she was almost running. Her shirt—she was glad she didn't have on a good silk one—was wet and sticking to her back and chest. And there was no time to slow down or look back; she could still hear Eddy and Tyrone behind her.

Maybe, if she started running, she could lose them. Maybe that's what it was going to take to give them the message. But she hadn't run in years. In fact, she didn't remember ever running.

As she passed the George Washington Monument, she heard several men calling her name. She looked right toward Cathedral and then left toward St. Paul—there was no way to escape— *"Latrice! Baby girl, where you going? Let me talk to you for a minute!"*

"Hey, girl, slow down! Let me holler at you!"

Latrice didn't even look to see who the men were. It was more than one; it could have been three. It could have been a mob! It was funny—no, it wasn't funny—that all these years she had joked about men chasing her, running after her. She had been wielding her mystical powers over men. Now, they were catching up with her! She could hear the feet of the monument men who were now in pursuit. And Eddy and Tyrone hadn't given up the chase, either.

"Come on, Latrice, girl!"

Maybe she bore some responsibility for what was happening to her now. She hadn't thought about the men, about how little self-control they had. She had just enjoyed toying with them. She knew they liked it—but then again, what was not to like?

Fat and sassy was a killer combination—she just didn't know how much. If she'd known, she wouldn't have turned loose all of who she was on them. But the truth was, she couldn't help how charming she was . . . she really couldn't. And she didn't make herself beautiful . . . it just was what it was. *Don't hate the player.* . . . Sure, she got her nails done, and she knew they mesmerized men. But still! And it sure wasn't fair to blame her for the junk in her trunk—she simply had made the most of what she had.

She didn't know the men would break down and lose their minds!

When Latrice crossed Mulberry, she could still hear them. They were getting closer. *"Mercy! Doggone, girl! It must be Jell-O, cause jelly don't shake that way!"*

"Hold up, baby!"

Latrice was flat-out running by the time she reached Charles and Fayette. *It must be true what people say about adrenaline, that it gives you power and dulls the pain.* She wasn't breathing too hard—she was panting from the run—but her chest wasn't gripping.

And her feet weren't hurting. That was really unusual, especially running in heels. But when a sister had to go, her feet had to go with her.

At this point, she didn't know who was behind her, but she wasn't about to stop until she saw water. The only thing was, her shirt was so wet on her—

Brinnggg . . . brinnggg! Her cell phone rang and startled her.

This was no time to be trying to take a call! Just let the answering thing pick up! *Brinnggg . . . brinnggg!* She heard her answering machine click.

"Latrice! Latrice-girl, pick up the phone! I know you're home!" It sounded like Randy calling—a mailman she'd been fooling around with for years. Why was he calling? Now the fools were calling her phone!

People had tried to tell her that her life was going to catch up with her. She should have listened when she had had the chance.

Latrice pulled at her shirt. And she was so sweaty. And her steps were getting shorter and shorter, as though her feet were tangling. The last thing she needed to do was fall. The mob would swarm her! They would devour her! Roaches on a piece of candy!

"Latrice! Latrice, pick up the phone! I'm not playing with you!" Randy's voice sounded funny. High-pitched.

She could see the harbor. If she could just get her feet untangled, if she could just keep running!

"Latrice, I'm not playing with you, girl! I said, pick up the phone!"

And she could still hear the men behind her. Their feet were pounding! They were yelling and screaming her name! *"Latrice! Latrice!"* Why wasn't anyone trying to help her?

"Latrice, if I have to come over there, you are going to be one sorry sister."

Was he threatening to stalk her? Randy sounded strange, and he had never seemed like that kind of person.

"Latrice, I'm not playing!"

He was sounding so weird.

"Latrice, you better pick up the telephone, with your sorry self! I know you're there. You're not fooling anybody."

She lost her concentration and fell forward. It was all over. Good-bye, Baltimore; good-bye, Maryland; good-bye, world!

When Latrice hit the ground, the first thing she tasted was carpet.

Piphtthhh, piphtthhh! She spit the fibers from her mouth.

"Latrice, pick up the phone! This is Thelma. I need to talk to you. I'm not playing!" The answering machine beeped time out.

Latrice rubbed her eyes open and looked around the room and at the blue sheets tangled around her feet. She blinked, trying to marry where she was seconds ago with the reality around her. If she wanted to play, this was not how she did it.

The phone began to ring again. *Brinnggg, brinnggg!* It was Thelma.

The only thing real was her tangled feet, Thelma's demanding voice, and the clammy shirt. It was wet and clinging to her like a sticky yellow candy wrapper on a pink Sunday shoe. First it was Tyrone begging on her front lawn, now men were invading her dreams. She shook her head. They were invading her *nightmares!*

"Girl, I just wanted to make sure you were up and on your way to meet us at the shoe store! If I'm going, you definitely have to be there."

THIRTEEN

South of San Francisco, California

Anthony pulled under a tree at a highway rest stop. He had to decide where he was going before he went any farther. He'd been traveling up and down the Pacific Coast Highway, stopping wherever it hit him, for a few weeks now. He got out of the car, stretched, then went to the trunk to unlock it. His hand-held computer should still have a couple of hours' worth of juice. He'd missed the one he'd had at work, so he'd purchased one of his own. He was glad he'd gotten the kind that could get on the Internet without dialing up.

He sat back in the driver's seat, but sat sideways with his legs extending out the door. He leaned his back against the guitar case. So, where *was* he going?

It was okay if he was a little out-of-sorts. He didn't wake up this morning thinking he was going to make a cross-country trip. He hadn't been planning for months, or even for weeks; it was okay if he was a little uncertain.

Anthony looked at his watch. Desiree should be home by now.

He shouldn't call, but maybe he should send her some email, just something casual to let her know he was okay.

No. It was a bad idea.

He looked at the trees reaching toward the sky. Each one was a different shade of green. He hadn't noticed that before. Actually, each tree seemed to be made up of a million shades of green. Anthony watched the families strolling on the sidewalks toward the brick, wood, and glass building. Many of them held hands, the sun bouncing off their hair. The children skipped and ran rings around the couples, seemingly taking eight steps to each one of their parents'.

Elderly people walked more slowly. Most of them wore visors and glasses or sunglasses, and thick-soled tennis shoes with white socks.

He was the only one that seemed to be alone.

Maybe he should have married Desiree years ago.

It would be nice to be married, wouldn't it, Anthony? We could have a big wedding.

Maybe someday, Desiree. Let's not mess things up. We don't need to rush, do we? Is there something I don't know about, some reason we need to rush?

No, I just thought. . . .

Well, let's just take it slow.

They could have been one of the couples with kids pulling at them. They could have been one of the happily frazzled pairs whose main goal each day was a good night's sleep. If he had committed to her then, they'd probably be together now.

I'm okay.

What he needed to do now was pick a direction. He was free; he could go anywhere he wanted. He leaned forward, his fingers poised to begin typing.

"What the . . . ?" The guitar case fell, hitting him in the back of the head. He turned to shove it back into place. That's all he needed, a cracked skull. As he shoved, the old clasp slid open and the cherry red of the Fender peeked out at him. Anthony pushed the clasp back together. He didn't have time to play around. It would be dark soon, and he needed to figure out where he was going—at least for the night. He'd been drifting long enough.

Maybe he should try the East Coast. Anthony typed *New York* into the dialogue box on the small computer screen and clicked *enter*. Immediately, the search engine provided a long list of responses. None of it talked about traveling or hotels.

Whack! The guitar case slipped and hit him again. This time, it opened wider so more of the guitar was in view.

It had been years since he'd played. He touched one of the strings and the fantasy came back to him, the one with him and long hair and Sly Stone. He pushed the case closed and shoved the guitar in place again. It was a stupid dream.

Anthony typed *New York* and *travel* into the dialogue box on his screen.

He looked at the guitar case, and then deleted the words.

He had time to be silly, for a few days at least. He didn't owe anyone anything. He'd worked hard and tried to do everything right. In the course of the last month, he'd lost his job, he'd lost Desiree—not to mention his townhouse. He was entitled to do something silly. It was his money.

Anthony typed *Sly Stone* and *California* in the dialogue box and clicked the enter key. He could afford to goof off a day or two. He hadn't been to L.A., which is where Sly most likely would be. He could take a trip south, hit some clubs, get some sleep, and take some time to plan his trip to New York. There were many beautiful women in New York.

There were not lots of responses to his query, but one looked interesting. Anthony clicked and opened the file. It was a news story, not really about Sly but about his brother

Freddie. According to the story, Freddie—aka Frederick Stewart—pastored a church in the Napa Valley. There was a picture of him, with a shorter Afro, playing the guitar. Anthony laughed. Wine country! Freddie preaching?

The Valley wasn't far up the road. He knew the way. He was sure he could get a hotel room this evening. He would get a hot meal and, who knows? He might be able to find Freddie Stone and listen to him jam. It was pretty funny to think of Sly's brother Freddie and their little sister Rose playing and rocking out to church music. Besides, if he waited around, he might be able to ask Freddie about Sly.

Anthony laughed as he powered down the computer and put it back in the trunk. He deserved a laugh. He switched on the car's ignition, backed out of his parking space, and headed for Vallejo. *Thank u 4 lettin me be mice elf again.*

In the dark of his hotel room, Anthony, wearing just his skivvies, pulled back the spread and climbed onto his bed. The sub he held smelled good. The meat was smothered in lettuce, tomato, hot peppers, and grilled onions. He opened it, nodded his head, and slid into place on the bed—his back to the headboard.

This was going to be a blast. He never ate in bed at home. He was free to do whatever he wanted to do—now.

Anthony sighed. *Who am I kidding?* He was still lonely for her, for the feel of her.

The left side, where he sat now, was always Desiree's side. How was he going to sleep without her?

I have to stop this.

Anthony picked up the remote and began to channel surf. Television would distract him. He stopped and laughed when he saw Pat Sajak talking to a brown-skinned woman with long blonde hair. Pretty cute. Not his type, maybe a little too old and a little too much hair, but cute.

Besides, it was the right show for him. That's what he was riding now: the wheel of fortune.

FOURTEEN

Bodega Bay, California

It hadn't been as easy to find a job as she'd thought. Naomi sat on the beach surrounded by newspapers held down by stones. Contentment blew off the bay waters and in the air, but she wouldn't have any of it until she had some financial security. She mentally counted what she had left and doubted that it would stretch—even though her episode of the show had recently aired—until she got her check from the *Wheel of Fortune.*

"Living in exile is not the answer, man."

She hadn't heard Ruthie walk up—if she had, she would have left.

Without asking, the girl plopped down beside her and tossed her a piece of fruit. "You're walking around in circles to avoid life, man. But you still got to come out." It had been so peaceful before she came. The sky was blue and calm. The water almost whispered as it rippled onto the sandy beach and back out to sea. There had been no one else around.

"You know how I got here?" The girl adjusted her shades, staring up at the sun.

Naomi had learned in the time that she'd been in Bodega Bay that it didn't matter whether she answered or not. It didn't even matter if she said she was too busy to listen.

"I was just like you—runnin'."

Naomi looked at Ruthie's stringy hair and her bare feet. What did she know about her life? They had nothing in common. Baltimore was about as far away from Bodega Bay as anyone could imagine. Ruthie had nothing in common with any of the girls or young women she knew.

Ruthie picked up a stick and began to drag it through the damp sand. "My family's in Malibu. At least, last time I talked to them or they talked to me, that's where they were."

Naomi didn't want to hear Ruthie's life story. She had enough drama of her own.

"You know how I got here?" Ruthie squinted.

It was obvious that Ruthie was going to tell the story whether Naomi wanted to hear it or not.

"One day my family came to visit and they left me here, like a puppy that messed up one time too many. I was inconvenient, so they left me."

Ruthie crunched into her apple. She looked up at the sky and then looked down again. She scratched her head. "Well, that's half of it. The truth is, I did my part to make them hate me. I stole, embarrassed them, got drunk, and said things." She looked away. "Some things I wish I could take back."

Naomi could imagine. Ruthie was irritating now. She could just imagine her as an arrogant, spoiled, rich brat.

"I started drinking when I was thirteen. I was a nuisance. I guess they did all they could. So when I turned eighteen, they left me. You know, like a pet you hope will die without you having to kill it."

Naomi didn't need to hear this. She didn't need to hear any stories about privileged girls who were out of control. She had her own problems, and if she wanted to hear a story about kids in trouble, there were lots of children—poor children—with stories in Baltimore. She didn't need to hear the ramblings of a fanatical Jesus freak, a modern-day hippie. What she needed was quiet so she could search the papers to find a job. What she needed was peace.

"What they didn't know, what they still don't believe, is about my cousin. He would sit at my family's table, sit across the table from me—so good, so perfect. 'Why can't you be like him?'

"He looked at me with clear blue eyes like he knew a dirty secret on me. Like if I told he would tell, 'she liked it.' And I was afraid they wouldn't believe me about my cousin, so good, so perfect. He didn't like me. And the truth is, I helped. I didn't give my mother the benefit of the doubt because he was so good and so pure, but maybe she would have believed me.

"And it wasn't about sex or power with my cousin—that would have been too personal. I was like shoes or a glass—no personality. I was available. I think that was why he was so offended, years later, when I finally told." Ruthie briefly closed her eyes, like she was holding back tears. When she was composed, she began to speak again. "I didn't matter. You don't have conscience over something that doesn't matter, doesn't exist. I was a convenience that had become inconvenient. He looked at me like I was White trash. Like I had been switched at birth."

Naomi stared at the girl as she spoke, trying to piece together the sentences. It was funny how the girl's voice, how even her speech patterns changed as she told the story.

"I didn't tell them at first. But every time they flew to Paris, every time they bought a gift for him, every time they were too busy buying stocks and cars, or making more money, I hated them. They should have been able to figure it out. They should have been able to guess.

"And when I told, finally, they were angry. '*If* it did happen, it happens to *everyone*. That was years ago. Why can't you let it go and move on?' It wasn't successful, it didn't fit my family's picture. Rich relatives don't molest one another."

Naomi looked at Ruthie and then back at the papers in her hand. Maybe the girl was making it all up. She hoped Ruthie was making it all up.

"I tried to do everything I could to separate myself from them. I changed my clothes, my hair, my friends. I drank. But acid was better, and cocaine was better than acid. Heroin was even better; it took me away, it filled the hole better, but it was harder to come by. Then one day they dropped me here: Bodega Bay.

"When money ran out, I stole from people here. I lied. Until one day I bottomed out." Ruthie stretched her arms wide. "At night, on the beach one night. I was ready to check out. But I cried first." She tilted her face up and closed her eyes again, as she must have that night. "'Hey, Man! If you're there, can you hear me? Can you speak to me? Man, if I matter, can you help?'" She dropped her arms. "And He did. That's why I don't care what people say. He shows up at wells, when you're abandoned, when you're partying, and even on beaches. Jesus is still making house calls, man."

Naomi felt embarrassed, like she was seeing the young woman naked. Why would she tell so much to someone she didn't know?

Ruthie shook her head. "I was so mad. I was so hurt— Jesus was the only one that filled the hole in me. It was as simple as asking for help. He put His arms around me. I know people don't understand, but it's the truth. Jesus is my family now. Jesus is my home, and He never leaves me.

"My family still doesn't want to hear from me. And I still have some days when I dream of castrating my cousin." She laughed, wiping her face. "But not every day." Ruthie adjusted the sunshades perched on her head. "Sometimes, I even wonder what happened to him to make him that way. You know, we don't talk about it, but boys get abused. I think about it, if that might have happened to him. And that we talk about the girls, but if we don't help the boys, what happens to them? They're still sick, right? Maybe like my cousin." She lowered her head.

Naomi tried to focus on the want ads. The words blurred together. She didn't come to Bodega Bay to help other people figure out their lives. She came to save her own life. She didn't want to answer Ruthie, but she heard words blurting from her lips. "The last thing I would be worried about is him. You need to be worried about yourself. Honestly, I think you're in denial. Your cousin raped you, your family abandoned you, and you're worried about them?" She shook her head. "I don't buy it."

Ruthie nodded. "I felt that way for a long time. But, finally, I had to stop focusing on being molested and abandoned . . . and I was molested and abandoned. I was used and left behind, you know? It hurts. I feel that. It's okay to feel that. But that's not all of who I am, you know? I had to learn—I'm still learning—not to focus on that, but on looking for God's love and the blessings He was trying to get to me in this place"—she swept her arms toward the surrounding countryside—"in this valley. I've learned to find joy in the valley, in the place where I am, right now. The sun does shine here." She held her hand up toward the sun. "You have to find hope here."

Naomi jerked at the newspaper pages that were flapping in the breeze. She didn't know why she felt so resistant to what Ruthie was saying. "You make it sound like such a happy ending. I want to believe in good things as much as the next guy." She pointed at the want ads. "But there is such a thing as reality. It's not a perfect world."

"I still don't have a job, either. You're right, everything's not perfect." Ruthie pointed to the sky. "But He never leaves me alone. And I don't have that hole in my heart anymore."

Ruthie resumed writing in the sand with the stick. "Some people say bad doesn't happen to you so good can happen. They're probably right. They're smarter than me and they didn't burn out their brains on drugs. But even if it doesn't make sense to other people, I always thank God for my cousin and that I got lost. I was lost before; the valley just wasn't deep enough for me to know it. And when I found my way home, I learned home isn't Malibu. Home isn't Bodega Bay. Home is letting your heart flow back to God, and the only way I found to get there is Jesus."

She smiled a Mona Lisa smile. "Whatever it is, He can make it better.

"Life didn't happen the way I planned. I don't know if it ever will, but that doesn't mean it can't be good." Ruthie stood to her feet and wiped the sand off her dress and then clapped it off her hands. "But you got to talk to Him. You've got to trust Him. You got to let Him get close enough to see into your eyes. You got to let Him get close enough to whisper in your ears. And you got to let Him get close enough to operate on your heart."

Naomi looked out her bedroom window. The sky was almost black, and the moon and the stars were so bright she couldn't sleep. She raised her head and punched her pillow. Naomi kicked off her sheets and then pulled them on again.

"But you got to talk to Him. You've got to trust Him. You got to let Him get close enough to see into your eyes. You got to let Him get close enough to whisper in your ears. And you got to let Him get close enough to operate on your heart."

She didn't want to talk, and she didn't need a crazy girl telling her about Jesus. She had been going to church before Ruthie was ever born. Most likely, based on the story the girl told, her family was too rich and too busy to bother.

"You've got to trust Him."

What did Ruthie know about trust? When did she ever have to worry about how she was going to pay the bills, or about a marriage, or a family? Everything had been handed to her on a silver platter that she threw away.

Naomi had trusted God and now she had nothing. No one had ever given her anything. She had worked for everything she had. Now she had nothing. Her marriage was gone, and her children had been ripped away from her. She had prayed to Him. She'd gone to church all her life, but that didn't keep trouble away.

Quincy had loved her, and then once she'd trusted him, once she'd let herself rely on him, he was gone. And the truth was, she didn't know why.

Naomi pulled the covers over her head. The moon was so bright.

Suddenly, she leapt from the bed. She slipped into jeans, a T-shirt, and beach shoes. The moon was bright enough for her to see her way down the stairs, onto the beach, and to find her way to a phone booth she had noticed near the bakery.

She knew the sound of him before he answered the phone. "Hello."

Naomi didn't need him. She didn't care about him. He had ruined her life. He had taken her children, stolen her children. She hoped that he rotted. "Hello, Quincy. It's me." Her voice betrayed her. There was still something about his voice—even after the divorce, after manipulating and stealing the kids, there was something about him that would not let her hate him up close. She could manage it far away, but when she saw him or heard him it was hard to do.

He cleared his throat. When he began speaking, he sounded defensive, like he always did lately—not the way he used to sound when they were younger. "Look, I don't want to fight with you, Naomi. If you're calling to say you're going to miss sending the child support payment, I'm not going to report it. It's not worth a fight. I just want to go on with my life." His voice sounded weary. "I'm tired, Naomi."

She needed to ask him why—why he left, why what they had died.

Naomi tried to make her voice sound pleasant. "No, I'm not calling about that." There was a long silence. "How are the kids?" It hurt to ask. To talk about them, to even think about them so far away caused her pain. To know they were part of her, a part of her that someone who didn't even know them had taken away from her—it was pain she tried not to think about or talk about.

"Fine," he said. "Asking about you."

"Well," she said. "Tell them I'll see them soon."

"I will."

When she thought of her children, she cried; and she didn't want to cry. She kept it brief. "Good. Thanks."

"So, what is it, Naomi? It's late. I know you didn't call for nothing."

She tried to giggle, to sound young. "Why? I can't just call you. I used to be able to call you. You didn't care what time it was. But it's not like that, now, huh?"

Quincy didn't sound amused. "I have to go, Naomi."

"No, wait." She needed to ask him, she needed to know. *Help me, God. I don't know what I'm doing here. Help me.*

"Naomi, I have to go to work in the morning."

Her heart was pounding. "What happened to us?" She was grateful for the darkness that covered her.

"Naomi, look. I have to go."

Fear was almost choking her. "I need to know, Quincy." She swallowed. "I've been thinking about it. I need to know what happened to us." She was not going to cry. "I just need you to tell me."

He coughed. He sounded uncertain. "You really want to know? Because if this is just about you needing to argue to feel better . . . I mean it, Naomi."

The way he talked to her—he did that a lot lately—as if she were the one causing trouble. "I don't want to fight." She looked at the moon again and told him where she was. "I don't want to argue. I was just looking at the moon. It's a beautiful place and a bright moon—and it looked like the night—"

"Like the night we met." He finished her sentence.

"Yeah." The waves rustled softly as they rolled in and rolled back out to the bay. "What happened to us?"

Quincy sighed. "You were trying too hard."

She tried not to get excited. It was over; they were divorced. But she could hear her voice raising in the lonely quiet of the night. "How can you try too hard to love somebody? That's what marriage is about, giving somebody your all. You're supposed to try hard."

He cleared his throat again, like he was trying not to sound afraid. "I don't mean you were trying too hard to love." She thought she heard his voice tremble. "I mean you were trying too hard to protect yourself."

She was supposed to protect herself, wasn't she? It was common sense. If she didn't do it, who else was going to do it? If she didn't do it, she was going to be like all those other people in the world who got run over. She could have been like her mother, but she wasn't about to let that happen. "Look, you knew I was independent when you first met me."

Quincy was quiet. She would have thought he had hung up, except she could hear the phone cord rattling. "Do you really want to hear this? I mean, I'm not trying to change you." He cleared his throat again, like he was trying to regain control of his trembling voice. "Not anymore. You get to live the life you want to live."

"If I didn't want to know, I wouldn't have called. But the truth is, I'm not going to let someone run over me . . . not at my job, and not in my home, no matter how much I love them."

"I'm going to tell you something, Naomi. Something I didn't want to tell you when we were together. Something I didn't have guts enough to tell you when we were together." He sighed again. "You're a bully."

She laughed. She felt as though her face had been slapped, but she laughed. "Yeah, right."

"I love you, but you are. I don't want to hurt you."

She shifted her weight and wrapped the phone cord around her index finger. Naomi wouldn't allow herself to sound hurt. She laughed briefly. "Yeah, and so I guess you thought calling me a bully would make my day?"

"See, see what I mean? Sarcasm is just part of it."

She thought of Ruthie on the beach.

And it wasn't about sex or power with my cousin—that would have been too personal. I was like shoes or a glass—no personality. I was available . . . I was a convenience. . . .

When Ruthie spoke, she understood the girl's feelings. She didn't tell her, but she had understood.

"With all I've been through, Quincy . . . you know my past. You know how I was abused, how my mother was abused. With what I've been through, how can you even fix your mouth to call me a bully? I'm the one that was bullied."

"Maybe at one time, Naomi." He sighed. "You're a beautiful person. I loved you." His voice quieted. "I still love you now, in some ways. And most of the times I didn't say anything because I knew what you'd been through. It was like walking on eggshells, I didn't want to be one of them—I didn't want to be one of the ones who hurt you.

"But the truth is, in order to keep yourself from being bullied, you *became* a bully. Like a lot of people, I guess, in order to protect yourself from the one that hurt you, you became that thing yourself."

Naomi felt like she was suffocating. She couldn't move, or she would have jerked the phone from her ear and slammed it into the cradle.

"You're a beautiful person. But you worked so hard to protect yourself, you never let anyone get close enough to see how beautiful you are. There was always a wall, and you standing guard like a sentry. Anyone that looked like they might be a threat to your heart, you cut them off at the knees before they could get to you."

She would not cry. She was stupid to have called in the

first place, but she would not give him the satisfaction of making her cry—not where he could hear it. "What was I supposed to do? Be like my mother and stand there and let people walk all over me, let them hurt me?"

Quincy didn't sound frightened or upset anymore. Instead, his voice sounded determined. "Maybe if I'd had the courage to say this to you before, we'd still be together. But I love you enough to tell it to you now.

"The truth is, Naomi, you wouldn't let anyone get near your heart." He sounded like he was shifting position. "You know the only time I ever felt like I ever saw, felt, or heard the real you?" He didn't wait for an answer. "It was when we were making love. That was good enough, at first. I kept hoping that who you were then . . . if I could make you feel safe enough, you'd allow yourself to be that more and more. But you weren't willing to try, Naomi. Anyone who touched your heart in any way was suspect—except maybe your girlfriends. Everyone else was suspect, and you either closed the door and withdrew the drawbridge, or you attacked. Even your own kids couldn't get to your heart, Naomi."

Now, he was being mean. He was just attacking her, using the kids against her, to hurt her. "That's not true, Quincy. You're just being hateful. I don't know why I called. I should have known you'd use the kids against me. You know I love them." She didn't want to cry, but her voice broke. "What you're doing is cruel. And you know it. Just like my father."

"I didn't say you don't love the kids. I'm saying that you won't let them get close—you won't let them touch you or get inside your heart. I'm saying you won't let them show you that they love you. You won't show them that you love them. You buy them things, you cook for them, but you won't be vulnerable in front of them. You won't let them see that you're vulnerable to them, that they can make you cry."

"I don't have to let people see me cry."

"No, you don't, Naomi. But for somebody that's always quoting the Bible, you don't seem to get it. Even Jesus let people see Him weep. Why? Because people needed to know He cared . . . He wasn't afraid to let people see He cared. That's love."

"I don't need *you* to tell *me* about love." She wiped her face. "I'm not going to let somebody see they can make me cry. Why? So they can use it against me and keep hurting me?" Naomi turned her back on the moon. "What? You wanted me to cry when all of you left me? You wanted to see me cry when you stole my children from me?"

Quincy sighed again. "That's one way of looking at it." He cleared his throat. "But maybe the kids needed to see that you cared enough to cry. Maybe *I* needed to see that you cared enough to cry." His voice lowered. "We cried a lot over you, Naomi."

"Don't be mad at me because you were too weak to control yourself." She didn't like the anger and derision she heard in her voice. But he deserved it. He had asked for it.

"Maybe I am weaker than you, Naomi. Does that make me inferior? Maybe my heart is more tender. Does that make you better than me? Smarter than me? You ever considered that the person who cries, who is willing to risk his heart for love, and maybe has to cry about it . . . did you ever consider that person might really be the stronger person?"

"I'm not crying for anybody. I'm not going to let anybody walk on me or make a fool of me."

"Right, Naomi. But what I think you have to ask yourself is—at the end of the day—are you happy alone? You're the big cheese, but are you happy standing alone?"

I don't have to listen to this. Still, she didn't hang up the phone.

"And you need to know I didn't take the kids, Naomi. I guess they just got tired of fighting, of trying to fight the bully who guards you so that they could get to their mother's heart." He sighed. "I guess we all got tired of trying."

A wave crashed. It startled her; she lost focus, and began to weep silently. "If I was so bad, why did you stay so long?"

"I loved you, Naomi. I kept hoping."

She imagined him twisting his hair.

"I *still* love you, Naomi."

When he said it, she realized it was what she wanted to hear. It was why she had called. "If you love me, how can you leave?" She tried to laugh through her tears. "You can't give up on love. No one can give up on love."

His voice was firm, but just above a whisper. "I guess you're right about me, Naomi. I'm not strong enough to keep fighting you. You're too good at what you do. You've injured me in too many places." His voice sounded very sad. "It's too late. I'm trying to put my life back together. We're trying to put our lives back together."

That was when she let her guard down, and she cried aloud. Naomi wept bitterly for all the years and moments it had hurt her to keep herself aloof so she wouldn't be hurt. She cried because with all she had done, with all she had missed, she was hurt anyway. And with all her pain, the truth was, she was still too afraid to risk asking him to let her try again. She cried because she was too afraid, too on guard, to let him know she needed to come back home. Naomi cried because she was too afraid, too well trained, to save her love, and she knew that this—not the divorce decree—but this call from a pay phone was the end of her marriage.

She and Quincy had loved each other. He had asked her to marry him. But the truth was, she wasn't ready, she wasn't prepared for the marriage.

"Anyone who touched your heart in any way was suspect— except maybe your girlfriends. Everyone else was suspect, and you either closed the door and withdrew the drawbridge, or you attacked. Even your own kids couldn't get to your heart, Naomi."

Her heart was too afraid, too hardened, when they married. He was right—she was too afraid to open her heart, even to her own children.

Quincy probably hadn't been prepared either. *"Maybe if I'd had the courage to say this to you before, we'd still be together. But I love you enough to tell it to you now."*

Naomi sank to her knees on the sand, and stayed there weeping until she had the strength to make her way home.

The sunlight in her bedroom awakened her. Naomi looked in the mirror. She had cried herself to sleep. From the look of things, she had cried in her sleep. The only thing she could remember from her dreams was being in a room saying good-bye to people whose faces she could not see, people who were seeing her off to begin a new adventure. She wanted to go, but she was afraid to leave.

They reassured her. "We'll see you again. Don't worry."

But when she awoke, her hands were clenched so tightly that her palms were red, and she was certain that it was the sound of her own sobs that awakened her. Her heart was pounding. It was not a nightmare, but that's how it felt.

She rose and looked into the mirror at her eyes. Maybe that's how it really was. Perhaps she was frightened of change, of good things that were entering her life.

Ruthie, with her blue eyes and tangled blonde hair, was not her daughter.

Naomi looked away from the mirror, fighting against what she felt tugging at her heart, against what she heard God's spirit whispering in her ears. As Naomi wrestled, a melody—a song she had sung in Sunday school as a child—played in her memory.

Jesus loves the little children . . .

Not only was Ruthie not her own child, she was not even one of the girls in Baltimore, in Chicago, in Harlem, or in Detroit that needed a mother to hold them and encourage them. Those girls hadn't had privileges like Ruthie; no one seemed to care that they were drowning. Why should she care about Ruthie? She didn't want to care.

. . . all the children of the world . . .

How was she going to open her heart to a stranger, to a strange girl, when she had lost her own children? How could she open her heart to someone else when she was too afraid to open her heart to her own children?

. . . red and yellow, black and white, they are precious in His sight . . .

As the song played, Naomi could feel the strings around her heart loosening. This was not Baltimore, Chicago, or even L.A. It was Bodega Bay, and Ruthie was the girl whose heart had been broken. Ruthie was the one before her in need.

When the knock came at Naomi's door, she didn't have to open it to know it was Ruthie. Naomi opened the door and looked at the girl. Ruthie wasn't what Naomi had expected; she wasn't the kind of friend that Naomi thought would be in her new life. There was nothing about Ruthie that reminded Naomi of Baltimore. But then again, this was Bodega Bay.

She missed her own children. No one could imagine how

much she wanted to hold them, to hear their voices, and yet how much it hurt to try to find a way out of the dark place to which their relationship had come. It was not the relationship with her children she had ever thought she would have. And the truth was, she didn't know if she would ever find the courage to search out a way back to their arms again.

Ruthie's words spoke to her. *"I've learned to find joy in the valley, in the place where I am, right now. The sun does shine here. You have to find hope here."*

Ruthie was a young woman who needed a mother. Ruthie wanted her friendship, and after hearing about Ruthie's life and how she came to be in Bodega Bay, Naomi felt ashamed of how she had treated her, how she had misjudged her. Ruthie was not her child—no one could replace her own children—but, she would find hope in the valley where she was.

Naomi opened the door wider and hugged Ruthie when she stepped through the door. "We've got a lot to do today." She put on hot water for tea. "We need to look for jobs."

Ruthie brightened and smiled. *"Life didn't happen the way I planned. I don't know if it ever will, but that doesn't mean it can't be good."*

"And one of my best friends is getting married. She's coming to California soon from Baltimore. People are coming from Baltimore, D.C., and even from North Carolina. The engagement was short so people are going crazy trying to get everything done. There's not much for me to do here. But whatever I do, wherever I go, I want you to go with me." Ruthie hugged her and began to cry. "There's going to be a wedding and you're invited."

FIFTEEN

Vallejo, California

Anthony strummed his guitar. It was Wednesday evening. He had spent most of the day sleeping. When he wasn't sleeping, he alternated between feeling sorry for himself and chiding himself for self-pity. Pity parties were pretty time consuming, so it had been a full day; and though he'd spent most of the day in bed, he was tired from his efforts.

He turned to the guitar case lying next to him on the bed. He searched briefly through the pockets for a pick. As he felt in one of the pockets, his fingers touched paper. It was Moor's wedding invitation. He had stuffed the envelope in the pocket to remind himself to call. He needed to beg his way out of the wedding. What good was he going to be to anybody as a best man?

Anthony gave up his search for the pick and strummed the guitar with his fingers again. He looked at the clock on the dresser, nodded to himself, and then set the guitar aside.

If he was going to be in Vallejo, holed up in a hotel, he might as well do what he had come to do. His Internet search had led him to Evangel Temple. Wednesday night was prayer and praise night. He didn't remember much about church, but everyone knew there was prayer on Wednesday nights. If it was the same as church had been when he was a boy, there weren't going to be a lot of people. Hopefully, he would see Freddie Stone—and maybe Sly—jamming with the church band. He tried to imagine Sly in rhinestone-encrusted, star-shaped shades, wearing banana-yellow bell-bottoms and matching platform shoes, shaking his Afro, and grinning wider than a river while he sang with the church band. *We shall come rejoicing bringing in the sheaves!* It was a lot easier to imagine him saying, *All you squares, go home!*

Freddie was the pastor at Evangel now, and one of Sly's little sisters was the choir director. *That should be some jammin' choir!*

In any case, he could sit in the back of what he imagined would be a small, weathered brick building. If things went well, he could stay and rock out, hear some real funk music—even if he did have to ignore the lyrics. If things went sour—if it was just a bunch of women and old people praying, moaning, and shaking tambourines—he would opt for Plan B and be the first one out of there. It was a low-risk venture.

Anthony picked up the directions he'd written down and headed out the door.

As he looked for a place to park, it was clear Evangel Temple was not made of bricks that had seen better days. It was not held together by crumbling mortar. It was not small, but was instead a large, modern-looking structure adorned with stained glass windows and a steeple.

He had been wrong about the crowd too. Though the service had started fifteen minutes prior, and though it was Wednesday night, people still streamed through the doors. By the time he parked and found his way inside, the only seats in the house were in the overflow room, the Fellowship Hall in the basement. Anthony wound his way through the corridors, led by an elderly, stooped janitor with thick eyeglasses and a bald head with patches of white kinky hair around his ears.

The old man looked Anthony up and down, smiled like he had a secret, and used his hand to motion Anthony inside. He followed Anthony into the cavernous room and switched on and then dimmed the lights. A large projection screen showed the images of what was happening upstairs in the sanctuary. There was no one else in the room.

"I hope you can find a seat," the old man wisecracked. There looked to be fifteen hundred empty, neatly arranged folding chairs in the room. "Make yourself to home, my man, my man."

Anthony stood still, trying to decide if he should immediately invoke Plan B.

"You might as well sit and give it a try, brother. It ain't gone hurt you none," the old man said like he was reading Anthony's mind. He pointed to a chair in front, but close to the doorway where they stood. "That looks like a good seat. You can take in the sights, but if you need to, you can make a clean, fast getaway!" The old man cocked his head and snickered, revealing two missing teeth.

Anthony nodded and laughed, hoping his face didn't look as sheepish as he felt. He stuck out his hand. "Anthony Carillon."

"Pops." The old man shook his hand. He smelled like Pine Sol.

"This is not my thing." He didn't know why he was explaining. "It's not that I don't believe in God. I just came to hear the band." Anthony laughed self-consciously. "Actually, I came to hear Freddie Stone. Well . . . honestly, I was hoping to hear Sly."

"Yeah? Sly Stone?" The old man raised an eyebrow, his eyes twinkled, his smile broadened, and he crossed his arms over his chest. "Oh, don't be embarrassed, Ant-nee. That's cool. Lots of people come here looking for the same thing."

The old man said Anthony's name like he'd heard it every day growing up. *"Hey, Ant-nee! Your grandmamma calling you!" "Hey, Ant-nee, you coming outside to play ball, man?" "Ant-nee, you better get in this house and do your homework, boy, before I knock you into next week!"* Anthony felt disoriented, like the past and where he stood now had kissed. Pop's voice was one from his old neighborhood.

The old man was still talking. "Looking for Sly Stone." The old man nodded. "No, don't be embarrassed. I been where you are myself, and back again."

Anthony quickly took a seat.

SIXTEEN

Jacks Creek, North Carolina

G arvin moved about her bedroom with her cordless
telephone glued to her ear. Ramona was on the other
end. Things were falling into place. Jonee was checking on a caterer. It looked as though everyone was going to
the California wedding.

"Garvin, girl, I can't wait to see you. My sweetness is even
excited and is taking time off so we can get there. We've
decided to drive and make a vacation of it."

It was funny to hear her friend call anyone *sweetness*. She
had mellowed more than Garvin would ever have imagined.
Ramona giggled in a way that said to Garvin that her friend
was used to, and comfortable, doing it. It was a laugh that
said she was comfortable in her new life, that she felt free.
She was not the Ramona that Garvin remembered, the
Ramona who had more creative ways of calling in for days
off from work than Baskin-Robbins has ice cream flavors.
Ramona's red finger waves and huge, gold hoop earrings had
been traded in for dreadlocks and cowry shells.

"My sweetness and I haven't been across country since we
took our bike ride."

It was that bike ride that had led to Ramona changing
her life and getting married. What had started out as a

disaster—Ramona knocked out cold, as if she were Miss Sophia in *The Color Purple*, only at L'Enfant Plaza Metro rail station instead of some hick town—had evolved into a rainbow cycle marathon.

There was no way of knowing how your life would turn out. Who would have ever imagined Ramona married to a preacher?

"We'll be there. Don't worry. We wouldn't miss it for the world."

As she hung up the phone, Garvin heard GoGo coming through the door that led from the garage to the kitchen. She walked from the bedroom to meet him, trying to determine if the sound of his footsteps meant he had been successful. She had sent her husband on a mission of the utmost importance; he had to talk Meemaw out of the bus idea. If anyone could do it, GoGo could. It was hard negotiating with Meemaw, but if anyone was going to be successful, it was going to be GoGo. Her grandmother was especially fond of Garvin's husband. Meemaw still took delight in teasing people by introducing GoGo, not as her grandson-in-law, but as her personal trainer. *He's my personal trainer! Um-hmmm!*

GoGo smiled at Garvin as she stepped into the kitchen. He reached into the cabinet for two glasses while, with his other hand, he opened the refrigerator and removed the pitcher of sweet lemonade. Garvin stepped up onto one of the stools on the counter side of the kitchen island. GoGo set the pitcher and glasses on the counter, then turned to scrounge for crackers and to rummage in the fridge for cheese.

There were still moments when it was all like a dream— moments when GoGo seemed like a handsome stranger instead of the man her legs tangled with in the middle of the night.

Garvin hoped that GoGo's impromptu snack fest was to celebrate his victory. The first thing she wanted to hear from her handsome husband was that they would not be riding a yellow school bus from Jacks Creek, North Carolina, to San Francisco.

After GoGo set the cheese and crackers on the counter, he returned to the refrigerator. He disappeared behind the door, and when he stood he held containers of red strawberries and green grapes in his hands. He hummed as he moved to the sink to wash them. Grabbing a knife from the drawer, he kissed her as he moved to sit beside her while depositing the fruit in front of her. Garvin leaned over to kiss him back. She touched his shoulder—he still had his professional football player physique.

He poured in silence, then sliced pieces of cheese and opened the crackers. It had to be good news. No doubt, this was a small victory feast.

GoGo picked up a slice of cheddar and sighed before he put it in his mouth.

Garvin's heart sank. She knew what the sigh meant.

"Meemaw thinks the small bus we have at the rec center should carry everyone. It would be cheap, and she thought it would be easy for me to drive since I'm already familiar with it." GoGo cleared his throat and kept chewing as he stared out the window.

She should have known not even GoGo would be a match for her grandmother. Meemaw probably cut him a piece of pie, batted her eyelashes at him, and had him committing to drive in a matter of minutes. "Oh, honey, you were our last hope."

He nodded, still looking straight ahead. "I know. But you know Meemaw; she wouldn't take no for an answer." GoGo picked up another cracker and nibbled at the corner. "Maybe we should have left well enough alone."

Garvin reached to pat her husband's hand. "It was worth a shot."

GoGo sighed and took a drink of lemonade. "I tried, you know?" He shook his head. "I didn't have a chance."

Garvin shook her head and then leaned it on her husband's shoulder. "No, none of us ever had a chance. We're going to be riding to California on a little yellow school bus. Hard seats. Closed windows." Her sigh was bigger than his. "It's not the worst thing in the world. We'll get through it."

GoGo kissed Garvin on top of her head. "Take a big drink," he told her and offered her her glass of lemonade. "That's not the worst of it." He took another big gulp from his own glass. GoGo picked up another cracker and another piece of cheese. When he finished chewing and downed another gulp of lemonade, he finally spoke again. "Inez Zephyr's going with us on the trip."

Garvin bumped her head on the counter as she slipped off her stool to the floor.

Meemaw hummed while she added sugar to the pitcher of tea.

Garvin reminded herself, as she touched the tender spot on her forehead, that she was not a little girl. She was not powerless to Meemaw's will.

Okay. So they were going to ride on a school bus to San Francisco. Okay. So GoGo was going to drive. Okay. All of them were going to be crowded on the bus together for days—Meemaw, Mr. Green, GoGo and herself, baby Princess, Monique and baby Destiny, Esther and Smitty and their two kids. Okay.

She could deal with all of that. She loved Meemaw. Her grandmother had raised her, and Garvin respected her. There really wasn't too much she was going to object about to Meemaw. But Inez Zephyr? That was too much for any two-legged creature to have to tolerate.

Inez wouldn't just ride the bus. No one would need to take photographs or make video recordings with her along. Inez would provide a running commentary. *I don't know why she wearing that dress, I wouldn't be caught dead in something like that!* And free of charge, Inez would make certain that no one ever forgot the event. She was exactly what the wedding did not need.

What was Meemaw thinking? This was worse than just riding a yellow school bus. Way worse! No one would want her on the bus. Inez would make an already bad situation impossible.

Garvin took a deep breath. She had to do something. Maybe GoGo had wilted, but she had been dealing with Meemaw a lot longer. Everyone thought Meemaw was in control, but there were times when she'd had to rein her grandmother in before things got out of hand. The truth was, maybe *she* needed to talk to Meemaw about the bus. Riding that way was going to be uncomfortable enough. But Esther, her beautician friend, and Inez together on a long bus trip might be an explosion in the making.

Meemaw's smile was as sweet as the tea she poured. "This wedding is going to be some kind of fun! All of us together on the bus! My, my, my, it's going to be a blast!" Meemaw shook her shoulders.

Oh, it was going to be a blast all right, but not the kind

of explosion Meemaw was counting on.

"Meemaw, I don't know if this is such a good idea."

Meemaw plopped ice cubes into the two glasses. "And it was so good for GoGo to come over here and volunteer to drive the bus."

Volunteer? Funny, but GoGo didn't quite remember it that way.

Meemaw was beaming as she settled herself into the cushioned kitchen chair across from Garvin. "I just didn't know which bus we would use, or where to get a driver we could trust. Then GoGo came up here like Prince Charming, and soon as I saw him, the plan all came together. Who better to drive us than GoGo?"

Garvin didn't know how her grandmother could smile so sincerely about having hoodwinked her husband that way. Meemaw knew she had gotten GoGo all twisted up in the game. Well, Meemaw wouldn't work her charms on her. They would not be riding on the bus, and no matter how they went, Inez was not going to the wedding. Garvin was not going to back down.

Her grandmother kept smiling and sipping. "He is the sweetest young man. Just as sweet as he was the day I met him. He found a good thing when he found you, but no doubt about it—you made a good choice when you said yes." Meemaw picked up a napkin and wiped the corner of her mouth. "How many husbands would have said yes when an old woman asked them to drive? He is just a special kind of man. He always has been, supportive and kind." Meemaw batted her eyelashes. "I don't know how you misread him all those years ago."

Garvin's face warmed. Maybe she shouldn't have come. Garvin touched the tender knot on her head.

Meemaw gave her a concerned smile. "What is that bump on your head, baby? Did you fall down?"

She was not going to be sidetracked. "Meemaw, I came over to talk to you about the bus."

"That's something, baby. I was just about to tell you we're having a meeting at the rec center to discuss just that."

Garvin began to rub her temples. Maybe it would be enough if she could just talk Meemaw out of letting Inez *ride* the bus.

Big Esther sat on the first row of brown metal folding chairs. Her tiny husband, Smitty—who sold the best snow cones in town—blueberry snow cones—sat next to her, their two children seated next to him. The other people who were going on the trip—Monique and Destiny, Mr. Green—sat a row behind them. Garvin sat down the row from Esther and watched her friend pat her foot. Inez was not one of Esther's favorite people—not on the street and certainly not in Big Esther's Beauty Shop. She had been seething ever since she heard the news that Inez *might* be riding the bus.

On Saturdays, Inez strategically stationed herself in Esther's shop so that she could see everything that passed by the window. Like CNN, she kept up a running commentary on the day's events—an unwanted line of patter that frazzled Esther so that she threatened every week to bar Inez from the shop. If it had not been for the love of Jesus, no doubt long ago there would have been a fight. Everyone said they would put their money on Big Esther if there was a grudge match.

Esther held her hand high, directing her gaze at Meemaw who stood in front of the room at a podium. "Miss Evangelina, I don't know if it's such a good idea to have Inez on the bus. You know how she gets on everybody's nerves." Esther looked down the row at Garvin, then back at Meemaw. "The long ride, the California sunshine, and all the hot air in Inez might prove to be just a little too combustible, if you know what I mean."

Meemaw continued smiling. "Well, Inez may have some faults—not that the rest of us don't—but whatever's wrong I know everyone here has enough right to make it all okay. There's room enough at the table for everyone to dine."

Garvin attempted to raise her hand, but GoGo held her wrist. "Don't do it, Garvin. Just let it go."

She frowned at him, wriggled her wrist away, and let her hand fly up in the air. "Meemaw, I agree with Esther. I don't think it's such a good idea for Inez to come to the wedding." She looked around the room. "And it's sure not a good idea for her to be on the bus. I don't think anyone here thinks it is."

Meemaw was still smiling. "Do tell."

Things weren't going so bad. It was just as she'd always thought. She just needed to take a firm hand with Meemaw. "I mean, why does she need to be there? What would she contribute?"

GoGo groaned.

Meemaw smiled sweetly. "You know, I'm glad you said that, baby. You're right, Garvina."

"That's Garvin, Meemaw." Garvin smiled at GoGo, patting him lightly on the shoulder.

"Sorry, baby. But you're right. Everyone should get a chance to contribute, to feel invited." Meemaw's eyes twinkled as she looked around the room. "That's why Inez and I decided she should bake the wedding cake!"

Garvin sucked in enough air to create a vacuum in the room. Esther turned gray. Garvin sputtered until she found her voice. Forget about barring Inez from the trip. The greater service to mankind would be to keep the woman away from the cake.

"First, Meemaw, nobody thinks Inez is such a good cook. And we all know she is no professional baker. Not only that, but how is the cake going to get across country without crashing? Not to mention that Inez doesn't have a car to carry the cake, and no car can get up Inez's driveway to get the cake because she sure can't carry it out to the road." Garvin was winded.

Meemaw nodded thoughtfully. "You're right. She doesn't have a car. It would be mighty risky trying to get a car up that old road. And, baby, you're right about her not being able to carry the cake out to the road. That's why I guess we're just going to pick up the cake and her on the bus."

SEVENTEEN

Baltimore, Maryland

Thelma stuffed her feet into the sixth pair of shoes she'd tried that day. She shook her head. "Uhhhh! This is hopeless. Absolutely hopeless. I don't even know why I'm trying."

Latrice tried to reassure Thelma with a smile. They had been hunting shoes for weeks now.

Thelma frowned as she dropped the eggplant-colored pump next to the shoebox. "This doesn't make sense, Latrice. I don't know why Mary has to rush the wedding." She picked up the shoe and held it near her face. "And I hate this color. Blue would go so much better with my eyes." Thelma had been frowning a lot lately.

The two friends sat in the middle of a busy shoe store in Randallstown surrounded by boxes, long rows of shelves, and dozens of other customers looking for the perfect footwear. Afternoon sun poured through the open glass window and shone where they sat.

Latrice looked across the aisle at Thelma. Mary was right—there was no getting used to seeing Thelma's contact-blue eyes floating in her brown face. She didn't understand why Thelma needed blue contacts to feel beautiful.

Latrice waved her hands in the air. Her long nails made

two fluttering, curved acrylic fans. They were hypnotic to men. "Oh, stop fussing, Thelma. Her prince came riding up on a trusty steed, and she's hopping on the saddle behind him." Latrice winced as she yanked her foot out of a maroon-colored, spiked heel shoe. "What's wrong with that?" As she talked, Latrice checked her long sculpted nails—it was time for a design change and she had lost a rhinestone or two. Maybe blue and white stars, this time, with a rhinestone in the middle.

"I mean it, Latrice. I don't know why Mary is doing this. She could be messing up her whole life. And you know what they say about African men. Why does she have to rush off and marry him? Why can't she wait? Why can't they just keep dating for a while? I don't think she's being reasonable."

Latrice bent over and held a pair of dark purple shoes against her feet. "No, I don't know what they say about African men. And don't tell me." She shook her head, sat upright, and laughed. "We've already been through this. Besides, it's hard to wait when you're being good."

Thelma rolled her eyes. "Being good," she mumbled. "Like little girls. Like we're not women who can make grown women choices. It's not like it's illegal." She rolled her eyes even more emphatically. "Well, if she's so good, I don't see why she has to rush now. And I certainly don't see why she has to rush off to *California* like a teenager—some of the girls I teach behave more maturely. If she's gone be a fool, why can't she be a fool in Baltimore?" She looked in another box of shoes and then pushed them away with her foot. "She should take more time . . . if only for the wedding. We don't have enough time to properly search for what we need."

Latrice picked up a wine-colored shoe and began to push the toe and heel together so that it gaped open. Then she placed her thumbs inside the mouth of the shoe to stretch it wider. "Mary's smart. She knows what she's doing. He makes her happy. He makes her come alive. All three of us—you, me, and Naomi—said Mary needed to get a life—to get a man. Well, now we can't complain because she has one."

Thelma huffed. The whites of her eyes, around the blue contacts, turned red. "Don't even mention Naomi's name. Running off, abandoning her dental practice. Who does that? That bird has lost her mind! What is it with people and California anyway?" She took the lid off of another box.

"Look, I can't say anything about Naomi, either. All I can think is that she must be having a nervous breakdown, and it ain't no time to talk about a sister when she's down." Latrice shrugged. "But, hey. She's grown, too, right?" She squinted at the shoe she was holding, as if giving it a look would make it loosen up. "But Mary's another story. She's happy. You see her face when he comes around. And you can't say he's not a tall, good-lookin', dark chocolate piece of the Motherland!" Latrice grunted as she wrestled to force her plump foot in the wine-colored pump. "Whew! I don't think I'm gone be wearing that shoe!" She reached in her purse for a tissue and wiped the perspiration from her brow. "And like I said," she giggled and shook her head. "It's hard to wait when you're being good."

Mary, the bride-to-be, appeared from behind a shelf, her arms piled high with shoeboxes. Well, it sounded like Mary, but her face couldn't be seen. She poked her hand out toward Thelma. "How about this one?" In her hand she held a bright blue T-strapped pump.

Latrice laughed. *Blue would look so much better with my eyes.* Mary had been hunting shoes way on the other side of the store, but had managed to return with the answer to Thelma's wish.

Instead of being grateful, Thelma looked more frustrated. "That shoe is definitely not eggplant, Mary. I don't think *you* know *what* you want."

Mary's voice sounded like she was smiling behind the mass of shoes. "I know what I want, but I also know what doesn't matter."

Latrice stood and grabbed a few of the boxes at the top of the pile.

Mary kept talking. "I want to be married, and I want my best friends at the wedding. Those things are mandatory," she smiled at Thelma and then at Latrice over top of the boxes. "But shoe color is optional."

Thelma put on her best teacher voice and leveled a correcting gaze at Mary, whose face had now appeared. "I think that you're rushing into this. You're not thinking things through. You don't have to be married to be happy. There's no need to jump off the deep end over this—over a man. You don't have to own the well to drink the water. It's not the fifties—you don't have to buy the bull to get the steak."

Mary simply smiled at Thelma, like she was looking at a resentful two-year-old.

Latrice could not help laughing. "I keep trying to tell her, Mary, that it's hard to wait when you're being good." She kicked the tight wine-colored pump from her foot and rubbed her instep. She shook her head at Thelma. "Buy the bull to get the steak? Girl, don't you ever try to be a writer." Latrice chuckled and waved a hand at Thelma. Then she pointed toward Mary. "Did you get me a pair of those blue ones? Maybe all the trouble I'm having has got something to do with the color." She giggled again as she admired her nails and plump hands. She wiggled her chubby toes.

Thelma looked like a blue-eyed rain cloud. "No, the trouble with you is not shoe color, it's the whole fantasy thing about love and romance—that a woman's not complete unless she has a man." She cleared her throat. "And what do you know about being good anyway? You're dating just about everything that wears pants in Baltimore . . . and I think you're working on the state of Maryland, now, too, aren't you?"

Mary shook her head and groaned. "Oh, Thelma!"

Latrice pursed her lips. *The comedienne Mo'Nique was right—if Thelma was their representative at this moment—skinny women were evil! Thelma had a lot of nerve!*

Latrice used her hands like a fan to cool her bosom and calm herself down. She wasn't going to let Thelma get her goat—it was just a case of the green-eyed monster getting a hold of her blue-eyed friend. "No, that's all right, Mary. Thelma's just trippin' today. We know how she can be. But we love her anyway." Latrice stuck out her tongue like a little girl. "I'm not going to bite. She's like one of those girls on *Jerry Springer*, just looking for a fight, but I'm not ringing the bell." She looked straight into Thelma's blue eyes. "And for your information, Missy—it ain't none of your business what I know, what I do, or who I do it with."

She leaned forward, frowned, and poked at the shoe she wore. "But what I will tell you is, you're right about one thing—the tightness of a shoe ain't got nothing to do with the color," she said trying to change the subject.

They laughed. Then, Thelma sighed. "I want you to be happy, Mary. But I don't want your heart to be broken. I don't want you to make a mistake. I don't think it's been long enough. And what do you *know* about him?" She paused and raised an eyebrow. "What if something is wrong with him?" She whispered. "What if something's not working? What if something is *missing?*"

Mary dropped several of the boxes of shoes she was holding. "What?"

"I mean it, girl. This is nothing to fool around with. You could be stuck with it for the rest of your life."

Mary dropped, along with the boxes she still held, to the seat beside Thelma. "You're kidding me, right?"

"No. I'm trying to be real."

Latrice rolled her eyes. "Right, Thelma. You haven't been rational for some time now."

"No, really. You have to think about it. Any man that's not . . . functioning . . . in these days and times . . . you know something has got to be wrong with the brother."

A chuckle bubbled from Latrice's chest. "Girl, you are scraping the bottom of the barrel for that one!"

"Latrice, girl," Thelma lowered her voice to a whisper, "you know it's one thing for a woman to say she's going to be celibate. But a man? Girl, please."

Mary slowly shook her head.

"Thelma, girl, you have cracked. For real."

Thelma's blue eyes flashed earnestly. "Latrice, if anybody knows, you know there is not a man in the modern world who's not making house calls if they can. All of them out there barking at the moon. There is no such thing as an honorable man anymore, if there ever was one. No woman should be living in a fairytale."

Thelma paused and then continued. "Why should I risk my heart and get hurt?" She stopped again, looked momentarily confused, and then continued. "Why should any woman risk her heart on a man just to get hurt? If a man is trying to play like he is all holy and pure, then look out, sister, something's wrong. You know men are dogs. And either the dog is doing some purring he's keeping on the down-low, or else his bark just ain't working no more."

Mary exhaled, somewhere between a sigh and a laugh. "Please, tell me you're kidding. Tell me that you, a well-educated woman—a woman who is teaching the youth of America, a churchgoing woman—do not believe what you're saying."

Thelma turned to look directly at Mary. "Yes, I do. And if most women were honest, they'd tell you they believe the same thing. Ask Latrice."

"Oh, Thelma."

It was hard for Latrice to catch her breath—she was still giggling—enough to speak. She took one deep breath and plunged. "First, Miss Thelma, no, I don't believe all men are dogs because if all men are dogs, what does that make us? 'Cause we're the ones chasing after them. And maybe we've been wrong—maybe we're getting what we get because we're getting what we believe."

It was Thelma's turn to roll her eyes.

"Second, Miss Thelma, I personally have not had a man pursue me that behaved with honor. I can agree with that." Latrice laughed again. She shook her head to clear away the image of Tyrone carrying a bag of hot dogs. "But, then again, I don't know if I gave any man a chance to be honorable. Or if I wanted a man to be, for that matter." Latrice chuckled and grimaced as she kicked off the shoe that was squeezing her foot. "But that doesn't mean that kind of man doesn't exist." She leaned forward, stretching for her tender toes. "I don't know any millionaires, either, but *they* exist. Maybe you have to be one to get one—maybe who we draw to us is a reflection of who we are.

"Third, I think that if anyone was going to be blessed enough to find an honorable man, I think both *you and I* would want that someone to be Mary." She looked Thelma directly in her blue eyes. "I think if any two people are praying that Mary has found her prince, then it's me and you, right? We're not drinking hater-ade." She looked at Mary. "We want you to be happy, Mary. We're glad you've found a good man."

Latrice thought she saw Thelma's chin tremble for a moment, then Thelma laughed. It was good to see her laugh. She'd been looking so stressed—no, she'd been looking and acting *uptight* the past few weeks.

Thelma kept laughing, covering her face. She laughed until finally she cried softly. She looked at Latrice and then at Mary. "I love you guys!"

Mary leaned over, briefly, to hug her. "We love you, too."

"I hate this!" Thelma laughed—not too loud—in between discreet sobs. Instead of looking like a stern teacher, she looked more like a confused child. "Everything's changing, you know?" She reached for her purse and pulled out a tissue. "Naomi has lost her mind and run off to California. Who's going to take care of her? What's going to happen to her?" Thelma looked at the shoes all around them. "You're getting married and leaving Baltimore, leaving us." Thelma pointed to herself and then to Latrice, "Who are we going to play makeover with, and who's going to nag us about living right?"

The look Thelma then gave Latrice touched her heart; her no-nonsense friend was capable of being vulnerable. Who would have thought it?

She thought of the three of them dragging Mary down the street to get her made over. When they were done, Mary had green eyes, the longest and brightest nails, not to mention long, lightened, store-bought hair hanging down her back. There had been months and months of dating drama. Now, after enough twists and turns to do any roller coaster proud, Mary was marrying her African prince. And Thelma was right; the four of them had shared it all. "Oh, girl."

This couldn't be the Thelma . . . wasn't the Thelma that had led the makeover parade down the street. This couldn't be Thelma whining. She was always in control and self-sufficient. It was funny, it was weird, to see her being emotional—or at least expressing some emotion other than I've-got-it-all-together-why-don't-you.

"And now all this." Thelma looked at Latrice. "Why does it all have to happen so fast?" Thelma shook her head. She had the sad eyes of an abandoned child. "I just wish everything would slow down!"

EIGHTEEN

Vallejo, California

For the past two weeks or so—it could have been shorter, it could have been longer, time didn't seem to be paying any attention to him—Anthony had been going back and forth between the church and the hotel. He'd been in the Vallejo hotel for some time now, and found a couple of restaurants that weren't too bad—actually, they were pretty good. And he'd found a stand where he could get a really good sub. Things weren't too bad.

He'd been able to keep from calling Desiree. Well, he'd called, but he had had the willpower to hang up in the midst of the first ring. The truth was, it wasn't about love. It couldn't have been—if it had been about love she wouldn't have let him go . . . she wouldn't have demanded that he go. Of course, the fault wasn't all hers. Maybe it never had been about love. He felt lonely sometimes; he missed the heat of her. Maybe what had held them together was sex . . . and their mutual love of the good life.

Things were pretty good, mostly. He'd dropped into the church a few nights. He always went to the empty fellowship hall. Pops Wilson, the old guy, was always there. Pops would pat him on the back. There was still no sighting of Sly Stone, but things weren't bad.

In fact, he would have stopped going to Evangel, but a couple of times when he was in the basement, he thought he heard a voice—he thought he heard Sly. He'd followed the husky voice, winding through the halls. There was never much to follow—just a few words here or there. *That's cool, man.* Or a sound as if Sly were going to let go of a funky scream. In the end, though, he always ended up running into or being tapped on the shoulder by Pops.

Anthony strummed a few chords on his guitar. *Everything's fine.* He hummed along as he played.

No, the truth was, he was confused. He went to Evangel, he stayed at the hotel because he needed some kind of routine in his life. He was confused. He felt ashamed, and there was no one he could tell. He had lost his bearings.

His reason for getting up at dawn had been his job. The basis for most of the decisions in his life—how he wore his hair, when he took vacation, where he lived, what clothes he wore, the kind of woman he chose—had been his job. When he was an executive, he had been decisive because he knew who he was and what he was about. Now about the only thing he knew was when he wanted to eat.

He tried to tell himself it was no big deal, that his job did not determine his worth or his identity. *Yeah, tell that to Donald Trump and the women on his arm!* But the truth was, Anthony could feel himself drifting. So he clung to the little routine he had: television—which he'd rarely watched before, eating, and Evangel and the search for Sly.

Wednesday night was his night. The small, skinny, stooped man was always there smiling *Back again, I see.* The smile just made Anthony feel as though he was more of a loser sitting alone in the Fellowship Hall watching church service on the screen.

Then Anthony would try to explain. "I thought I heard someone."

"Hearing voices, my man? Flying?" Pops smiled like the joke was on him.

"No, I'm here looking for something, for someone. I told you." Anthony used the voice he had used at the office to get people back in line: civil but not cordial.

"Don't feel shame, my brother."

"I'm not shamed. I told you I was looking for someone. I told you that the first night."

"I know." Pops was still smiling. "You find him?"

"No." Anthony didn't know why he kept answering. Why he kept coming.

"No?"

It felt as though Pops was playing with his head. "I told you I was looking for—"

Pops finished his sentence. "Yeah, man. Sly Stone. And you still ain't found him. Well, you keep looking. If you don't find what you looking for, you for sure gonna find what you need, man." He nodded. "Why don't you go upstairs? Get a little closer. You can't get a good look at the band from here."

"This is fine."

Pops held up two fingers. "Peace. Stay cool." He was like a sixties throwback. The old man had walked away nodding and grinning.

Anthony looked around the motel room. All this searching for Sly Stone was ridiculous. What difference did it make? He was blowing money for nothing. If he was going to find Sly Stone, wouldn't he have found him by now? Instead of hunting for a phantom, what he needed to find was a job. Not that he needed one right away, but it was just that it would keep him from feeling unglued.

Going back and forth, it was what he had been doing for weeks now. Anthony fingered the frets of his guitar. It was hard to relax, to stay cool. He felt useless. Sometimes he thought of the men and women he'd fired, if they were able to handle it any better than he was now.

He tried not to pick up papers and look at the want ads. He tried not to go to the web site of the firm he'd worked for—he tried not to check their employment openings online. He was better than all that. He was taking this time off to find himself. To enjoy himself.

He played a few lines from "Proud Mary". *Left a good job in the city. . . .*

Secretly—though he didn't know who *cared,* maybe he was trying to fool himself—instead of relaxing, he had been on two job interviews. He knew the script, he had interviewed many people himself. He thought everything was fine, until the interviewers asked him why he'd left his last position. He was in control until they turned that hard unflinching eye on him, until they raised an eyebrow and asked why.

He had an answer. He was prepared. He'd written it down and practiced it so that he could say it to them, face-to-face. But, somehow, when they asked the question, it wasn't as though they were asking. It was as if another voice, a bigger spotlight was asking—as if the universe was asking. "So, what was it, man?" And when he tried to give the corporate response he had crafted, the universe—laying on its side, chilling on a galaxial sofa—laughed. *"Come on, man. I mean really? I mean, between you and me. What was the cause, bro?"*

And because the universe was infinite in its insight, since it was all-knowing and all-seeing, he could not lie—not even to himself.

He couldn't lie, but for weeks he was silent. He just wouldn't answer. He didn't have to incriminate himself.

Then things would bubble up. Things he could only say to himself. Like when he had terminated people when his stomach told him don't do it. He had fired people when the company said they were no longer suitable, and he had beat back the voice that whispered to him that it was all about money, about not wanting to pay the pension. *What about my family? How are we supposed to eat and pay the mortgage?*

It was business, nothing personal. He had laughed at jokes and people when his conscience had tried to tap him on the shoulder and had told him not to. He had done things for money—*I've got a condo and a car to pay for, don't I? I've got to protect my career*—and played the harlot. He had hoped the universe hadn't seen, wouldn't catch up; he'd pretended the universe really wasn't ethical. *For the love of money.* He'd pretended that the universe was really on a hustle just like him. *We got to get paid!* He'd gotten privileges and walked past people who had been cheated out of theirs and pretended the universe was colluding with him.

Now the universe was lolling on a couch and jeering at him from the other side of the room while he sat in front of an interviewer.

"You should have known better, man." The universe chided him. *"You should have known payback time was coming."* The universe shook its head and laughed. *"Why would people think they can mess over people, children—cheat them—and it never catches up? Why do people think they can lie and laugh and get away with it? Why? Just 'cause I don't make them pay up right away? Man, I'm always watching. I been making a list and checking it three times. Santa ain't got nothing on me. No, I just sit and wait until the tab is so big, 'til you so far behind in what*

you owe, you can't never pay up. I wait until you dug in so deep, until it's a valley and there ain't no way out. Then, I come to call." The universe cackled. *"Don't you know the tune? If you dance to the music, don't you know you got to pay the piper? Ask yo' mama."*

So Anthony still had the taste in his mouth for a job, for money, for walking down a hallway filled with people who looked up to him. But the universe wasn't letting him off the hook.

Anthony parked his car outside Evangel Temple and walked in the back door with the others going inside—only when they took the stairs up to the sanctuary, he took the stairs down to the Fellowship Hall. Right now, he was sure. He was going to find what he was looking for.

He looked around the darkened room and then at the screen. He hardly ever paid attention to the sermon. He looked briefly at the man at the podium dressed in a robe. Mostly Anthony daydreamed about playing guitar with Sly's band, or he thought about how he had come from an office on top of the world to an empty room at the bottom of a church.

"We all know the story of the prodigal son, don't we?"

Anthony looked at the preacher on the screen. He didn't look like Freddie Stone. But, then again, who knew what Freddie Stone looked like now. Anthony always imagined him with a large Afro and bell-bottom pants. But, more likely, he was a gray-haired old man like Pops.

The preacher was nodding as he spoke. "We all know the story. You know the story of the young man." The preacher waved his arms dramatically. "He wanted it all, and he wanted it all now!" The preacher picked up a handkerchief from the podium and wiped his mouth. "'Daddy, give me everything that's due me. Give me all my gifts now!'" The preacher laughed. "I know it kind of reminds some of us of our own kids now. 'Mama and Daddy, give me this and give me that!'" The congregation laughed with the preacher. "It makes you want to holler, throw up both your hands!" They all shook their heads and laughed.

The preacher couldn't have been Freddie Stone, Anthony decided. He was much too young.

"So, the ungrateful young man goes off and lives a riotous life. Drinking." The preacher pantomimed a man drinking. "Cavorting and carousing!" The congregation laughed as the preacher pretended to dance. "'Til pretty soon all that he had was all gone. You know the story: He found himself in mud, in slop, living with pigs. One day everything's fine. He's on top of the world—living in the palace, working in the big house. But before you know it, the brother is living in the pit. He's lost his Lexus and he doesn't even have a hoopty. He was eating caviar and drinking Dom Perignon, now he's fighting the pigs for slop . . . and the pigs are winning.

"And we think to ourselves, 'We could have told you, brother! We could have told you how this story was going to end. Didn't you know the commandment that says honor thy father? Didn't you know wild, thoughtless living was going to dry you up?'"

On the screen, Anthony could see some of the choir members nodding affirmatively as the preacher spoke. Funny, but he felt the preacher's rhetorical questions were aimed at him. But the preacher and the choir members were wrong. Anthony wasn't drinking. He wasn't doing drugs. He wasn't spending money wildly.

Anthony's thoughts didn't quiet the preacher. "Now, I

could jump to the end of the story and tell you how the father took the son back, how he welcomed him back home. And I could tell you how the older brother was jealous of how the father welcomed his younger brother. But I don't want to tell you that part of the story because I don't want you to be mad at me today." The preacher shrugged dramatically. "I want you to be my friends, so I won't remind you of how mad we get sometimes when God, our father, brings a murderer back home, or when he brings our crack-addicted sister back home after we've had to raise her kids." He shook his head. "No, we're not going to touch that." He exaggerated his movements, pretending to walk stealthily. "We're going to tiptoe around that one today. We'll talk about that another time."

Anthony looked around the dark room. Sly wasn't here. He hadn't been here any of the times he'd visited. He was crazy for sitting here subjecting himself to this. But he didn't leave.

The preacher leaned over the podium. "So, no, I'm not going to fuss at my children or your children about being disrespectful and greedy. I'm not going to tell them that they are on the road to ruining their lives. And I'm not going to fuss at myself or at you for being mad about how the Lord seems to always be blessing people who have messed up and don't deserve to be blessed." He stood up straight. "What I'm going to talk about today is how glad I am that our Daddy takes us back home. Because you see, most of us are prodigal."

The preacher was quiet for a moment as he looked around the room. "God gives us all these gifts up front. He gives them and He doesn't ask us how we're going to use them. And the truth is, most of us don't ask Him, 'Father, how should I use these gifts you've given me?' The truth is, most of us go off and squander our gifts on the world, doing what seems good to us—you know, making a little money, getting a few things. We ain't hurting nobody. But few of us are asking our Daddy what we should do with our gifts. Few of us ask, 'God, how do you want me to live my life?' Then, when our life is hard, when we end up having cast our pearls before swine, when we're on our faces, about to throw in the towel—if we're blessed—we come to ourselves and remember we can go home to our Father. If we're blessed, we get grown enough and wise enough to acknowledge that we can't figure it all out, that He knows more than we do."

The preacher used his hands, pretending to dust off his robe. "We pick ourselves up—our dirty, dejected selves—and we rush home hoping that the Father will take us in. We're not good enough for a place of honor, but if He just will let us feed the cows, or carry the slop jar, that will be good enough." The preacher lifted his head, threw his arms wide, and smiled broadly. "But, oh, the joy! The joy and surprise when we find He's been waiting for us—oh, when we find He's been waiting for us to come to the celebration! Oh, the joy that floods our souls when we realize He's been waiting for us to come home!"

NINETEEN

Bodega Bay, California

Naomi sat in the backseat, the wind whipping her blonde ponytail as she, Ruthie, and Mona the baker gunned south down the road to Vallejo in Mona's beat-up Ford. Naomi touched her hair. The black roots had taken over—the tail was about the only thing still yellow—and she needed the weave tightened and a touch-up. If her friends could see her now!

All the car windows were down and anything not tied down was flapping. Ruthie's cheeks were pink. She bopped her head to the music.

Mona yelled happily over the blaring radio: "It's my pleasure to have you ladies ride with me!" She looked at Naomi in the rearview mirror. "It's better to have a crew than to make this trip alone."

The wind was so strong, all Naomi could do was nod in response. *Soon as I have money, I'm going to send for my car. Right after I get my hair done!* Since the show had aired, she'd begun to make mental lists of the things she might buy, thinking of things that might be a good use for her money.

And my children? I want to see my children. But what if they don't want to see me? She let the blowing wind quickly whip the thoughts away; they were too painful.

Mona was still talking: "I've been making this run twice a week for years, you know? And soon as I found out our friend Ruthie here needed a ride so she could get to the volunteer center in Vallejo, well, I said, 'Why sure, hop aboard!' Right, Ruthie?"

Ruthie held up two fingers, still singing, in response.

"So, when Ruthie told me you were going with her, I was pleased as punch."

Naomi nodded, still trying to hold her ponytail. She wasn't sure this was such a good idea. What was she going to do at the center? What she needed to be doing, more than flying up and down the road, was looking for a job. If she was going to look for a job, she was certain she didn't want to do what Ruthie was doing, working with children. What could she do? She'd just be in the way.

But she was trying to be friends with the girl, to be better than she'd been before. She could make the trip this one time. What would it hurt?

The Vallejo All-Volunteer Center on Toulumne Street was next to a grocery outlet store at the corner of Toulumne and Tennessee. While people walked in and out of the salvage store pushing loaded buggies, people—mostly women and children—milled in front of the center.

"There's a few doctors that volunteer here twice a week," Ruthie explained as they walked through the front doors. "I just come to help out." Ruthie tossed her stringy hair. "Some of the families don't have health insurance and can't afford a doctor. Some have Medicaid, but even then a lot of doctors won't take Medicaid patients. The docs here don't have a lot, and they need more. But they do what they can."

Naomi followed behind Ruthie, who stopped to hug groups of kids. Mothers, many with their hair braided or their heads tied with scarves, brightened when they saw her. The children followed behind Ruthie, winding their way through the large chair-lined room. It seemed that life followed her; wherever she went, gray silence disappeared. The children giggled and danced behind her as though she were the Pied Piper. They followed her around the large room. It was filled with gray-colored, curved plastic chairs—a type of waiting room. Ruthie's smile and the bright colors she wore seemed to bring the area to life.

As she circled the room, Ruthie plucked storybooks from chairs, from the counter at the front of the room, and from off the floor. She gathered the children in the corner of the room. They sat cross-legged around her as she began to read.

The children, and even Ruthie, who looked scruffy standing outside, looked themselves like a page from a storybook. They were smiling and wide-eyed. Many of the children were snaggle-toothed. Naomi smiled at the picture. It had been a while since she'd thought about clinics or dentistry. She had not imagined anything like this when Ruthie had invited her. As she began to look with her dentist's eye, she could see more than missing teeth. She could also see signs of decay. If they weren't receiving medical care, it was likely that they were also lacking dental care. She thought of Baltimore and the career she had left behind for a chance on *Wheel of Fortune*.

Naomi found a chair close to the place where they were gathered. As she sat and listened, a little girl crawled onto the chair next to her. Naomi looked down at the little girl. She smiled and took Naomi's hand. Perhaps there was a place for her here after all.

TWENTY

Vallejo, California

Anthony strummed a twanging rhythm on his guitar while Pops stirred a couple of boxes of macaroni and cheese. The steamy, greasy, salty smell of boiling polish sausages let him know that dinner would soon be on the table—or on the two wooden TV tables that sufficed. He looked around the room at the ratty carpet and down at the cot he sat on. It was a long way from his San Francisco townhouse.

In that time, he hadn't done anything but play.

He still hadn't figured out why he'd said yes to the old man's invitation. The message about the prodigal son, the one the preacher at Evangel Temple had taught, was still running through his mind. It was after that message, when he was leaving the church, that Pops had first stopped Anthony and invited him. *"Come on by my place and get a little something to eat, brother."* Since then, though he still lived at the hotel, he'd been dining on only the best—hot dogs, burgers, canned spaghetti, and packages of ramen noodles at Pops'. Occasionally, there was also Spam and Vienna sausages, meat products, or alleged meat products Anthony hadn't eaten in years. Maybe he'd just needed company while he thought about what the preacher had said.

"*Because you see, most of us are prodigal . . . most of us don't ask Him, 'Father, how should I use these gifts. . . .' Few of us ask, 'God, how do you want me to live my life?'*"

Anthony's plan had been to leave if he hadn't found Sly Stone at Evangel Temple. He'd told Pops about his plans to go to New York if Sly Stone didn't materialize.

"Life is a trip, man. You in a tight spot," Pops had told him. "You got a lot on your mind. Most times the answer ain't to run. You got to stay right where you are and dig. Ain't no running. You got to stand still and keep digging until you find the gold in who you are. Keep playing 'til it comes back to you."

So Anthony, because he didn't have any other plan, had taken the old man's advice. He practiced licks on his Fender while the old man pontificated.

"Yeah." Pops had laughed. He was always laughing, as though he knew about the pyramids and every other mystery in the world. Pops pointed at the guitar. "You can play for your supper."

He was a strange old man, and Anthony was unable to shake the feeling that there was something familiar about him. Anthony looked around the pad, as Pops called it, while he played. There were peace signs on the wall—it had been years since he'd seen any of them. There were also loud-colored psychedelic posters on the walls, a lava lamp on a side table, and a yellow fish net, heavy with star fish, hanging from the ceiling. There was a large purple beanbag chair. And hanging on the wall, on a nail, were a pair of gold, star-shaped sunshades. The old guy was as weird as his pad, like some outdated rock star. Anthony chuckled to himself. This whole thing had been crazy. The idea of finding Sly Stone . . . it was crazy. He looked at the old guy stirring the pot, at the peace signs and the glasses on the wall. He might as well face it—Pops was probably the closest he was ever going to come to finding Sly Stone.

In between cooking and smiling, Pops spoke in metaphors and riddles. "Man, I know what the preacher was preaching about. You know, about the prodigal son, man. The truth is, you don't know who you are, man. You think you rolling. You think you got it all together and that you're cooler and hipper than everybody else. Yeah." Pops nodded. He nodded a lot. Pops snapped his fingers and laughed. "Yeah, baby."

He poured the hot water off the noodles and then added the powdered cheese to the pot. "That's what I'm talkin' about, baby!" He pointed at the pot. "This is real, right here. Everyday people food."

Pops turned the blue flame off underneath the pot of sausages. "We all looking for something, baby. We can't find what we looking for, man, 'cause we blind. But it's in our faces. What you looking for is in your face." Pops nodded and giggled. "Yeah."

He was whacked out, but he was harmless. Actually, Pops had a good heart. He was generous, and it was nice to be around someone who gave without wanting anything in return.

"We can't see that we're digging our way in a hole, man. Even when people try to tell us, we don't hear. 'No, I'm okay. It's Betty Jean and Michael over there that's got the problems. Not me.' So we keep doing what we're doing and digging in until we're way over our heads. The hole is deep, man."

Anthony moved his fingers from fret to fret. He'd stopped trying to figure out what Pops was saying. He just listened: precious gems from the brain of a burnout.

"Man, I was cool for sure. What did I need Jesus for? I didn't even know who the cat was, the rule maker. Crashing my party; I was on top of the world."

Anthony looked around the room. If this was on top of the world, he didn't want to be there.

"What did I need religion for? My stuff was sweet. I was a good person. I gave to the poor—tossed a couple of dimes in the cup when my pocket was full. That was for losers and old people, man. Let my mama do that."

Pops began to dance, waving his hands in the air, his back stooped. He was a strange sight, but Anthony could not get over the feeling that he knew the old man from somewhere.

"I was cool, grooving and doing my own thing, 'til Jesus got up in my face." Pops slapped his knee. "And He didn't get in my face until I was in a valley so deep I couldn't get out, and it was time to pay up. Or, at least, I didn't hear Him until then." Pops looked up at the stained ceiling, and then down at the floor. "I was on top of the world. Then just as fast, the party was over. Then that cat reached down and saved me. People can laugh at me all they want about how I feel about Jesus. They're just laughing 'cause they don't know they in a hole yet. When your back is not up against the wall, but in the wall, when you're going down for the count and somebody comes in and saves you, man, you thanking that cat all the time. You don't care what nobody says."

Pops reached in the cabinet for the two cracked plates he owned. "I dig the cat, man. Give to the poor. Feed the hungry. Open your doors to strangers. Love those that hate you. Turn the other cheek. Church helping church. Church loving church. Forgive and love. Turn the other cheek. Love your brother. Wash your brother's feet. And your brother is everybody—all shapes, all sizes, all colors, all nations. That's Jesus, baby. That's the real Jesus. People couldn't take Him, baby. And they ain't foolin' nobody—white-washed walls. They couldn't take Him then, and some folks still can't take Him now."

Pops reached for two glasses and poured water from the refrigerator into them. "But it still trips me out, man. He still inviting us back home." He nodded, grinning. "Yeah, baby!"

Pops slid his wiry frame into his seat. "Jesus wept," he said. He pointed with his fork. "Dig in, man. Let's eat."

TWENTY-ONE

Baltimore, Maryland

S o, I think everything turned out all right. The blue shoes are nice, right? And I think you can wear them again, don't you?" The restaurant candlelight reflected in Mary's eyes.

Latrice smiled at her friend. With only a few days before the wedding, it was probably going to be their last visit to Phillips Restaurant, probably even their last visit together to the Inner Harbor.

Thelma smirked and looked away.

Latrice nodded. "It's going to be fine, Mary. It's going to be a beautiful wedding."

Mary reached across the table to touch Thelma's hand. "No ruffles, no flounces. I promise. It's going to be beautiful, right?"

Thelma still looked like a spoiled child instead of the schoolteacher she was. "Sure. Beautiful. There's nothing more beautiful than a wedding."

Latrice enjoyed being the one to give Thelma a correcting glance this time.

Thelma sat up straighter in the booth. "I just have to get used to it, that's all. Maybe if I had more time, if you all had been dating here instead of your flying back and forth to

California." She poked at her drink again. "I just don't think I would know—that I would know so soon whether I was ready to marry."

"Look, I've got a letter from Moor." Mary gushed as she pulled a letter—sage green paper in a matching envelope from her purse. It was pretty obvious that she was trying not to join Thelma in her blues. "Want me to read it to you?" Not only was it a letter from her love, but it also changed the direction of the conversation.

Thelma grimaced. "Do we have a choice?"

Mary began to read aloud.

"'My Dearest FuFu—'"

"FuFu?" Thelma was frowning. "What kind of name is that?"

"It's the name of one of Moor's favorite foods." It was obvious that Mary wasn't letting Thelma's negativity spoil her party. She cleared her throat and began again.

"'My Dearest FuFu, there is no way to describe how much I miss you. When I see the stars, the sun, or the moon, they are nothing to me. I would pull them from the sky except they promise to shine day and night on the one I love.'"

Latrice leaned forward, laying her chin atop one of her hands. As Mary read, she could imagine Moor and hear his voice, his exotic accent, as Mary spoke the words.

"'I was a fool to fight God for so long. When I am with you, I know that the good Lord has given me my heart's desire.

"'"O my dove, in the clefts of the rock,
In the secret places of the cliff,
Let me see your face,
Let me hear your voice;

For your voice is sweet,

And your face is lovely."'"

Mary looked up. "That's from the Song of Solomon."

She smiled, then continued reading. "'My dearest one, our wedding date is soon, but my heart says it is too far away.'" Mary looked at Latrice and Thelma, smiling like Christmas.

Latrice was feeling fluttery. "Girl, girl, girl."

"I know!" Mary was almost squealing.

Thelma pouted and shook her head in disgust.

Mary continued reading. "'Soon you will come to me. Soon we will be one.'"

Latrice fanned her with her napkin. "Mercy!"

Mary pressed the letter to her bosom. "I know!"

Thelma rolled her blue eyes.

Mary pressed on. "'My family is so far away. Only my grandmother—my heart, my wise one—can come for the wedding, but she will make up for everyone and tell the story when she returns home.'"

Latrice imagined the high mountains of Lesotho in southern Africa as Mary read. She imagined the wildflowers, bold and bright, waving in the fields as Mary had described what Moor had shared with her.

"'And because I am new in California, I only have one friend. But Anthony is a good man and will be there as my best man. I have also secured a church. It is only available for three hours for the ceremony, but I believe it will be enough.

"'While we are apart, I pray for you each night, as I will pray for you when you are in my arms. "Great Father, bless my beloved. Do not let her dash her foot. Wipe worry from her brow and lift trouble from her shoulders. And, Lord, make me fit, teach me kindness, that each day I will bring her joy."

"'I love you, my FuFu. I pray and wait none too patiently until you come. The seas of my passion await you. Love, from the one who adores you. Moor.'"

Thelma pursed her lips. "We still don't know anything about *him*—Moor. So he can write things on paper. So what? All I know is one day you are happy and single, the next minute you're married. Who knows what happened in between? Who knows what has you convinced this is the man of your dreams?"

Mary smiled at her. "Do you want me to tell you a story?"

"Wait!" Latrice wiggled on the bench until she was comfortable. She dropped her napkin across her lap, and then slid the shrimp and cocktail sauce across the booth closer to herself so she could dip and eat without looking. "Okay, girl, go ahead."

Thelma sighed.

"In San Francisco, at the Bay, there are restaurants and shops, like here. But there are more boats, and somehow it seems saltier, bluer—maybe it's the air. I can't explain it. But anyway, it was sunny and we were running from place to place and laughing.

"Suddenly, out of nowhere, it was raining. And the first thing I thought was, 'Oh no—'"

"My hair!" Latrice finished for her.

Mary laughed. "That's right. You know how we are about our hair. But then I thought, so what. If he doesn't like me because of my hair. . . ." She blushed. "It was me that was worried about it, he didn't notice. He didn't care." She batted her eyes. "He doesn't care."

Thelma's expression was cynical. "So, that's how you knew? Because he didn't freak when he saw your hair nappy?"

"It wasn't just my hair. I mean, it was pouring. I was wet and squishy, and I fell on the way back to the car and was out of breath. I was a mess, and my skin had broken out while I was there. I was a mess."

Thelma's eyebrow raised. "And?"

"I know it's probably nothing to you. I know falling down is not exciting. It would be exciting and convincing if I said we went out in a limo, he bought me diamonds, and we danced all night."

Thelma took a sip of her drink. "Something like that."

"To me, it was beautiful because it wasn't like that. He looked at me—with my pimply, wet, fat, kinky-haired self, like I was the most beautiful woman he had ever seen. When I fell and was feeling all embarrassed—'cause you know how you feel when you're overweight and you fall—he lifted me and kissed me on my forehead and on my cheeks. 'Are you harmed, my sister, my love, my beauty, my queen?' he kept whispering. Moor took off his shirt and began to wipe the dirt away from my hands, off my knees, and feet. And I thought about something."

Latrice realized she had been holding a shrimp mid-air the whole time Mary spoke. She tried not to look too enthralled.

Thelma didn't sound so convinced. "What?"

"Every time he whispered those things to me, I became more what he spoke. Maybe I just believed it more. He kept calling me, 'my treasure, my crown.' He was speaking to me, to who I really am—not to my hair, or my clothes, or even to my body. He was speaking to the inside of me, the part of me that never changes, the part of me that is eternal. I was drowning in his voice and in his eyes—it was a kind of rapture. It scared me how I felt."

Latrice could feel herself blushing. When was the last time *that* had happened? Her *blushing?* She shook herself.

"And it came to me that the true test of love is not how much someone loves you in your perfection, but how much they adore you in your imperfection.

"Of course, a man loves me when I'm a size seven, and when my nails and feet are perfectly manicured."

Mary flashed her hands at Thelma and then at Latrice. They were definitely much more groomed than the hands she had presented before last year's makeover. Girlfriend was even wearing polish! Latrice nodded her approval.

Mary continued talking. "Of course, a woman loves a man when he has great wealth and owns a Benz. But the test is, can I trust the person enough—can I be fragile enough to reveal the flawed parts of me, to allow that person to wash the dirt from my feet, or to touch my wounded places? That's love. Can I be his friend, and allow him to be my friend? Can I show him what I show to both of you?" Mary poked at the appetizer in front of her. "We kiss men's scars. Most of us don't give them a chance to kiss ours."

Thelma's chest rose and fell. "So, that's it? He wiped your feet?"

Mary smiled and shrugged. "It was a lot to me. It was beautiful to me."

Thelma looked around as if she was searching for their waitress, then settled back and casually took another sip of her drink. "I guess I was just looking for something more, like you can't wait or have to rush because he's swept you off your feet and you're burning with desire! Something!"

"Well, it's that too."

"I don't get it, Mary. I thought you would have something more."

Latrice tried to be quiet. Mary was a big girl, she could take care of herself. And she knew Thelma didn't really mean any harm, but. . . .

Thelma continued. "I just thought, at least . . . it's probably our last supper together . . . that you would be able to give us the details, the skinny. I mean you've preached to us about the rules—"

Latrice nodded. There had been lots of conversations among Mary, Thelma, Naomi, and her about men and about being single in the church. Some of them funny. Some of them uncomfortable.

Mary interrupted, "I said I think we ought to *think* about how we live our lives. I never tried to tell anyone how to live. I just suggested that we think about it."

Thelma continued. "I just thought you'd tell us about how you all did it," she laughed, "or avoided doing it. You know, how all this works." Thelma smiled nonchalantly, but just beneath the surface it looked to Latrice that Thelma might have been more interested than she wanted to let on. "You know? How to be single *and satisfied*. I thought you'd at least leave us, before you go, with Mary's rules for dating. A word for all us women still stuck in Single Land."

Mary tilted her head and then smiled thoughtfully, sadly. "I don't have a word. Unless the word is that I'm excited. The truth is that I'm also as afraid of going into this new place—moving to a new city, living with a new man—as you are afraid *for* me."

Thelma turned her head away briefly.

"Some days, I'm packing and thinking this is everything I've been waiting for, everything I've wanted. I've taken all the singles' classes and prayed—I'm ready. And I'm not kidding you, the thought of being able to make love to Moor on our wedding night—well, let's just say a sister is not too opposed to the idea."

Latrice laughed. "As long as you've been celibate, girlfriend? I know you're right!"

Mary laughed softly, then looked intently at her and Thelma. "But one second later, I have my eyes squeezed shut. I'm on the floor in a ball, I'm crying to myself and my hands are balled so tight. Then I don't want to go—I want to stay where I am.

"I guess it's like babies being born. You've got this comfortable place. You know the smells and the sounds."

When Mary looked across the table into her eyes, Latrice thought of all the years the four friends had known each other—since college. They had teased each other, prayed for each other, played the dozens, laughed, loved, cried, argued, and danced their way through almost twenty years. Between them, they had collected memories of football games, boyfriends, shared private jokes, and college graduation. They had met as girls; now they were women.

"Where I am, I feel safe and protected. I love it here. Baltimore is my home. I know the rhythms with you all. You're my sisters. I don't want to leave you. It's like leaving part of me, part of who I am." Mary laid her hand atop Thelma's hand. "But the truth is, I also know I have to go. You know I have to go. We can't let fear, fear that something bad will happen, fear of some valley that will appear, keep us from walking into our new lives."

Thelma moved her hand, like she needed to pick up her napkin.

Mary looked back and forth between them. "I know

where I'm going is a good place. I know Moor loves me. I love him. He's a good man. But in my heart I'm crying out, leaving part of me behind. You," Mary looked at Thelma—who hung her head—and then at Latrice, "are part of me." Mary laid her hand over her heart. "We're one, the four of us. And I need to know—I need *you* to give me the gift of knowing that that will never change, no matter how far apart we are." Mary touched Thelma's hand again. "You're not the only one who's afraid, but my fear is outweighed by my trust and my love."

Thelma turned her head again.

Mary laughed. "As for the rules."

Latrice nodded. They were going to be okay. They really were. They were going to survive the change. "Yeah. That's what I want to hear." She dunked her shrimp in cocktail sauce. "Tell me the rules! Do you hold hands? Do you kiss? Do you need a chaperone? Do you even date? Do you just pick somebody and jump the broom? Girl, inquiring minds want to know!"

Thelma looked back as Mary giggled and continued, "Girl, if I had the rules, I would write a book."

Latrice slurped on the shrimp she was holding. She enjoyed the plump saltiness of the meat mixing in her mouth with the sharp sweetness of the sauce. No point in letting the little fellow go to waste. "I know that's right!"

"The only rules I know are kingdom rules. And the kingdom rules for dating are the kingdom rules for everything else."

The waitress brought their food. Thelma picked at the deviled crab in front of her. "And the kingdom rules are?"

She raised her hand. "No, stop. Never mind. Stop in the name of love!"

Latrice hushed her. "Be quiet, Thelma. Stop blocking. I really want to hear."

TWENTY-TWO

Vallejo, California

Anthony played—first he fingered some chords, and then he found his way to a rhythm. He hummed. *I want 2 thank you 4 lettin me be mice elf again.*

"Oh, I like that, now." Pops began to hit a step in the tiny Vallejo apartment. The old man flapped his arms behind him like a chicken. He shook his head—and what there was left of his wiry white hair—in time. "Oh, you got something there, brother. You bringing back memories now!" Pops grabbed his sunshades off the wall and stretched out his arms like he was on stage playing to a crowd.

Anthony was feeling better about his playing. It was coming back to him now.

He looked at the old man and laughed. It would be a trip if Pops turned out to be Sly Stone. Anthony laughed and shook his head. That was impossible.

"Ain't no 'bout a-doubt it, man." Pops danced some more. "What you say you were doing down there in San Francisco?"

Anthony laughed while he played. "Earning a living."

"I know that's right." Pops was still cutting the rug. "Seem like artists don't ever have enough to get by, man." The old man stopped and looked around. "'Course, I don't ever earn enough to get by now."

"Why don't you invest some of it?"

Pops grabbed his stomach, laughing. "Man, I don't have enough money to buy no stocks." He pointed around his apartments. "Look at this pad, I ain't got no long green. Investing's for rich cats, man."

Anthony stretched his fingers and lifted his wrist to reach a chord. "I thought you called them fat cats."

Pops sat down at the table nearby. "There's a difference. See, rich cats got it legit, baby. Fat cats steal. You dig? But like I said, I still ain't got *no* money to invest—legit or otherwise."

"You don't have to do it by yourself." Anthony found his way back to the rhythm. "Get some friends together. Invest as a group."

Pops reached and stopped Anthony's hand. "You know all about this money stuff, huh, brother?"

"Like I said, I was making a living."

Before Anthony knew it, he was walking into Evangel a few evenings later—not to find Sly Stone, but for a meeting Pops had set up at the church. The room he entered was small. Inside were all the church janitors, and a few of the cooks and maintenance men. All in all, there were fourteen people. This was sure not San Francisco. There were no suits and no power ties. There wasn't even any coffee.

He'd brought newspapers with him. He turned to the stock listings. "Go through. See what you like. You can do research. Find out a stock's history. Making money is not a mystery."

"It is to me," a woman in braids, who was wearing a blue

uniform, answered. "I ain't never had two dimes to rub together."

Anthony sat down with them. "If you can work together, you can invest. And if you get enough money, or if you have a big enough group, instead of just buying the burgers, you can own the franchise." Soon he forgot where he was and to whom he was talking. They were no longer janitors and cooks, but businessmen and businesswomen.

As they rode along in the car, on the way home, Pops turned the radio until he found a classic rock station. He settled back in his seat. "Dig it, man. You gave a whole lot of people hope tonight, brother."

Anthony checked the rearview mirror and then shrugged. "I didn't do anything."

"Yes, you did. What you did was groovy, baby. You brought your gifts back home."

Anthony looked at Pops and then back at the road. He'd drop Pops off, then head to the hotel.

"It's like the prodigal son, baby."

How many times was he going to hear that story? "Yeah, sure. The prodigal son." Anthony laughed. "I don't think you'd call what I was doing living riotously. I wasn't a drunk and I'm not a philanderer. I have one woman . . . I *had* one woman." He didn't want to think about Desiree. He wouldn't think about her.

"That's what a lot of people think 'cause they don't look deep, man. Like the preacher said, it's really a story about you and about cats like me. You know, we cool. We got a lot of gifts. We think Daddy's a square, the establishment. He don't know nothing about real life. You know, trying to be a man. So we break away.

"We got it in our heart to do something, to have an adventure, to live the dream."

Pops was right about that. He didn't want to be like a lot of the men he saw in the 'hood. Sitting on the corner, year after year, they never went anywhere. The color of their hair changed, the uniform changed, but they were still in the same spot. He had wanted something different.

"Only, we don't know, God ain't mad at us for that. He likes wild men. He ain't mad at us for wanting to take life and squeeze it for all it's worth, man. He just don't want us to forget who we are and where we come from." Pops nodded. "And see, we're just like that prodigal, 'cause our Daddy gives us all our gifts up front, baby. He lets us make the choice, you dig? That's why I love that cat, man. It's like you with the guitar. Music just come out your belly, baby."

Anthony laughed. "Well, I've seen you cutting some steps around the apartment, Pops. You could be on the stage, man."

"You think so?"

"Oh, yeah. I know I could see you playing for people. Making them happy. It would be a blast, man."

The old man invited him in so they could talk. They pulled into the apartment parking lot, got out of the car, and Pops began to dance as they walked up the sidewalk. Something about his moves, as it had seemed so many times before, was familiar.

When they walked in the apartment door, Pops was still talking. "But music ain't all you got." He turned the lights on. "What you did tonight, giving people an understanding of money—you gave them hope. That's ministry to the poor, baby. You ain't handing out soup. You giving them knowledge, baby." He took some pots from the cabinet. "You got all these gifts, took them out in the world, and the world used you, and then spit you out. But you learned a lesson tonight, baby—just like I did." Pops reached for two cans of spaghetti. "Daddy will always take you back home." He set the cans on the counter.

Anthony cleared his throat. He sat on his cot.

"What brought you here?" Pops asked.

Anthony didn't like where this was going. "You know I didn't come here to get preached to, man."

Pops opened the first can. "No?" He dumped it in a pot.

"I told you. I came here looking for Sly."

"Is that all?"

"That's all."

"You just quit your job, left your home and your woman to find Sly Stone?"

It was none of Pops' business. If he'd gone to the hotel, he wouldn't have to hear all this. "Yes."

"See, we get fooled. We think we okay because we got women—or a woman—and a little bit of money." He snapped his fingers. "Man, that can be gone in two seconds."

Pops picked up the second can, opened it, and dumped it. "You're just looking for Sly?"

Anthony didn't owe the old man any explanations. It was none of his business. "Yes." Why did Pops have to grill him? Why couldn't things just stay cool?

Pops took a wooden spoon from the drawer and began to stir in the pot. "Well, I don't think you're looking for Sly Stone. See, man, I think you're missing the picture." Pops leaned one old, frail hip against the counter. "We're being lulled asleep, we're being fooled. We think the greatest adventure of our lives is getting a job and making money. But that ain't it."

Anthony kept playing. There was no point in getting worked up over anything the old man had to say. "Well, what *is* it?"

"You looking for your great adventure. And the greatest adventure ain't about money. It's the story of the good king, and the evil prince who is willing to ruin the kingdom so he can have everything, and the good son willing to do anything to save his father's kingdom and all mankind. The greatest adventure is full of angels and demons—it's a wild ride, baby."

As Pops spoke, Anthony could see the kingdom in his mind. It was like a fairytale: there were mountains, green valleys, and desolate plains.

"In the great adventure, the evil prince running all over the place, man. He's ruining people's lives, stealing from them, murdering them. The good prince is willing to do anything to save the kingdom. But to do it, he has to leave his throne, to leave his place of safety, and come to earth to fight the wicked prince. When the good prince comes, he's got to come with nothing . . . 'cause see he comes in a way the wicked prince would never suspect. The prince gives up everything and comes into this world to be born in a stinkin' stable, undercover. Most people don't even recognize him."

Anthony imagined the good prince being born in a poor place, maybe a stable, maybe amongst pigs like the prodigal son. He was certain he had heard the story before.

And, lo, the angel of the Lord came upon them, and the glory of the Lord shone round about them: and they were sore afraid.

And the angel said unto them, "Fear not: for, behold, I bring you good tidings of great joy, which shall be to all people. For unto you is born this day in the city of David a Saviour, which is Christ the Lord.

And this shall be a sign unto you; Ye shall find the babe wrapped in swaddling clothes, lying in a manger."

"So when people recognize the good prince, it ain't because of his jewelry—all that's gone. You recognize him by his love. 'Cause see, he looks like everybody else. He don't look like a prince or a king."

Anthony imagined a heavenly prince walking the earth as a common man. It was hard to picture.

Pops slapped his knee. "While he's here, he invites people to take part. That's the real adventure of your life. People get to choose sides. Part of the adventure is choosing sides, the other is figuring out what role they're supposed to play. Some people are musicians, some are warriors, and some tell the story, but everybody is supposed to invite someone else."

Pops smiled. "You join the story by saying, 'I believe!'"

Anthony stopped playing. It sounded familiar. He had heard the story before. *For to us a child is born, to us a son is given, and the government will be on his shoulders. And He will be called Wonderful Counselor, Mighty God, Everlasting Father, Prince of Peace.*

Pops was still smiling. "And get this, to fool the wicked prince—the enemy—the people that fight for the good prince fight with weapons the evil cat don't understand. See, he thinks they comin' with anger and swords, but the weapons of their warfare are faith, hope, and truth. And our greatest gift and weapon is love.

"So, the good prince lives among us for thirty-three years. While he's here he does a lot of good. He tells us the way back to the kingdom. He heals people and sets people free. And while he's here, he's beaten, betrayed, and makes the ultimate sacrifice—he dies to save us from the delusion that our lives have no meaning, dies for our sins. Through his dying, we come back to real life. He goes home again, but the story ain't over. The wicked prince still wants to win, still trying to fool us into believing we ain't nobody, we don't matter. So the good prince, who is now king of kings, invites us into the battle."

Anthony stared at Pops. He had heard the story.

"Only the wildest thing is, the story is real. And even wilder, it's not just a story for telling. But, man, you can be part of the story—you can play a part in the battle between good and evil. The gas is that it's real!"

Anthony looked at his guitar, at Pops, and then around the room—at the posters, the peace symbols. It all felt surreal. This was the last conversation he ever thought he would have been having with anyone, not to mention that he would never have imagined himself in a place like this psychedelic shack.

"You been on a trip the whole time. 'Cause He's real and He's coming again. When the prince comes again—only now as King of Kings and Lord of Lords—He's coming as a bridegroom. As a bridegroom on a white horse and His name is Faithful and True. You're invited to the wedding. All kinds of people are invited to the wedding. When that wedding comes, it's gone be something else, baby!"

Pops said it was real, but it felt as though it were a dream. All this talk of princes and kings and bridegrooms—it was a wild and fantastic story.

A thought nagged at him. He had heard a story before about a prince and bridegroom, about an invitation and a wedding.

The old men . . . they call me Prince. . . . I need you to be best man at my wedding!

Moor's voice haunted him.

Anthony jumped to his feet. It had been weeks since he'd thought about Moor! It had been weeks since he'd thought of the wedding and the invitation. He'd never called. Anthony dug in the inside pocket of his guitar case where he'd put the invitation so he wouldn't forget to call and give his regrets. He opened it and looked at the date.

It was too close. How was he ever going to get there on time?

Pops shook the pot and stirred again. "Oh yeah, brother, I think you're looking for a great adventure. I think you're trying to find your way back home."

TWENTY-THREE

Baltimore, Maryland

Latrice waved her hand at Thelma. "Hush and let Mary talk." With just a few days before the wedding, it was probably their last meal at Phillips and she wanted to hear.

Thelma wasn't going to surrender that easily. "Don't hush me, Latrice. Like you are really interested in Mary's rules. Right! Tell me anything."

"No, Thelma, you hush." It was like they were five years old.

"No, you."

Latrice waved Thelma away. "Go ahead, Mary. Ignore Thelma. What rules?"

Mary's smile said how much she loved them, how much she was going to miss them. "You know, 'Love the Lord your God with all your heart and with all your soul and with all your mind.' And 'Love your neighbor as yourself.'"

Thelma nodded. "Um-hmm. Like Sunday school. The greatest commandment and the second." She raised that famous eyebrow. "And. So? What does that have to do with dating?"

Mary continued, counting on her fingers as she spoke. "You know, 'Do unto others as you would have them do unto you.' Then, love people like Jesus loves us—you know, minister to others. But when the Lord said it, I don't think He only meant strangers, or people in church, I think He also meant those we love. Sometimes we're the most careless with people we love, people we're dating—we take advantage of those relationships. Be a servant instead of trying to get your way and be first." She tapped another finger. "And be Jesus' witnesses in Jerusalem, Judea, Samaria, and all of the world— and that includes the people we love, or even people we're dating." She shrugged. "That's it. Those are the rules."

Latrice looked at the shrimp in front of her, at the cocktail sauce, at Mary—who was calmly adjusting the napkin on her lap—and then looked into Thelma's confused blue eyes. She felt better that she wasn't the only one confounded. Both of them broke out into laughter.

Thelma cleared her throat and spoke up. "Mary, I don't know. Am I the only one missing something here? I mean, I got the Sunday school lesson, but I don't know what those commandments have to do with dating. If I was going to take your advice and decide to be celibate—which I am not—I still don't know whether to pet or not to pet. I still don't know the rules."

"That's the thing. There are no rules."

Latrice dropped the shrimp she was holding. "I knew it, she doesn't know!"

Mary went on, "That's what I finally figured out. There are no special rules. Not for dating. Not for anything else."

Thelma's smile was somewhere between victory and being perplexed.

"People make up rules because that's what we like. It's safe. We don't have to think—it lets someone else do the work for us. But the truth is, if we love God with all our hearts, we're going to want to live lives that please Him. That will be in our hearts. We'll want to please Him when we date."

Latrice was trying to sit still, but frustration wouldn't let her. "But that's why people want rules—to be sure that what they do pleases God." She looked at Thelma. "Why do I feel like I'm stuck in a never-ending loop?"

Mary smiled. Her calm only made it more frustrating. "What pleases God is us asking Him, seeking the answers in the ways He has taught us."

Latrice was certain her face said that she wasn't getting it.

Mary continued. "But none of this makes sense unless you believe the Lord and trust what He teaches—to me it changes everything."

Latrice clicked her nails together. "Mary, girl, you are going to drive me to drink."

"See, I think the reason why it's confusing to us is that we know what we want from relationships—really. We're just distracted by the thing that looks like it." Mary laughed.

Latrice bit her lip.

"What most people really want from dating, or relationships, is love."

"That's debatable." Thelma narrowed her eyes. "Maybe that used to be the fantasy women were buying."

"But see, I don't think it's just a fantasy. I think that the desire for love is part of who we are—it's human. We can pretend like we don't care. We can try to be cynical. But the truth in our hearts is that most of us really date, or whatever, because we are looking for love. Young girls, old women— we're all looking for the same thing. We're afraid to hope enough to admit we want it, but the desire is still there. Only we have confused the physical indicators with the real thing."

"And the physical indicators are?" Thelma laughed sarcastically.

Mary began to count on her fingers again. "If he loves me, he buys me things. If he loves me, he holds my hand. If he loves me, he takes me to dinner and buys me cards. If he has sex with me, he loves me."

Thelma's eyes grew bigger. "I like those things. Who doesn't like to be wined and dined? A man that does those things is paying attention and taking out time—spending his money. What's wrong with those things as indicators?"

"What's wrong is that they're physical indicators. But they're not spiritual indicators." Mary tilted her head. "Come on, we've all been through it. A man can make dinner for you or take you out and not love you."

Latrice thought about Mary's dates with Reggie and Floyd. They were definitely not about love.

Mary continued, "He could go through those motions and still not love you. Somebody can do those things and not care. Someone can do those things and beat you or talk bad to you. No matter how much stuff he buys you, if he beats you or talks to you like you're dirt, he doesn't love you—not God's kind of love.

"Love is spiritual, and the spiritual indicators are—" Mary began to count on her fingers again—"that he loves me like Christ loves me, which means he wants to serve me, to heal me with his love, to put me first—he listens to me. If he loves me, he speaks and prays words, and has thoughts and hopes that restore me. If he is kind and patient and forgiving with me. If the words he speaks to me speak life to me. And the truth is, those are the things that I find in my baby, Moor."

Latrice giggled. It was nice to hear Mary speak of Moor that way. Very nice.

Mary's face seemed to glow. Her eyes looked and her voice sounded as though her lover was present, sitting with them in the booth. "No other man has spoken to me that way. And the truth is, that when Moor speaks to me that way, when he is gentle with me, it makes me drunk with love. So, in return, I want to speak and offer him love that lifts him and encourages him.

"And the truth also is, that the kind of love he offers me is intoxicating, and I do burn with desire—so it is physical. It's not just one or the other. It's the spiritual leading the physical, not the other way around." Mary shook her head. "As grown women, we have been letting our bodies make decisions for our spirits. And we're teaching our daughters to do the same thing."

Thelma raised an eyebrow. "Well, with all that burning, sister girl, and all those trips back and forth out of town, I don't see how you and Moor are waiting until your wedding night. Why wait? You're engaged."

Latrice sighed. Thelma was hopeless.

"Truth be told, there were times when I didn't want to wait—if it was left up to me, we wouldn't have. But when I wasn't strong, when he wasn't feeling strong himself, he would look at me with such love in his eyes, such honor and say, 'I want it to be right. I want God to know that His love and your love are precious enough to wait and honor you and Him.'"

Latrice waved a shrimp in the air. "That's what I'm talkin' about, girlfriend! That's a man right there!"

Mary gently rubbed a finger over the letter she held. "I love him and desire Moor because *all* of who he is—not just his body—ministers to all of who I am as a woman. Somehow, the way he loves me, talks to me, and treats me, witnesses to me about God's goodness. His influence in my life moves me closer to the person I want to be. And I want my life and love for him to be the same. Because our lives shouldn't just witness to the world, our lives should also witness to those we love."

Latrice could feel the depth of Mary's love as she spoke. Something had changed about her—there was a maturity, not old, but a kind of wisdom.

"Do you know that Moor whispers prayers to me? Has he held my hand? Yes. Has he kissed me? Yes. But in the midst of it, how he treats me honors me and God. And when I fell, he was so tender. It wasn't champagne or a diamond—anyone can buy those things, but a good heart is priceless. And when I look into his eyes, his heart, I want to pour myself on him. I trust him, I trust God in him enough to let him see the nakedness—not just physical, but emotional and spiritual—of who I am."

Thelma laughed. "Finally, we get to the nakedness."

Latrice waved her hand at Thelma. "Girl, you are too silly!"

Mary laughed, "Yeah, girl, finally I'm naked." She smiled at both of them, then continued talking. "Learning to love, to trust, to give, to have faith, and to forgive—are the more excellent way the Bible talks about. If you focus only on whether to hold hands or not, or whether to kiss, you miss the point. Like it says in the Song of Solomon, we are waking passion, waking love before it's ready. Focus on the more excellent way and love will wake when it's time." Mary smiled ruefully. "And the truth is, what's wrong with my girls—"

It was the first time since the engagement that Mary had talked about the girls at her church. They were precious to her—tough Cat, wounded Agnes, and preppy Pamela. Mary's silence about the three girls she met with each week, the teen-aged girls she had given her heart, said that she was worried about them. Latrice hadn't thought about how they were taking all this. Who would be their champion now?

"What's wrong with our daughters—whether it's my girls or Lil' Kim or Paris Hilton—is that passion has been awak-ened in them before they are ready. They've never gotten to live as young, tender girls. All they know is sex. Our culture uses sex to sell them everything—hair dye, books, clothes, movies, cars, and more. And we don't care that we're awak-ening their sexuality before they're ready."

Mary looked down, quiet. "I didn't mean to preach." She lifted her head and looked at both of them. "But we're like them. We didn't get to be fragile princesses." She smiled. "But I'm getting to be one now because of Moor, and because of the Lord."

Thelma smirked. "Right!" She looked away. Her face looked as though she were thinking, *"Don't you think it's too late now?"* She turned back and touched Mary on her hand. "I believe in Jesus, but—" It was a warm touch, her eyes were sincere. "I can't believe all this fairytale stuff for myself. But for you, I hope it's true. It looks like it worked out for you. But for the rest of us. . . ."

Latrice drained her drink and stared at the bottom of the glass like more tea might appear. There were no more shrimp to keep her occupied. It was now or never. "Well, since it's our last night, our last supper. . . ." She looked at Mary. "There's something I've been trying to keep . . . there's some-thing I think I need to tell you . . ." Latrice tried to think of some way to make it funny. "There's something I need to say."

Thelma moaned, "Mercy! What now? I can't take much more! Don't even say you're pregnant, Latrice!" Thelma's blue eyes were wide open. Several patrons turned to stare. "I'm not playing. I can't take it. If that's what you have to say, then just don't say anything."

Pregnant? That was a joke. Latrice tried to pretend people weren't staring. "No, that is not it, Thelma. Will you calm down?"

"I'm just saying—Mary is running off to get married, Naomi has lost her mind, and all I need is for you to be pregnant. That would be it. Just pack up and go home! Lights out! Party over!" Thelma rolled her blue eyes.

"Well, that's not it."

"Well, good. So," Thelma looked like her old self. "What is it? A new man? Some new men?"

"Not quite." Latrice drummed her nails on the table. Maybe she shouldn't tell. Maybe it was none of their business. She looked at her two friends. How could something like this not be their business—it was surprising that she had kept it from them this long.

Latrice took the plunge. "I am no longer—how can I say this delicately? I am no longer *available* to men. I have removed myself from the menu . . . so to speak."

Mary choked on her drink.

Thelma's jaw dropped, so her mouth was a gaping circle.

TWENTY-FOUR

Bodega Bay, California

Naomi walked toward Ruthie sitting alone on the beach. She was pleased to see her. Nothing had changed about how Ruthie looked, or even how she behaved. Her hair was still stringy, her clothes were still too bright, and her flip-flops were still ratty. Ruthie still said embarrassing things—*I'm groovin' with Jesus!* But like the children at the clinic, Naomi's life was brightened by the girl's presence.

She couldn't say everything was perfect. She was still divorced, things were still rocky with her kids. And she was probably going to miss Mary's wedding. But her life had changed.

It was like the simple Scripture she had been reading earlier. She could recite it now. It was from Proverbs 24. *Without warning your life can turn upside-down, and who knows how or when it might happen?* Each morning when she awoke, she read a verse or two. It was something she hadn't felt like doing in years.

A few months ago, she had been in Baltimore. Then, she didn't envision herself traveling to Sonoma County Valley and living on the beach with the wind blowing her hair. She certainly didn't see herself with a friend like Ruthie. She hated her job and thought God had abandoned her.

She had given up hope. But Ruthie, with all the girl had been through, had reminded her to trust God—to have faith and to trust His love.

"I've learned to find joy in the valley, in the place where I am right now. The sun does shine here. You have to find hope here."

Ruthie had given her the courage to keep believing that her life could be something more—that there was hope and a reason to take another step.

Ruthie—who at first always looked as though she was begging—had actually given her so much more. Now she had something to share with Ruthie.

Naomi dropped into place on the sand next to Ruthie. She looked at her own bare feet. She was a long way from high heels and suits, but closer to the person she really wanted to be. She put her arm around Ruthie's shoulders, around her daughter's shoulders. They both looked out at the gently blowing water of the bay. There were seals barking in the distance while gulls flew overhead.

"I've been thinking about when my check comes."

Ruthie sighed. "What? Thinking you'll move back to Baltimore?"

Naomi laughed. "No, I was thinking I'll have enough money from the show to do some dentistry at the Vallejo clinic, if you help me. We'd have to start small, just a couple of days a week until we can get a grant. I'll have to send for my car so we can get back and forth. But it will be a start." She smiled at Ruthie, whose eyes were shining brightly. "And if you think you're up to it, you can get your dental assistant's certificate. You're great with the kids."

Ruthie shook her head. "How can I do that? You know I

don't have a job. I don't have any money."

"I'll pay. I've got enough to do that."

Ruthie looked away. "I can't let you do that. I can't take your money. It wouldn't be right."

Naomi reached her hand and touched Ruthie's hair. "Hush, child." Naomi smiled. "Besides, it's like you told me. Like in the Bible: it's gleanin', man!"

TWENTY-FIVE

Baltimore, Maryland

"Wha-wha-what? What are you talking about, Latrice? What is wrong with you and Mary?"

Latrice picked up her water glass and began to inspect it. The last thing she wanted was to ruin their last dinner together at Phillips. People were staring. "There's nothing wrong. Mary's getting married—which is not a rare disease. She's turned in her passkey to the singles' club, but she's still Mary. She's still our friend." Latrice, though she felt uncertain, couldn't help but enjoy the confusion she could see in Thelma's eyes. "And I've called all my keys back in, but I'm still your friend."

Thelma looked like she didn't know whether she was coming or going. Latrice loved Thelma, but it would do her good to not always have all the answers. "You and me are still in the same club—I'm still single, but just not *quite* so *available!*"

Mary's face fluctuated between beaming pleasure and surprise. "Latrice?"

Latrice looked at Mary and laughed. "Don't look so innocent, Miss Thing. Weren't you the one preaching to us all last year about how we ought to be virtuous, about how if we loved God we would keep His commandments?" Latrice inspected the glass again and then twittered. "You ruined it for me, okay?"

She tried to whisper so that the customers sitting near them wouldn't hear. "I'd be out with Tyrone and just about to get my groove on—not to mention that he was my dependable supplier of Dog House hot dogs and just as things were about to get good . . ." She raised her hands in the air and began to sway from side to side. Suddenly she dropped her hands. "Oops! Up pops your voice, Miss Mary, talking about Jesus!" Latrice shook her head as she thought. "Or I'd be out with Eddy after a walk by the Harbor. He'd be massaging my hands and my feet the way I like." Latrice closed her eyes and smiled. "I'd be thinking of paradise." She could see the moonlight on the water and remember, later, the feeling of Eddy's warm hands on her feet. Her eyes popped open. "And just when I was about to surrender . . . Oops! Up comes some Bible verse and a Word from the Lord!"

Latrice couldn't hold back; she laughed out loud. "Then I was out with Terrence. We came back to my place to get cozy. We had the bubble bath and everything. I turned the television on to put on some nice music on one of the cable music stations. Instead of Luther, there was Trinity–5–7 singing, 'My body is God's temple.'" She fanned herself again. "It was kind of like the Jenny Craig of chastity was following me everywhere I went. I gave up, girl. It was working my nerves." Latrice touched a hand to her stomach. "A sister couldn't eat!" She laughed at herself. "And you know that's bad!"

Mary laughed.

Thelma's mouth was still open.

Mary leaned forward in her seat. "Just like that, Latrice? Cold turkey?"

"It wasn't something that I was trying to do. It wasn't like I felt like God didn't love me, or I didn't love God, or any of that stuff. It just kind of happened. I don't know." Latrice nodded. "But, yeah, cold turkey. I figured wasn't no point in playin' around. 'Cause you know, if I smell cake, a sister is gone take a bite!" She thought of her dream. "But it hasn't been easy. A sister has been having nightmares about men chasing me through Baltimore! And Gerald Levert—he was in the dream—kind of. And Negroes have been calling me on the phone begging." She smiled and wiggled her flashing nails. "But what's new?"

Thelma finally got control of her mouth. "No dates at all, Latrice?"

"Well . . . no, I mean, yes. I'm not getting my groove on anymore."

Mary looked dumbfounded. "Wow."

Thelma's blue eyes narrowed. "You mean no one?"

Leave it to teacher Thelma to spoil the party. Latrice tried not to look guilty. "Well, I am seeing someone." She looked at Mary. "But it's all on the up-and-up, girl. Even dieters get a little celery, you know what I mean?" She waved one of her plump hands.

Thelma smirked. "Hah! I thought so! I knew you couldn't hold out!"

Mary shrugged. "Well, I'm proud of you, Latrice."

"So, what's your piece of celery's name?" Thelma's eyes were glittering. She leaned forward. " 'Cause it may be celery now, sister girl, but it's going to be fried chicken later."

Latrice pretended to be enthralled by the glass she held. "Don't be so nosy, Thelma."

"Come on, Latrice. Give up the name. Denzel? Is it one of the Baltimore Ravens? Ray Lewis? You always had a crush on Ray, and I hear Deion Saunders is in town now. Who is it? Give it up."

"No, Miss Nosy. And for your information, Denzel and Deion Saunders are married."

Thelma smirked. "Like that ever stopped you before! I know a nun when I see one." She looked at Mary and then back at Latrice. "You're no nun."

Latrice huffed and set the glass on the table. Thelma was not going to leave her alone until she got the name. "Floyd. Okay. You satisfied? Floyd." There was silence and Latrice hoped, somehow, they would not remember.

"Oh no!" Mary frowned and then began to laugh. "I don't know if this is quite what you call progress." She laughed louder.

Thelma looked at Mary, confused.

Latrice knew why Mary was laughing. Mary was thinking about her own date last year with Floyd, the king of ribs and sauce. It was one of Mary's last dates before she had met her prince, her fiancé Moor.

Latrice tried not to laugh, but it was hard. She looked around. The customers near them were trying to pretend they weren't listening, but their ears seemed to have grown three sizes.

Mary was snorting now. "Not Floyd and the ribs!" Mary held her stomach. "Not Mr. Saucy!"

Latrice surrendered and began to chuckle. "Well, if I can't walk on the wild side, at least I can go to the Rib Shack and get a good meal!" She could feel herself shaking as she laughed. "Those ribs are *good*, girl!"

She reached across the table and touched Mary's hand.

Everything was changing. It was a little sad. But, it was even funnier for someone to think of her as a nun. "Like Quincy Jones said in the song, 'nothing stays the same.'" She giggled. "But, I think *nun* might be going a bit too far!"

———

Latrice had washed her hands five times. They were withered, and if she wasn't careful, the rhinestones glued on her fingernails were going to dislodge and wash down the drain.

She knew everyone was laughing. She laughed sometimes herself. She knew no one believed it—she wouldn't have believed it herself.

Latrice looked at her hands and then at her reflection in the mirror and cracked up. Who would have ever thought the player would be giving up the game?

But truth be told, she enjoyed Floyd the rib king, with his saucy self. He made her laugh. No, he wasn't the handsomest prince or the brightest bulb in the city, but he made her laugh and he was right about one thing—the Rib Shack did make good ribs! She smelled her hands again—and she was wearing the sauce to prove it.

Floyd held doors open for her. He told her that she was beautiful. He thought she could do anything she set her mind to do. And when she told him about not having sex with him, Floyd took off his hat. "I wouldn't never stand between a lady and her commitment to the Lord." Who would have thought Floyd would turn out to be a gentleman?

No one knew, but at moments when she got weak, when sex was calling to her and she was ready to holler back, it was Floyd who reminded her—like Boaz talking to Ruth in the Bible—that she was a virtuous woman.

"Oh, Miss Latrice—" he had taken to calling her Miss

Latrice after she had told him about being celibate "—you don't want to do that. You're a lady. You deserve a man to marry you first."

When she looked at the calendar and counted the months—and sometimes at night when she couldn't sleep—what she was doing seemed foolish. It seemed impossible. But Floyd would hug her. And the funny thing was, he seemed proud of her—which made her proud of him, because most of the men—like Tyrone—laughed when she told them. Not that she could blame them. Her saying she was going to abstain was like Flavor Flav saying he was giving up his gold teeth. It was like Colonel Sanders giving up fried chicken.

Still, it touched her that Floyd believed in her. Twice when she was ushering, she had thought she'd caught glimpses of him, through the sea of people at her church, heading for the balcony.

She just wasn't too sure about the maroon hair dye he wore on the wiry hair that circled the bald spot on top of his head. That was the one thing—she couldn't stop staring at his head when they were together. But what Latrice knew in her heart—though she would never admit it in front of Mary, Naomi, and especially not in front of Thelma—was that Floyd was growing on her.

When the phone began to ring, she wiped her hands on a towel, then walked to the kitchen to answer. "Hello?"

"You may have Mary fooled. But you know I know better. I've got my eye on you. You can't fool me." It was Thelma pretending to be the wicked witch.

"Nobody's trying to fool you. Who could fool you, Matlock? I mean, who could fool you, Thelma?" Latrice laughed at her own joke.

"Very funny, Latrice. So, I guess now you're going to take

over the role as goody-two-shoes. Okay, so Mary's getting married, but you? Now *you're* trying to tell me you think you're better than me."

"I'm not saying I'm better than you." Thelma was trippin'; the best thing to do was to try to placate her.

Thelma would not be calmed. "I know you're not. 'Cause you and I both know that if I brought a piece of choice, one hundred percent, pure grade A beefcake over there and set him on your front step, you'd snatch that brother inside and the lights would be out before either one of us could say betcha by golly wow!"

"Thelma, why are you making such a big deal out of this?" If she had just kept her big mouth shut, she would be in her house in peace.

"Because I know you're smarter than this, Latrice."

"Oh, Thelma."

"The others—Mary may not be able to think for herself, but I know you know better. And if I don't know anything else, I know you are more of a player than any man I have ever known. You got the crown, sister girl. I know when you hear the song, you know the beat. You know what time it is."

Latrice looked at the Bible laying facedown on her kitchen table. She'd left it there last night.

When you hear the song, you know the beat. When you hear the song, you know how to bow.

Thelma's words reminded her of the passage she had read last night in Daniel. She sat down and opened the Bible, scanning the words in Daniel Chapter Three as Thelma talked.

King Nebuchadnezzar made an image of gold, ninety feet high and nine feet wide, and set it up on the plain of Dura in the province of Babylon.

The king had commanded all the people—people of every nation and language—that when they heard music of any kind, they were to bow down and worship the idol or be thrown in a fiery furnace.

"What I'm learning, Thelma, is that when I hear the music, I need to sing a song back to God."

"What are you talking about, Latrice?" Thelma laughed. "You must be drinking out of the same cup as Mary."

"You know the story in Daniel, about Shadrach, Meschach, and Abednego? You know about when they were taken captive from Israel to Babylon?"

"Oh no, Latrice, I know you are not giving Bible-study lessons now."

"Don't try to be funny, Thelma. You know I believe in God. We both do, so don't even try it. I've seen you get your shout on, too, sister girl."

Thelma quieted. "Okay, Latrice. So, what about Shadrach, Meschach, and Abednego?"

Thelma followed the words on the page with her finger. "Well, when I was reading the story, I realized something. You know, when the king of Babylon Nebuchadnezzar made the golden image of himself and told people anytime they heard music they should think of him? You know what he was trying to do? He was trying to change people's minds."

"Girl, what are you talking about? Not only are you trying to act like Mary, you are starting to sound like her."

"What I'm saying is that the wicked king wanted people to associate music with him, like he created it. So any time they heard music, they would think it was his and act like him—wicked and dirty."

"So?"

"Well, until that time, when people heard music, they

thought of God. And the truth is, God is the Father of crea-
tion. Music is meant for worshiping God—all music. And
think what it would be like if, when we heard *any* kind of
music, we praised God.

"It took the wicked king thirty days to change people's
minds. Read it for yourself. It's right there in Daniel Chapter
Three."

*Therefore, as soon as they heard the sound of the horn, flute,
zither, lyre, harp and all kinds of music, all the peoples, nations
and men of every language fell down and worshiped the image
of gold that King Nebuchadnezzar had set up.*

Thelma sighed like she was bored. "So what's your
point?"

"My point is, it worked. That was thousands of years ago.
But all those years ago, Nebuchadnezzer changed the world's
mind, and even now people hear certain kinds of music and
think evil. Even now some people hear music and bow
down."

"But we weren't talking about music. We were talking
about you getting your freak on."

"And that's what I'm talking about. 'Cause it came to me
last night, that somewhere along the way, instead of giving
God credit for creating sex and even for creating marriage
and thanking Him, something has changed. Now we think
of evil when we think of sex. We think the devil created
romance and we bow down to him."

Thelma was quiet on the other end. "Well—" she said
finally—"I've got to go. I smell something burning in the
oven."

Latrice picked her way through the racks of dresses.
There was no sale like a sale at Nordstrom. Mary held one of

the blue shoes they had chosen, while she and Thelma waded through the racks to find something suitable.

Mary lifted a hanger, turning the dress front and back. "And I don't know what to do about Naomi."

"Naomi?" Latrice stopped moving dresses. "When did you hear from her?"

Thelma answered. "She called me." She continued pushing dresses. "California dreamin'. We'll have to figure out something later."

Latrice didn't think it was possible to try on more dresses than they had tried shoes. They did. But it was worth it, though. The three of them stood in line at the cash register, blue dresses draped over their arms.

"Well, that's it. I'm satisfied. I thought if we could just get this done, everything would be okay. 'Cause we know everything is going all right in California." Mary smiled. "And the dresses are nice, don't you think?" She looked at Thelma. "You can wear it again."

Latrice waited for Thelma to say something smart, to give another reason why there shouldn't be a wedding—maybe the shiny dresses, or the color.

"Mary, I was thinking about your girls, you know the girls at your church, at New Worshippers."

Latrice shifted from foot to foot. It was not a nice thing to try to make Mary feel guilty about leaving the girls. Thelma knew how much the girls meant to Mary. If there was one thing that could give her second thoughts about marrying and going to California, it would be the girls.

If she couldn't help, why couldn't she just let Mary be happy?

Thelma carried on, as though she couldn't see the worry in Mary's eyes. "I wondered who was going to take over. . . ."

It was late Wednesday afternoon and, as usual, Mary was rushing to meet her class. Hiking the hill from Old Frederick Road to New Worshippers was no joke. This climb was going to be one of the last ones she made.

She looked at her watch as she huffed and pushed through the glass doors. "Late again."

Down the hall, into the elevator, and down to the floor where she and the girls met. Mary checked her bags, and took a deep breath outside the door of Room 31. "Well, this is it." She pushed the door open.

Inside sat three girls—three young women—as different as any three could be. One of them, wearing spike heels, and sporting a rhinestone watch that matched her nail tips, looked up. She tapped her watch. "Late again! Miss Mary, you're going to miss your own wedding."

"Thanks for the vote of confidence, Cat!" Mary smiled as she slung her bag down on her desk. "As you all know, I'm going to be leaving soon for California. We've already met your new teacher. But Agnes, Pamela, and Cat, I wanted you to meet two of my very best friends." Mary pointed toward the door. "Ladies, meet Thelma and Latrice."

Latrice was still trying to catch her breath after struggling up the hill behind Mary and Thelma. As she looked at the three girls and at Mary, she wondered what Thelma, after a sudden turn of conscience while they were shopping at Nordstrom—*"I wondered who was going to take over . . . I thought maybe Latrice and I could help. . . ."*—had gotten her into.

TWENTY-SIX

Vallejo, California

Anthony stared at the television in his hotel room while he dressed. It kept him company. He turned and looked at the invitation to Moor's wedding lying on his bed. Though it was too late, he wanted to call and give Moor his regrets. That would be easier than going back to San Francisco to a wedding. Thinking of the city made him remember what he had lost—his job and Desiree.

But it was too late. Instead, earlier he had unpacked one of his suits—he hadn't worn one since leaving San Francisco—and taken it to the cleaners to be pressed.

He turned back to watch the television while he buttoned his shirt and tucked it into his pants. It was Wednesday night, and though he still wasn't sure why, he was on his way to Evangel. And he had promised Pops that tonight he was going to sit in the sanctuary, in one of the front rows. *"You ain't never gone see the band downstairs, man. If Sly was in the band, you wouldn't know it, would you? Come on up. Sit down front."* That promise and the coming wedding had his stomach churning.

He'd left his guitar at Pops', while rushing to get to the cleaners.

"Congratulations, Naomi from Baltimore!"

Pat Sajak's voice interrupted his thoughts. *Wheel of Fortune* was on television . . . a repeat episode. He recognized the contestant, the Black woman with blonde hair from Baltimore.

Though he was still staying in the same ratty hotel, a lot had happened to him since the first time he had seen her. "Well, Naomi from Baltimore, I still don't have a job." But he was friends now with someone he never would have known in his old life. He was playing guitar every day and each day music was becoming more a part of him—or a re-awakened part of him. There was a song he played over and over. It was a melody that had come to him. It woke him up at night and insisted that he rise from his bed to play.

"I like that, brother! It sounds like a love song." Pops had nodded his head along with the tune when Anthony played it for him. "You got any words?"

He had shaken his head, hoping to change the subject.

What was he going to do with a love song?

Things were changing, but Wednesday night was still Evangel night.

When Anthony finished dressing, he clicked off the television. "See you later, Naomi from Baltimore."

The sanctuary was larger than he had imagined. It was designed like the church that he remembered from his childhood: three sections of pews, one behind another, that faced the pulpit. But instead of the wooden lectern there was a clear Plexiglas podium. And the floor, from where he entered at the back of the large room, tilted downward toward the pulpit as he walked past row after row.

He'd gotten there early, and as he moved forward, he watched the band members tuning their instruments: drums, a saxophone, a trumpet, a keyboard, and a bass guitar.

When the band quieted, an older woman went to the microphone at the podium and began to read Scripture. "'This is the day that the Lord has made. Let us rejoice and be glad in it.'" People stood to their feet, clapping in agreement. "I'll be reading Psalm 150." As soon as she finished, the band began to play.

Anthony nodded his head in rhythm. The melodies and the beats they played were a long way from what was played at his grandmother's church years ago. But many of the words were the same.

Take me back.
I wanna go back.
Take me back
To the old landmark!

Most of the crowd was on their feet, clapping in time, smiling, and swaying from side to side. Anthony joined them—he might as well enjoy himself; that was what he had come for. If he wasn't going to find Sly, at least he could enjoy the music.

A door to the side of the band opened and Pops—still in his janitor's uniform, but wearing the star-shaped sunshades Anthony had seen hanging on the old man's wall—danced out the door and to the microphone. The crowd, still singing the song of praise, clapped louder at Pops' appearance, as though they had been waiting for him.

Pops was grinning and strutting just like in his apartment. He sang like Anthony had seen him do so many times, but now he stood before a microphone. "Owww!" Pops shouted. "Take me back!" he joined in to sing with the band.

Anthony cheered. He had the feeling he often had when Pops was around, as if he had dreamed all this before. It was like his daydream. There were no bell-bottom pants and no Afros, and the words were different, but there was music, and lights, and people. Anthony could feel himself smiling. It was a long time since he'd smiled. He shook a triumphant fist in the air and shouted. "Yeah!"

Pops beamed at him and waved for Anthony to come on stage, to join the band.

Anthony shook his head.

Pops waved again while he continued doing his apartment dance and singing, "Take me back!" He was a wild man. He yelled into the microphone: "I played with a band once. You all know that."

Anthony looked at the gray tufts of hair around Pops' ears, and the star-shaped glasses. *"What you been looking for has been in front of you the whole time."* It couldn't be, could it?

Pops was smiling and shouting into the microphone: "I was making funk music, then. But I learned, ain't nothing wrong with praising the Lord!"

The crowd shouted back in agreement.

Pops danced his way to the side door, opened it, and stepped out of sight while the band continued playing.

Anthony could feel the pounding of the drums in his stomach.

When Pops reappeared, he was holding Anthony's guitar over his head. "Come on up here, man!" Pops yelled into the microphone.

He had intended to stay with the congregation. Maybe it was seeing his red Fender, maybe it was the drums, or the star-shaped sunshades—Anthony moved from the pew. Then he was up front with the band. He hit a few licks and he was breathless. The excitement swelled his heart.

"Take me back!" Pops called.

TWENTY-SEVEN

Baltimore, Maryland

Latrice wondered, for the tenth time, how she had let Thelma talk her into this. Maybe it was her friend's pleading blue eyes. Or, maybe it was how excited Mary had looked about the whole thing.

"I think you all would be perfect! The girls will love you!" Mary's face had beamed as though she were five and it was Christmas morning. "They've got a new mentor coming from the church, but it would make me so happy to leave you all with my girls. You two are a piece of me—a living, breathing, junk-talking—" she'd laughed and put her hands on her hips —"piece of me with them."

Latrice had felt unsure about hiking up the driveway to New Worshippers, let alone meeting with the girls who were now in front of her. She didn't have anything against anyone who wanted to go to New Worshippers, but eight thousand members was about seventy five hundred too many for her. And the building was so big, so carpeted—it was nothing like the wooden-floored, wooden-pewed church she had been ushering in since she was a little girl.

She had too many things going on in her own life. What time did she have to spend with some sassy young girls? Because she could tell from the way they looked that at least two of them were sassy—in different ways—but still sassy.

Mary was gushing. "These are two of my very best friends, Thelma and Latrice."

Thelma's reaction surprised her. Latrice would have thought that Thelma would be aloof, but her blue eyes were sparkling. She was smiling brighter than Latrice had ever seen—but, then, she had never really seen Thelma around kids.

She, on the other hand, was feeling like a fish out of water. She could wink, wave her nails, and bring a man to his knees. They couldn't resist her plump perfection. But sassy girls? That was a whole different story. "Hello."

Two of the three girls sat behind a long table that faced the front of the room. The third girl, the one who had spoken to Mary about being late, was standing at the front of the room. She was definitely sassy.

Mary looked at the girls as though they were living treasure. Her smile was on high-beam—it could have cut through fog.

"So, Thelma and Latrice, this is Agnes." Mary pointed to one of the girls sitting at the table.

"Hi." The girl gave a quiet little wave. Agnes was very pale with dark blonde hair swept up into a ponytail. She looked briefly at Latrice, then at Thelma, gave a quick smile and then lowered her head, slightly.

"Next is Pamela."

Pamela tossed her head full of curly black hair as she spoke. "Hello, Miss Thelma and Miss Latrice! Welcome to New Worshippers!" Her diction said that she was from the suburbs, her skin and hair said she was probably bi-racial, and her personality was definitely bubbly.

Latrice gaped at the perky girl's behavior. Good thing it

was afternoon; Pamela's personality was way too bright for a morning meeting.

"And this is Cat." Mary pointed to the young woman—the sassy one—standing near the front of the room.

Cat pulled down her shades and looked Thelma and Latrice up and down. "Whassup?" she said as she pushed her shades back in place.

Short skirt, spiked heels, enough lip gloss and attitude for about twenty girls—Cat was definitely sassy. Latrice looked at Cat's nails—they were long, hooked, and painted a bright pink. At least the child had good taste in nails.

But it was hard to see, at least on the surface, why Mary was so excited about the girls.

Cat tapped her watch. "Miss Mary, can we get started? I'm supposed to teach today."

The other two girls—Agnes and Pamela—got more chairs. Latrice sat behind Agnes.

Cat pulled off her shades, then wrote a few words on the blackboard:

Luke 15:11–31 The Prodigal Son

She turned to face them and began to read, "'A certain man had two sons. And the younger of them said to his father, "Father, give me the portion of goods that falls to me." So he divided to them his livelihood. And not many days after, the young son gathered all together, journeyed to a far country, and there wasted his possessions with prodigal living.'" Cat continued reading until she had finished the story.

It was surprising. Looking at the girl, Latrice never would have imagined her to be the kind of girl who went to church, let alone the kind of girl who would open the Bible. She remembered Mary telling her, Naomi, and Thelma that the girls were teaching class, but she never imagined anything like this.

Cat laid her Bible on the small table in front of her. She shifted her weight to one leg and put one hand on her hip. "First of all, I figured I better figure out what *prodigal* meant." She laughed. "I hear people saying it all the time, but I don't remember anybody explaining it." Cat nodded when the other girls agreed. "It means extravagant living, or lavish spending." She looked at Mary, who was smiling at the girl proudly. "I thought, hey, that's like the rappers, you know? They're making lots of money, driving big cars, lots of bling-bling, big parties, big liquor, lots of girls—" she smiled and raised and lowered her hands —"or boys!" She turned to the board and underlined the word. "Our brothers and sisters are living prodigal. You know, like the lifestyles of the rich and famous—living large."

Mary, Thelma, and the other two girls laughed in response.

Cat continued. "But the part of the story that really got me was about when the prodigal brother came back home . . . it tripped me out how mad his brother was, you know the good one that stayed home." She took her hand off her hip and shifted her weight. "You know, how mad he was that his father was happy to see the prodigal brother come home. And I thought, that is keeping it real. It's hard sometimes not to be jealous, you know?

"First of all, you tryin' to do right, and you see people you know are doing wrong and living it up." She laughed and adjusted her shades, mugging for the class. "It's hard for a sister to keep up her image!" Cat stood straighter. "Especially when you're trying to do the right thing, you know?" She touched her hair. "This 'do costs money." Cat held up her hands. "It takes some cheddah to keep these nails tight."

Latrice looked at her own nails. No doubt, the sister was right.

"But I'm a church girl now. I'm trying to be—as Miss Mary says—a good ambassador. So, I got a job. But I'm a teenager, so it doesn't pay much and it takes up most of my free time." She smirked and shifted her weight. "While on the other hand, there are lots of girls getting money smart, you know what I mean? They got boyfriends that are hustling, or they're hustling themselves. They're playing men for money. They're shaking their booties—whatever it takes. But they got lots of chingy and they are having fun." She nodded. "It may not be right, but it sure looks tight."

Latrice looked at Mary. She was hanging on the girl's every word.

"But I'm working hard, I'm coming to church, I'm studying the Bible, I'm putting up with people being smart with me because they know I'm going to church now. So, when do I get my reward? Okay, I'm willing to wait, 'cause I know in the end everything's going to work out for me, and the people living the high life are gone be sorry some day."

The girl shifted her weight. "Then, all of a sudden, one of those people that's been living it up gets saved. It's all over the neighborhood. It's all over the news. Now they're saved—like the football players that get saved—and everybody is all over them. The preachers are all over them, the newspapers are all over them, and they get to keep their money and houses too. And nobody comes and pats me, or the usher who's been ushering for years, or the man who's been cleaning up trash and gum after church services—nobody throws a party for us.

"If Missy Elliott, or Lil' Kim, or Mary J. Blige, or P. Diddy says they're saved, then people go crazy." Cat waved her hands. She dropped them. "But then, there are some of us, who have been trying hard all the time—we just don't get it." She put a hand on her hip. "For real, what we get is mad." She waved her hand. "You know a lot of church folks get mad about it—faces get tight. And, truth be told, we get mad at God because we think it's not fair. I'm just trying to be real. Why do the bad people get the good stuff and they get to come home and sit in the front pews? That ain't right. The people that's been doing right for years don't ever get invited to the VIP seats. They don't ever get the prize."

Latrice looked at Thelma. She was leaning forward in her seat, really listening to Cat.

"But the truth is—I had to admit it to myself—that it's jealousy. It's like your Daddy is giving your brother or sister something more than He gave you. And what we really think that means is that He loves that person—the one with the bling-bling—more. And we hate that. I hate that. I don't want God to love somebody else more than He loves me." She shrugged her shoulders. "I've had enough people in my life that I thought should love me, who don't. I don't need that from God. I don't want to have to compete with other people for God's love."

Cat nodded. "And, truth be told, when I finished the story, I was kind of ticked off, you know? But then, I thought about what the Bible says about God's ways not being our ways. And I realized, the prize is not really money, cars, or VIP seats. That's not the prize. The prize is close relationship. And because God has a close relationship with someone else, it doesn't stop Him from having a close relationship with me. He's got room enough to love everyone.

"The prize is not stuff. You know, the truth is, I don't know why God gives people stuff; probably because it's for a million different reasons. Some people need it because they have low self-esteem and maybe God is trying to make them feel better, some people need it because they're going to do good things for God's kingdom, and other people have it just because God loves seeing His people blessed. I don't know. But I do know that I looked at the other son—not the prodigal—and saw that he had everything too—but he was mad. He was mad because he was looking at the wrong thing and thinking the wrong thoughts. He was staying home to earn his Daddy's love. He didn't need to do that—Daddy loved him right or wrong." Cat looked down at the Bible, and then back at them. "I guess he wasn't sure—I guess sometimes we're not sure of our Father's love. Nothing could separate him from his Father's love. He had everything his brother had and more—he got to be with his Daddy every day, to feel that love every day. If the good son wanted to go out and party, he could have. His Daddy would still love him."

Cat closed the book and silently looked at each person. "Me being mad about somebody else's situation is not going to change anything. The prodigal son was wasting money. But I guess we're wasting time, opportunity, and love, when we choose to be unhappy in the presence of our Father's love. He gave us His Son. So, now, how we gone act?"

TWENTY-EIGHT

Jacks Creek, North Carolina

M ary?" Garvin expected her cousin to be jittery.
They had made lots of calls over the summer—
thank goodness for flat calling rates.

The wedding was so close now. Things were falling into
place. Jonee had made arrangements with relatives in California to cater Thai food for the wedding. Moor, the groom-to-
be, had not only chosen a minister—one of the associate
ministers at the church he attended in San Francisco—but he
had also made arrangements for the small wedding ceremony
to be held at the church. Meemaw, though Garvin wasn't too
thrilled about it, had settled the transportation matter. The
North Carolina contingent was traveling by bus, and that
same bus was going to transport the wedding cake. As bad an
idea as everyone else thought the cake idea was—except for
Mary, who thought Inez's offer was sweet—Meemaw wasn't
budging. It was settled.

The only other thing that still troubled Garvin was
Mary's bridal gown. Meemaw had made a lot of progress. But
though she was close to finishing, she still wasn't done.

Everything was close enough, though, to being on schedule, that Garvin was as calm as she was able to allow herself
to be. But it was her cousin's wedding, and Garvin expected

that Mary would be worried about the details. It was a calm Wednesday evening; she thought she would call.

"Garvin?" Mary's voice sounded surprisingly calm.

"I thought I should call to check in—the wedding's only one week away!"

Mary giggled. "It's the strangest feeling, like it's a dream, you know? I believed it would happen, I know it's happening. But at the same time, I can't believe it."

Garvin remembered feeling the same way when GoGo asked her to marry him. He spoke to her from the Song of Solomon.

> "'Set me as a seal upon your heart,
> As a seal upon your arm;
> For love is as strong as death,
> Jealousy as cruel as the grave;
> Its flames are flames of fire,
> A most vehement flame.
> Many waters cannot quench love,
> Nor can the floods drown it.
> If a man would give for love
> All the wealth of his house,
> It would be utterly despised.'

"Marry, me, Garvin."

She didn't remember saying yes to GoGo; she had simply melted in his arms.

Mary was still bubbling. "He is what you dream of, you know? Moor is what you pray to God for at night, in the quiet, when no one is around. He is one of those prayers you whisper, but are afraid to hope will be answered."

"Yes, I know."

"And he loves me. When we are together, sometimes I

catch him looking at me and there is so much tenderness in his eyes—it is like a dream."

"I'm happy for you, Mary."

"Did I tell you about how he proposed to me?"

Mary had told her at least ten times, but it was a beautiful story and it gave her cousin pleasure. "No, Mary, tell me."

"I had been flying back and forth to California to visit him."

"I remember."

"It was a cool San Francisco day. You know, you can never tell when they're going to happen—the cool drifts in over the water. Anyway, we had pulled off our socks and shoes and were walking on the sand. The water was too cold to wade in, even though it was summer. But the sky was so beautiful, and the sand, and the water. When was I going to get to do that again? So, I dipped one foot in—really just my toes. I felt like a little girl. It was so cold, girl. When I stepped back, I stepped into Moor's arms and he began to whisper to me:

"'*Entreat me not to leave thee, or to return from following after thee: for whither thou goest, I will go; and where thou lodgest, I will lodge: thy people shall be my people, and thy God my God: Where thou diest, will I die, and there will I be buried: the Lord do so to me, and more also, if aught but death part thee and me.*'"

"His accent was so beautiful, Garvin, and his heart so sincere. I had read the passage so many times, but it was alive on his tongue. Moor is so like a dream. When he asked me, how could I say anything but yes?"

"How could you?"

They talked about the arrangements. "I'm getting my hair

braided so I don't have to worry about it." And they talked about how the time had flown. "It's almost here." When they had finished, Garvin felt at peace and wondered at the strangeness and beauty of love.

TWENTY-NINE

Jacks Creek, North Carolina

It was the middle of August, and thank goodness the air conditioning was working. The bus was big enough for all the luggage to be stored in the back. Some black netting kept it from sliding around and separated the bags from a spot that held a fifty-gallon cooler. The wedding gown, the beading finished just the night before, lay covered in a garment bag on its own seat. There was also room enough on the bus for people to spread out, but not enough space to avoid each other. Without air conditioning, there probably would have been a funeral or two before they ever got to the wedding.

Meemaw sat in the second row on the left-hand side opposite the driver. On her lap were spread maps and a few yellow highlighter markers. Her Bible lay on the seat next to her. If no one else was going to enjoy the trip, it was obvious that Meemaw was.

The plan, once they got to California, was to swing by Bodega Bay to pick up Naomi and her young friend Ruthie. Garvin didn't know Naomi well, but she was one of Mary's best friends, and it seemed she had already moved to California and lived in the beach town not very far from San Francisco.

"Why sure we'll have room on the bus for them. We'll just swing right by," Meemaw had told Mary during the last call Garvin had had with her. Garvin suspected that Meemaw was excited about the stop. It gave her grandmother opportunity to do more map reading, planning, and an excuse to stop in the Napa Valley, along Highway 80 before traveling on to Bodega Bay.

"Are you all settled, Meemaw?" Garvin smiled down at her grandmother.

"I am looking forward to this!"

Garvin was sure that Meemaw meant she was looking forward to the trip as much as the wedding. Her grandmother, in addition to the maps, was dressed for adventure. She had a gold sun visor atop her curly silver hair. Her eyes were masked by large, dark sunshades, and her royal blue jogging suit was covered with gold fleurs de lis that matched the visor and Meemaw's tennis shoes. She was ready for business.

Esther's husband, Smitty, sat in the seat immediately behind GoGo, ready to take the wheel or offer a little road conversation. Behind Smitty sat Mr. Green, who was wearing one of the yarmulkes he only wore on special occasions—and whose seat just happened to be across the aisle from Meemaw's.

After making sure the four of them were ready, Garvin moved to the back of the bus to check on Monique—a new semester would be starting for her in college by the time she came back from the wedding—and her daughter Destiny and Garvin's daughter Princess. Across the aisle from them, Esther sat with her daughter, putting the finishing touches on the girl's cornrows. When she had finished, she sent the girl to sit in a seat further ahead with her brother.

Garvin slid onto the bench next to her. "Well, this is it."

Esther shook her head. "I'm just hoping you will keep her away from me. Inez can worry the husk off of corn."

Garvin smiled and nudged Esther. "Ready to rumble?" she said in an exaggerated wrestling announcer's voice. She laughed. "Just like the WWE Smackdown!"

"See, you always playin', Garvin. You play too much." Esther looked pained. "And I don't see how crazy Inez is gonna carry a wedding cake from North Carolina to California, anyway. That thing is going to be all smashed up, not that anybody wants to eat it anyway."

"I think the plan is to put it in that cooler back there."

It was hard to believe that she and Esther had been friends for so many years. Now their daughters were jumping rope, playing jacks—or video games—together as they had. Garvin hoped that they had as many years of love, laughter, and teasing as she and Esther. "Oh, Esther, it's going to be all right."

Esther patted her foot. "At least one thing I can give thanks for—that child Mattie is not coming. Thank the Lord! Because as much as Inez gives me hives, Mattie worries me even more."

Garvin laughed. "Don't worry. Mattie's not scheduled to be on the ride. Everything's going to be okay."

"All right. That's what *you* say. But I wouldn't cry at all if this bus rolled right on past Inez's house."

Of course, the bus didn't roll past Inez's. Meemaw made sure of that.

The Zephyr place was on a road off the state road that only locals knew about. It was easier to see in the winter. But in the spring and summer, the leaves—from the trees that crowded the sides of the road—hid it. Drivers found the road as much by intuition—or faith—as by sight. The road was paved with tar and was usually sprinkled with a few unlucky possums or raccoons. The pavement ran out thirty feet or so before it reached the driveway that led to the Zephyr home. The dirt was firmly packed though, so the bus rolled over it easily.

GoGo, wearing a black baseball cap pulled low on his forehead, stopped at the end of the driveway. "Here we are."

Garvin walked to the front of the bus and stood near Meemaw.

"Here we are," GoGo said again. "I guess she's expecting me to blow the horn."

Meemaw pulled off her sunshades, but kept inspecting her maps. "She's expecting you to drive down there and pick her up at her door."

Smitty, who probably had been quiet because he knew it was best, piped up. "No way!" He looked at Meemaw, then sat back in his seat and pulled his own red baseball cap lower on his head.

Mr. Green, who'd been Meemaw's friend since they were young adults, weighed in gingerly. "Now, Evangelina, I'm not sure that's such a good idea. This bus—" he pointed—"and that road. . . ."

Meemaw kept reading.

Garvin stooped lower to see out one of the bus passenger windows. The driveway, if one could call it that, that led to the Zephyr house was full of deep ruts that seemed to start and end abruptly. It really wasn't a drive, but a large and long patch of the yard—at least fifty feet—that led to the Zephyrs' front porch. Strewn along the drive were automobile carcasses, many of them missing wheels, or doors, or windows. Half of them, their hoods wide open, were without batteries or even motors. All of them were covered with dirt and rust.

The ghosts of the cars cried out that they had fought the path and lost. They were there like signs and skeletons in Dry Gulch warning others away.

GoGo tried again. "One of us can get out and help her back to the car with the cake."

Meemaw didn't say a word. She kept reading.

GoGo must have been feeling reckless or desperate. "Meemaw—"

Meemaw turned her head and gave GoGo *the eye.* She didn't use it often—she was usually more quick on the draw with cookies and hugs—but Meemaw's eye was famous. Her look was known to quiet rowdy children in grocery stores and freeze them in place.

GoGo was desperate. Garvin thought she saw Smitty and Mr. Green shaking their heads, trying to warn him. "Miz Evangelina, I don't think we ought to go down there. If the bus gets stuck—"

"The Lord will make a way," Meemaw said, finishing his sentence.

GoGo opened his mouth as though he was about to reply. He looked at Meemaw, then at the drive, and then back at Meemaw, who was still giving him *the eye.* The duel was over. GoGo started his way down the drive.

The bus, a new bus, shimmied and slid from gully to gully. The transmission made a grinding sound as GoGo rocked the bus from first, to overdrive, to reverse, and back again, in order to avoid the mechanical road kill surrounding it.

By the time they got to Inez's home, GoGo was sweating.

Inez stood on the porch holding three plastic-wrapped rectangular pans of graduated sizes. Next to Inez, Mattie Zephyr held a red, out-sized, lidded plastic mixing bowl.

Garvin thought she heard Esther moaning in back.

A translucent white plastic grocery store bag filled with odds and ends dangled from Mattie's arm.

Inez was smiling fit to beat the band. Meemaw got up to greet her. "You come on here, Inez, so we can get this show on the road." Meemaw nodded. "I see you bringing Mattie with you."

Esther groaned louder.

Inez shook her head. "No, she just helpin' me get my cake fixin's on the bus."

Garvin thought she heard Esther whisper, "Hallelujah!"

Garvin got off the bus to help. Inez was still beaming. "This is gone be something special, Miz Evangelina."

"I know it is, baby."

"I've been workin' on it all night long." Inez tilted the cake pans for Meemaw to see. "I loosened the cake, but I'm leavin' them in the pans for safekeepin'."

Garvin lifted the red bowl from Mattie's hands.

"That's the frosting. My own special recipe. I'm gone steal away and put it together and ice it when we get there."

Meemaw patted Inez on the back. "I've got my teeth set for it, baby."

It was funny to hear Meemaw call Inez *baby*. It was easy to forget that Inez wasn't much older than Garvin and Esther. Esther always said that Inez looked older because minding other people's business was such hard work.

Mattie ran into the house and came back holding a large piece of white cardboard. She handed it to her aunt. In a few minutes—after Mattie and Inez hugged and kissed—they were all packed and onboard.

It only took an hour for GoGo to work the bus out of the Zephyr driveway.

Inez sat midway back in the bus, near the wedding dress. Without asking, on her way to sit down, she had unzipped the bag. "Is this the bride's gown? It sure is pretty." She zipped the bag back and sat down. "I guess she didn't have money enough to buy her own gown."

Garvin slid onto her seat next to Esther just in time to hear her say, "Help me, Jesus! I can feel trouble coming!" Esther patted her foot. "If I see her touch that gown again, I'm not going to be responsible for what I do!"

Garvin told herself she was not going to worry.

THIRTY

It was a long way from North Carolina to California, and they had already spent two nights in hotels along the way. So far, things had been peaceful except people had taken to looking toward the back of the bus whenever there was an abrupt stop or sharp turn, as though they were expecting a *cake-quake* at any moment. But climbing the steep hills was the worst.

Meemaw sat up front, maps in hand, and a smile on her face.

Garvin told herself she was not going to worry. It was very early Saturday morning, the day of the wedding, but they were making good time. There would be time, once they got to San Francisco, for Inez to ice the cake, for everyone to get dressed, and most importantly for the bride to retrieve her gown.

The Baltimore group was already in San Francisco, Garvin had learned when she spoke to Mary by cell phone. Mary had spoken to Moor by phone, while Mary and the bridesmaids were stashed away at a hotel out of sight. Garvin looked at her watch—Jonee, Ramona, and her husband's flight from Washington, D.C., should be landing soon. A few hours behind them should be the flight that carried Moor's grandmother on the final leg of her journey from Lesotho.

Mary had sounded very calm. Garvin reminded herself not to worry.

Sacramento was the westernmost point on the journey—they had traveled on U.S. 80 West through Lincoln, Nebraska; Cheyenne, Wyoming; and Reno, Nevada. Once they got to Sacramento, it was south through northern California—Davis and the Napa Valley to San Francisco, with a side trip to Bodega Bay. The mountains had been steep along the way. Garvin, while she kept Esther distracted, also saw GoGo's shoulders get tenser with each mountain the school bus climbed. He strained to hold things together in the valleys, to keep the little bus from moving too fast. While he, the other men, and Meemaw watched the road, everyone else—except the children—looked back at the luggage area and listened to the sound of the cake-filled cooler sliding forward until it bumped against the compartment wall. It held there until the bus began to climb again. Then the cooler slid back until it bumped against the rear door. They were still on schedule, but hours had passed with the cooler sliding back and forth.

Whenever they were on level ground, and heads turned forward, Inez reassured them. "Honey, that cake is fine. I wrapped it up myself."

The cake may have been fine, but the set of GoGo's shoulders and the whine of the transmission told Garvin the mountains and valleys were taking a toll on her husband and on the bus.

"Oh, don't worry," Inez said every time the cooler slid back and forth. "I got it packed in there. It's safe, and good, and cold. You can believe that."

"Help me, Jesus," Esther whispered every time Inez spoke.

Inez sat midway and Esther stayed in the back. That's how it was until Inez felt the urge to make a trip to the back. "That sure is a pretty dress." She pointed at the bag holding Mary's gown. "It kind of reminds me of Starr Jones' dress."

Esther mumbled into Garvin's ear. "I am not going to bite. I am not going to bite. I'm not saying a word!"

Inez went on talking. "I just hope the bride is not wearin' Payless shoes. 'Cause with all that money, Starr Jones didn't need to be wearing Payless shoes. But that's what she was wearin'. I read about it. And I don't have all her money, but I wouldn't be caught within ten feet of some Payless shoes. But I know that's what she was wearin', because I know Payless shoes when I see them."

Esther's foot was tapping to beat the band, but she was quiet until Inez went back to her seat. Then she spouted like a teakettle. "Garvin, if you don't keep that woman away from me . . ." Esther huffed. "She wishes she had one Payless shoe, let alone a pair." Esther mumbled until the rhythm of the road and the passing trees seemed to calm her down.

It was still calm on the bus. The men talked and laughed. Meemaw read her maps. Everything was going smoothly. Garvin told herself there was no need to worry.

Again, Inez came and sat on the bench in front of Esther. "I sure hope this lady, Mary, has a nice wedding. But at least Starr Jones got married. Oprah ain't even married." She rolled her eyes. "Who knows when she's gonna get married. Of course, at home, they say he won't marry her. I didn't say it, but that's what I've heard. It's a shame, too, all that money Oprah got and can't get a man."

Esther's foot was tapping out *Flight of the Bumblebee* and her jaw muscles were flexing.

Inez continued. "You know her boyfriend is from down home, don't you? It's a shame. She need to get married."

Garvin could feel Esther stirring. "So, Inez, why is Oprah's life any of your business? Why do you care whether she gets married or not?"

Inez looked like Esther should have known the answer. "Because I care about her."

Esther slapped her hand over her mouth.

Inez continued. "I care about her." She nodded emphatically. "That's right! And with all that money she got, I just don't want her to end up in hell. 'Cause you know money will go to your head and send your behind straight to hell."

Garvin could hear Esther mumbling something about "your head."

Inez settled in for a long conversation. "It's just like when preachers get a lot of money. It's the root of all evil." Inez put her feet up. "Probably her boyfriend was cheating on her— that's probably why Oprah ain't married."

Esther stood up, as if the blast Garvin had been trying to stave off was about to happen.

"You know what? I don't want to hear another word, Inez. I'm so tired of hearing about preachers being strung out on sex, trying to sleep with everybody, eating chicken, and grubbing money. Blah, blah, blah. Get a new story. Get a new preacher!"

Esther's engine was revving. "Being saved ain't about pointing fingers at everybody else. Being saved is about learning how to shine the light on your own messed-up self. When you in church, the message is not for the other people on your pew; it's for you, honey. You ain't got no business judging them—not Starr, not Oprah, not anybody else. God is talking to you, baby doll, with your messy judgmental self. You want the church to get right? You want the world to get right?" Esther put her hands on her hips. "Get right yourself!

"Ain't none of us perfect, but God loves us anyway. And if anybody ought to be glad about that, Inez Zephyr, it's you!" Esther raised a finger in the air, as though she had more to say. But she froze.

Garvin looked up to see Meemaw giving Inez and Esther *the eye.*

Esther wilted and slid into her seat.

Inez ducked her head and slinked away.

There was an uneasy truce between Esther and Inez that lasted the rest of the journey west. An unofficial school bus demilitarized zone was in effect between them. Esther made sure she got off last at bathroom and restaurant stops. Inez made certain she boarded the yellow school bus last when it was time to reboard. Meemaw, in between marking her maps and joshing with Mr. Green, kept her eye on the entire matter.

Up front, the whining of the engine got louder and GoGo's shoulders got tighter. Smitty and Mr. Green were leaning forward as though they were helping him drive. By the time they passed through Sacramento, the bus was moving more slowly, but GoGo's arm motions, as he worked the gears, became more frantic. So Garvin wasn't surprised when the school bus pulled off the road and onto the shoulder, sounding like it was laboring to breathe.

Garvin decided it was time to worry.

GoGo and the two other men circled the bus, shaking their heads and clicking their tongues as if they were doctors.

Garvin tried to sound calm as she trailed behind them. "Do you think we're going to make it?"

Her husband shook his head. "It doesn't look good."

Garvin sighed, and continued sighing as they reboarded the bus.

"The good news is we're not very far away," GoGo explained to everyone. "We're in the Napa Valley. The bad news is we're not going to get there on this bus."

Garvin slumped onto the seat next to Meemaw. She felt her grandmother's arm encircle her shoulders. "Don't worry, baby. The Lord will make a way."

In short order, Meemaw had the women and children off the bus and striking out for a broad-branched tree in a nearby field. When they reached the tree, she nodded. "Just like I thought, this is a fig tree." She tapped her maps. "There are orchards near here, and I heard that sometimes a tree will grow wild." She looked around. "The day's not too hot, and this tree will give us good shade while we wait."

Hours passed and a tow truck had not come. Garvin had called Mary, who told her to call Naomi, who didn't live too far away. "And, Garvin," Mary had said just before the call ended, "don't worry."

Naomi had sounded efficient and in control. She'd called back after being contacted by Mary, arranging for their pickup and the bus's towing. Garvin looked at her watch. There was no tow truck in sight. She touched her hand to her temple. She was going to remain calm.

The men were still with the bus, their heads disappearing under the hood. The women and children were scattered in the shade of the fragrant tree. A gentle breeze blew underneath the boughs.

Inez leapt to her feet. "I need to ice the cake. We're running out of time!" She scurried toward the bus, jiggling as she went.

"Wait, Inez!" Garvin scrambled to catch her. What Inez needed to do was to sit still. What good was it going to do to ice a cake in the middle of nowhere?

Meemaw grabbed the tail end of Garvin's shirt. "Let her go, baby."

"But, Meemaw, it's just going to be confusion."

Meemaw nodded. "Let her go. Inez just needs to be doing something."

Esther chimed in, "Yeah, causing confusion."

Garvin exhaled. "We all need to sit still and be calm."

"Calm is not the same thing to everybody." Meemaw pointed up at the fig tree. "See these branches?" She lifted her Bible from beside her, opened it, and began to read. "'Now, learn this parable from the fig tree: When its branch has already become tender and puts forth its leaves, you know that summer is near. So you also, when you see all these things, know that it is near—at the doors!'"

Garvin listened to Meemaw speak while she watched Inez dragging and bumping the cooler along the ground.

"It's a funny story to me." Meemaw smiled. "You know that the fruit doesn't come on the tree, it's not ready for harvest, until the branches get *tender*. It seems like it would be just the opposite, don't it? Like the branch ought to be hard and strong to hold the weight of the fruit?" She read a portion of the parable again. "'When the branch has already become tender. . . .'" Meemaw closed her Bible.

Fifteen yards or so away, Inez began to lift the cake pans from the cooler.

"The parable is about the end times: We'll know it's

harvest time when the branch becomes tender. I think that means flexible and sensitive, like the Lord is when He's dealing with us . . . like He was when He was here. And I think that means we have to be the same way. Being hard, strong, and unyielding ain't always the answer. Being flexible may not look stronger, but it don't matter what it looks like. What matters is what it *is*. We've got to be tender enough to bear all the fruit the Lord wants us to bear—not just the fruit we like."

Inez unwrapped the largest sheet cake and tipped it gingerly onto a rectangular cardboard sheet covered with aluminum foil. The cake fell perfectly into place.

"We're the branch, you know." Meemaw pointed around at all of them. "We're the tender church."

Garvin could feel her shoulders beginning to relax. She sat down next to Meemaw and watched as Inez opened the bowl of frosting, stirred it, and began to ice the first layer of the cake.

"And I've been thinking that this story is not just about the end, but it's about how we live our lives. Strength is a good thing, but strength and being in control might also mean being tender at the right times, being flexible. Every person in our lives can be part of the harvest for the Lord's kingdom to come. But sometimes, if we can't bend—if we can't be flexible, if we can't be sensitive—we'll lose them."

When Inez had finished icing the first layer, she flipped the next sized layer from its pan, gently laid it atop the larger bottom layer, and began to frost it.

Meemaw patted Garvin's hand. "Then maybe in our own lives, we miss the fruit of it, if we can't learn to be flexible. We'll break, and miss out on good things in our lives, if we can't learn to be tender and bend. Just be flexible. If Inez needs to ice the cake to feel better, let her."

Young Monique joined them, while her daughter skipped with the other children not far away. Monique used the back of her hand to move the hair that blew into her face. "Do you think we're going to make it to the wedding in time?"

Meemaw nodded. "Baby, I know the Lord is going to make a way."

Garvin looked at Monique and then at Inez. She wanted the kind of heart that Meemaw talked about: she wanted to be flexible and forgiving, but Inez sure didn't help. She was the queen of celebrity gossip, not even considering that the people she spoke about were flesh-and-blood people with feelings.

Her biting tongue didn't only attack celebrities and pastors. It was hard to forget that years ago Inez spread rumors about Monique. And there was no doubt that, in a town as small as Jacks Creek, Monique had heard the rumors too.

. . . *"Oo-oo-oo! That child looks like a ghost!*

"You know they never said for sure who her daddy was, but look how light she is. Those funny eyes and hair. I know that child is mixed for sure. . . . Her mama's family was light, but that child is way lighter than the rest of them . . . . And you know what else they say. You know about the baby. That's right, Monique got a secret baby. I don't know all the details, but they said it was messy. Something about a pickle jar."

Of course, that was one thing about Inez—she was an equal opportunity gossip. Her hurtful insinuations weren't aimed only at Monique.

Poised near the front window in Esther's Beauty Shop, Inez talked about everyone.

. . . *"Look! Look at all those Mexican children coming up the street. They are taking over."*

"Inez, how could three people be considered all?"

She had spread tales about Meemaw and GoGo, too, tales that had reached Garvin's ears. Positioned at that same window from which she had launched many of her juiciest stories, Inez had begun the tale that changed all their lives.

"Look who's coming now! GoGo, child! That red car and that black man . . . um-um-um. And you know where he headed—straight for Miz Hightower's, straight for Meemaw's. . . . Somebody needs to tell Garvin."

Garvin looked at Inez, who was still bustling with the cake. It was difficult—even as kind as Meemaw was—to understand inviting Inez to the wedding.

Meemaw reached and affectionately squeezed Monique's shoulder. "I know the Lord is gone make a way because this wedding is special. The whole time, I've been thinking that it's not just an everyday wedding." She smiled. "I guess ain't no such thing as an *everyday* wedding. But I keep thinking this one, and maybe all weddings, are like the wedding when the Lord Jesus comes back for the church." Her eyes twinkled. "Can't you just see it? Everybody's invited! And that's why I been inviting everybody to *this* wedding."

Garvin shook her head. "I'm still not convinced, Meemaw."

Her grandmother waved her hand in affirmation. "Baby, I've been studying it. Lately, when I've been studying my Bible—"

Garvin and Monique both laughed.

"Studying? Meemaw, when have you had time to do anything lately?" Monique teased.

"Yeah, Meemaw, I can't imagine that." Garvin agreed.

Meemaw laughed. "I guess I have had my hands—and my lap—full of beads and wedding dress." She clapped her hands together. "I have been kind of snowed in, ain't I?"

Then she continued earnestly. "But I've been reading the parables in the Bible, you know, the ones about the wedding. We supposed to invite everybody! Just like we inviting people to this wedding, we supposed to invite everybody to be part of the Lord's kingdom, to be part of the Lord's wedding, whether we like them or not."

Meemaw nodded. "We supposed to invite people to the wedding that don't deserve to be there . . . that we think don't deserve to be there. 'Cause the truth is, we don't deserve to be there ourselves." She pointed to her chest. "We supposed to be inviting the uninvited, we supposed to tell them that the King of Kings has requested their presence. He has asked for them by name. We need to tell them that they may not have the right clothes, people might not like them, but they're still invited. If they get on our nerves, we still supposed to invite them. Prisoners, sick people, doctors, lawyers, drug addicts, prostitutes, policemen, teachers, Black, White, Brown, Red, Yellow—everybody—even Inez. They may not be ready now—they may not have on the right clothes or have oil ready for their lamps, they may not be studying or living right—but we still supposed to invite them."

Meemaw looked like she did sometimes at church, when the spirit was especially high. Her eyes were shining and her face was glowing. "Whether we choose to say yes or no to the Lord's invitation, we are all still invited. We're all invited because God loves us and is inviting us no matter what our condition. If we love God, we got to be like He is, and invite like He does. Jesus invited people while they were still sinning—the woman at the well who was shacking up, Zacchaeus who was stealing poor people's money because he was a powerful man—which God calls an abomination. The Lord invited the lepers, the poor, the ignorant, and He invited the high and mighty.

"We don't want to invite people just because we don't like how they talk or how they dress, how they act, or what kind of music they sing.

"We invited to the wedding because the Lord loved us first. Just like we prepare for earthly weddings after we get invited, we got to get prepared for the Heavenly wedding. Some of us are prepared—or we think we're prepared. Most of us get the invitation and we're not prepared, but we can get ready, and *they* can get ready, while we're all waiting for the bridegroom to arrive.

"We got to learn to love that way. You know, to do what God says and invite everybody to the Lord's wedding, to invite everybody—even those that offend us—into the Kingdom. Then once we invite them, let—as I been saying: Let whosoever will come. Let each man or woman work out his or her own soul salvation. This is the invitation for everybody. We're loving first before people love us; we're inviting first, then let every man and woman . . . let each person make himself ready for the marriage."

Garvin looked at Inez bowed over the cake. *Let whosoever will come.* It was still hard to reconcile inviting someone like Inez to the wedding. Garvin turned to look at Esther, who was not far away, laughing with the children. And if she *could* somehow tolerate Inez enough to invite her, she wasn't sure Esther—who had had to tolerate years of Inez's gossip—was willing or able.

When Inez had finished frosting the rectangular layers, Garvin had to admit that the cake looked better than she ever would have imagined. It was almost like some kind of white fortress, or an unusual castle. Inez rummaged in the white plastic bag she had brought with her.

The cake looked surprisingly nice, but it was still a disaster waiting to happen. Garvin pointed in the direction where Inez worked in the distance. "But, Meemaw, how is she going to carry that cake? How is she going to get it to the wedding?"

Meemaw nodded and smiled. "She got it this far. Let's be flexible and see what Inez can do."

Inez pulled decorations from the bag. From a distance, it was hard to make out what they were, but some of them seemed to shine. She opened one small tub, smiled, mumbled to herself. Inez pressed what appeared to be silver beads on the cake, making a design.

Meemaw stood to her feet. She held a hand down to Garvin. "Come on," she said to Garvin and the rest of the group. "Let's take a walk and leave the artist to her work." She and Meemaw walked ahead. Monique joined Esther and walked behind with the rest of the group.

Meemaw looked up in the trees as they walked. "The end's getting closer. There are wars and rumors of wars. Men are lovers of themselves. But we still ain't tender."

Meemaw pulled a leaf from a tree. "The bridegroom, the Lamb of God, ain't come because the bride ain't ready. She ain't prepared. People are smarter now about the Bible—I mean regular people—than I've ever seen in my lifetime. We know the rules—got them in order and we can recite them by heart, but there's no heart in what we recite. Like the Pharisees and scribes, we're big on 'don't do's', but short on compassion. We're looking good on the outside, but stinking on the inside—whitewashed walls."

She took Garvin's hand. "I know Inez Zephyr gets on people's nerves. Her mama was just like her. She talks about everybody—rich and famous, or not—it doesn't matter to her."

Garvin turned to look back at Monique. She was a lovely young woman. Inez had even spread rumors about Monique and GoGo—who was then the talk of the town. It was Inez who stood at the window in Big Esther's Beauty Salon spreading rumors about the girl's family. None of them knew then how heartbroken Monique was. It was a miracle how things had turned out.

Garvin turned back as Meemaw continued talking. "She does the wrong things—most times I think just because she's looking for attention and friendship. But I know," she smiled at Garvin, "that don't make it any less irritating. I know; her mama used to work my nerves."

Garvin laughed. "Really, Meemaw? I can't imagine you getting irritated with anybody."

Meemaw leaned closer to Garvin. "Oh, child, yes! Oo-oo! Inez's mama and her grandmamma! Lord, have mercy! And I tell you, I wasn't able to do what I'm asking you to do. But you further along than I was at your age."

It was hard to imagine Meemaw as anything other than what Garvin always remembered. It was hard to believe that she had ever been anything other than patient, kind, and loving.

"Oh, honey, when I was young, I was a spitfire. I see a lot of me in you. I was always trying to control things." Meemaw laughed again. "But I learned. I'm just trying to give you the benefit of all my years.

"No, I wasn't patient. I was like some of the other people. When Inez's grandmamma said something, I was like Esther—ready to jump down her throat. But when I think back, if I had been a little kinder and a little more patient—

if I'd looked at her heart instead of listening to what she was saying—maybe I could have helped her." Meemaw chuckled. "Maybe Inez wouldn't be like she is today."

Meemaw stopped, closed her eyes, and took a deep breath. She opened her eyes. "It sure is pretty here." She turned and pointed back. "And that fig tree makes me think. We know the rules. But if we really *follow* the rules, the rules say we have to love everybody, even those who get on our nerves, even those who hurt us. And I don't see us doing that. The rules say we have to be forgiving to people that don't deserve forgiveness; we have to have compassion and understanding. The rules say we have to give mercy instead of seeking revenge. That's what's missing. Our hearts are still hard; that's what makes us brittle—like an old, hard branch—and not ready to bear much fruit." Meemaw shook her head. "The bride's not ready."

Garvin held her grandmother's hand. She looked up at her face—Meemaw was beauty and grace.

"See, baby, it took me a lot of years to understand that we are all imperfect. I read it, I said it," she pointed to her heart, "but I didn't get it here." She looked toward where Inez was kneeling, working. "God uses backbiters, liars like Jacob, harlots like Rahab and the woman of Samaria, thieves, womanizers like King Solomon, and even murderers like King David and the Apostle Paul. We're not ready—we're not tender—because we still don't want to let any of them in the kingdom . . . unless we're talking about us. We have to have enough tenderness and compassion to have patience for other people's walk with the Lord. And we have to have enough hope in our hearts to believe God is going to work it out for and with them—just like He's working it out for us."

Garvin leaned her head on Meemaw's shoulder. When the

others caught up, they all turned to walk back.

The grass was green, and if she allowed herself not to think about time and all the things that were going wrong, it was a beautiful day. Meemaw was right, again. Taking the walk and stretching their legs, and their hearts, was just what they needed.

From fifty yards away, even the yellow school bus looked beautiful.

Garvin stopped and used one of her hands to shield her eyes. "It's the tow truck!" she yelled, and they all began to run! As they got closer, Garvin could make out a fifteen-passenger van in front of the truck.

It was going to be okay. They were all going to live happily ever after! It was all wonderful!

Until Esther screamed!

"Oh, Lord, Inez has got the gown!"

Inez was holding the gown, halfway out of its bag, in the air near her cake. She was all smiles, looking at the cake and then back at the gown.

It all happened in slow motion.

Meemaw yelled, "No, Esther!" as Esther, covering the fifty yards like the best of running backs, made a running dive for Mary's gown. She managed to tackle Inez and snatch the gown—mid-air—from Inez's hands.

Then Esther, Inez, the frosted cake, and the beaded gown all met in a tumbling heap on the ground.

PART THREE

The Wedding

The Wedding of the Lamb

"Then I heard what sounded like a great multitude, like the roar of rushing waters and like loud peals of thunder, shouting: 'Hallelujah! For our Lord God Almighty reigns. Let us rejoice and be glad and give him glory! For the wedding of the Lamb has come, and his bride has made herself ready. Fine linen, bright and clean, was given her to wear.' (Fine linen stands for the righteous acts of the saints.)

"Then the angel said to me, 'Write: "Blessed are those who are invited to the wedding supper of the Lamb!"' And he added, 'These are the true words of God.'"

—THE REVELATION OF THE APOSTLE JOHN,
CHAPTER 19:6–9

Anthony threw his jacket on top of his guitar on the passenger's seat. He'd argued with himself about bringing the guitar, finally deciding to carry it as some sort of comfort.

He was anxious about the wedding. He hadn't talked to the groom. And this was his first trip back to San Francisco since his big loss—the loss of his job and the loss of Desiree. None of it was stuff that would boost a guy's ego. If carrying the guitar made it a little better, so be it.

Anthony backed out of the motel parking lot and quickly jumped on Highway 80 headed for 'Frisco. Traffic on the highway was calm. The only excitement was a yellow school bus parked on the side of the road. The hood was up, there were men standing on the bumper, their heads bowed over the engine.

He turned on his blinker to pull over.

Anthony immediately clicked it back off. There were plenty of men, and he didn't know much of anything about engines. He wouldn't be much help. Besides, if he stopped, he was definitely going to be late for the wedding.

Garvin was hysterical.

It took some time before Naomi could get the story out of her. "Wait, Garvin. Wait! I can't understand you." Eventually, Naomi learned that there had been a human collision.

Garvin was calling from her cell phone. The yellow bus had broken down, and there had been an accident by the side of the road. "All Meemaw's beautiful, intricate beadwork!"

According to Garvin, the two members of the wedding party involved in the mishap were shaken but okay; the cake and the gown had not managed to survive.

"The one good thing is," Garvin said between sighs, "not much more could go wrong."

Garvin didn't get any better when Naomi passed on her news. Mary had contacted her to say that the groom's grandmother's flight had been delayed three hours. While Mary and the bridal party waited in a hotel room, Moor and his party had gone ahead to the church.

The couple didn't want to get married without Moor's grandmother, so they were going to miss the window of time scheduled for the church wedding. The caterers were threatening to leave. "Things don't look good."

Naomi moved the phone away from her ear. Garvin was howling and sobbing hysterically.

By the time Meemaw picked up the phone Garvin had dropped, Naomi was in charge and had a plan.

"I guess everyone was right about not taking the bus." Meemaw was crying now too. "Everything's ruined." Naomi could hear women's voices in the background.

"Inez, you always got to ruin everything!"

"No, it was you tackling somebody like Mean Joe Green!"

Meemaw stopped crying long enough to yell. "If you two don't stop fighting, I'm gone show you that fat meat is greasy!"

When the room quieted, Meemaw sighed and then began crying again. "Lord, we have ruined the child's wedding!"

It was a strange introduction, meeting Meemaw—the woman who had a reputation for cheering everyone else— now reduced to tears. It was strange for Naomi now to be consoling someone else. "Maybe not." Naomi echoed Ruthie's advice. "Don't worry. Hang loose."

Anthony knew he should have arrived earlier. He knew he should have called. As he parked, his heart racing, Moor was the only person on the front steps of the church that he recognized. Besides Moor there were twenty or so people milling about—some in suits and dresses, some in caterers' uniforms. Their faces were anxious. Anthony jerked on his suit jacket as he ran for the steps.

Moor's face was distressed. "Everything has gone wrong. It is all off!"

There was a man standing near him in a clerical collar. "It's not off, just delayed. Watch. The Lord will make a way."

A woman with dreadlocks standing near the preacher, who appeared to be his wife, nodded. "He didn't bring us this far to leave us. We have to trust Him."

Naomi thought of Ruthie and repeated the encouragement she'd given to Meemaw, to Mary, and the bridal party. "Hang loose. Take some time. Straighten yourselves out, and try to be here by six o'clock this evening. The bus driver knows the way."

When Naomi hung up the phone, she ran up the steps and knocked on Ruthie's door. "I need your help. We've got a Bodega Bay wedding to throw!"

They made several phone calls and then ran out the door.

"It is all ruined! It is a disaster! Maybe I was never supposed to marry. Maybe I rushed things!" Moor shook his head. "My grandmother's flight is delayed, I cannot marry without her, and the church cannot change our wedding time!" He was worried, his arms flailing, and his accent made it difficult to understand what he was saying.

"Then I had no best man."

Anthony tried to explain. "I'm sorry. I . . ."

Moor pointed at two older men and a young, blond-haired man standing near them. "Now I have three!" He shook his head. "My wife and her bridesmaids are in a hotel, crying! The bus carrying my bride's gown and our wedding cake is broken down on some highway north of here." Moor waved his hands in the air. "Some crazy yellow school bus, broken down by the side of the road!"

Anthony's jaw dropped. Not the bus he had seen by the side of the road? It couldn't be!

The white-frocked caterers stood off to the side whispering among themselves.

Moor began to wring his hands. "It is a disaster! It is over!"

Two old men patted Moor's back.

"Oh now, Prince! Get a hold of yourself, now! This ain't like you to fall apart. If the Lord got us here, you know everything else is gone be all right!"

The other old man nodded. "I hate to say it, Prince, but Blue's right. Like the lady said, I don't think He brought us this far to leave us."

Blue nodded. "Brighty's right. Why, I remember the time when you swooped out of nowhere like a big Black angel—"

"This ain't no time for stories, Blue. We got to calm the man down." Brighty nodded. "It's gone work out, Prince!"

Moor would not be comforted. "Even if we get everything together, who will marry us? We don't have time to find another preacher." With open palms he slapped the top of his head in frustration. Blue grabbed his arms.

The woman with the dreadlocks smiled. "Why, my sweetness can marry you." She pointed at her husband the preacher. "Just about anybody can marry you in California!"

Moor shook his head. "We have no music—"

Hmmmm. Hmmmm.

Moor's cell phone vibrated loudly enough that the whole group could hear. He listened closely. "Are you sure? Are you certain?" He ended the call and looked around the group. "It was my wife-to-be. We must retrieve my poor grandmother from the airport. Then we are going from here to someplace called Bodega Bay."

Naomi and Ruthie walked through the door of the beach store. There were colorful beach balls, surfboards, and swimsuits. They walked to racks that held dresses, shirts, and sarongs. The bridesmaids couldn't wear gowns if the bride didn't have one.

Whatever they did, they had to do it quickly. They had almost no money and even less time. A wedding in just a few hours? It was going to take a miracle.

Naomi found a white embroidered beach shirt for the groom, and three blue and white cotton beach shirts. Ruthie found one beautiful white embroidered sarong and three ankle-length white cotton dresses, all on sale.

"But they can't all wear white," Naomi said.

"No worries," Ruthie said. "Leave it to me."

―――――――

Anthony moved his guitar to the trunk. Two of the caterers, who whispered in what he believed to be Thai, rode in the car with him. Moor, the three wise men, and the others waiting on the church steps had also piled into waiting cars. They had decided to all stay together. They would go to the airport to retrieve Moor's grandmother. Then they would all make their way to Bodega Bay.

At this point, anyone speaking was whispering. It was too weird a plan to discuss aloud.

Naomi took a deep breath. The bridegroom and his entourage had already arrived and dressed—or undressed. Shortly thereafter, the bride and her party had gathered and completed their preparations.

By the time the chartered bus arrived carrying the North Carolina party—the truck towing the yellow school bus was close behind—the sun had begun to set. Someone had gathered logs and already started the two fires.

A silver lobster pot dangled on a pole between two sticks above the smaller fire.

The wedding party stood near the larger fire.

Inez and Esther—who still eyed each other suspiciously, while they kept a civil distance between them—and Garvin and Meemaw each held their hands to their mouths as they stepped off the bus.

"This is beautiful," Monique cooed as she stepped to the ground. The children oo-ed and ah-ed as they watched the bride.

White baby's breath was wound in a crown around Mary's head. Puddin's veil, attached to the tiny flowers, fluttered in the evening breeze. Mary's braids hung down to her bare shoulders. The flowing white sarong she wore against her beautiful chocolate skin picked up gold reflections from the fire. On one wrist she wore a thick gold bracelet, like the one that adorned her ankle. On her other wrist was a bracelet made of shells. In her hands was a bouquet of baby's breath, twisted twigs, and wild orchids.

Naomi, Thelma, and Latrice—the bridesmaids—were dressed in blue and white. Individual blue patterns—simply and quickly tie-dyed by Ruthie—adorned each dress. Sprigs of baby's breath were in their hair, and they held simple bouquets made of the same. Like the bride, their feet were bare.

The groom—also barefooted—wore black slacks and a white embroidered beach shirt. Next to him, his groomsmen—three wise men from Baltimore—wore blue jeans and the blue and white beach shirts. The shirts fit snugly around the two older men, but dangled loosely from the thin frame of the younger groomsman.

Ramona's dreadlocks were twisted to form a crown. Her husband stood in front of the party, ready to officiate, while a man, Anthony, sitting on a rock, played guitar.

"We have come here today to join this man and this woman in holy matrimony."

An elderly woman—the groom's grandmother—smiling broadly, was dressed in traditional African attire. She stood between the bride and groom and held their hands.

The ceiling of the chapel above them was infinite. The colors had shifted from blue to gold and rose. Now the sky was slowly turning black, with millions of tiny stars. "Who gives this woman?" the pastor, Ramona's husband, asked.

"I do," the old woman nodded, looking pleased with herself.

. . . Meemaw, smiling and crying while she watched the bride and groom, stood arm-in-arm with Mr. Green who wore an intricately embroidered yarmulke.

The floor beneath their bare feet was sand—rocks polished and ground in a way that would have taken men millions and millions of years.

The tide moved in slowly. The waves scrambled in and out while the trees that surrounded the beach clapped their hands with joy.

Once Mary said, "I do," Moor leaned to kiss her. He enfolded the bride in his arms, and she surrendered her lips to his. One of the bridesmaids, the one with long nails sighed audibly, "Oh, girl!"

"You go, FuFu!" the one with blue eyes said.

After the perfect kiss—lingering, but not too embarrassingly long—the joyous celebration began.

There was boiled lobster for everyone. On a table nearby, there was a half sheet cake decorated with balloons.

While everyone ate, Garvin pulled Naomi aside. "I-I-I can't believe this." The light from the fire made her eyes sparkle. "How did you do all this?"

Naomi smiled. "It's gleanin', man!"

"What?" Garvin's eyebrows knit together.

Naomi looked across the beach at Ruthie, who was sitting on a rock next to the young man that Naomi, earlier, had learned was named Ali. Monique sat with them and they laughed together. Naomi laughed. "Nothing. It's just something I learned from a friend." She breathed deeply. "It was a miracle."

"It turned out beautifully. I don't think it could have been any better."

"We never know how things are going to work out."

Garvin looked at Meemaw sitting on a log next to Mr. Green. There was no doubt that this wedding was her grandmother's dream come true.

Inez stood beside Esther—the uneasy truce was holding—cutting the cake Mona the baker had provided, while Esther handed out cups of punch. Bob the fisherman—assisted by GoGo and Smitty—lifted freshly boiled lobsters and steamed shrimp onto Thelma and Ramona's waiting plates, while Jonee and her relatives served a hot, spicy concoction—chicken with curry sauce, lime juice, fish sauce, hot peppers, and fresh steamed vegetables ladled over rice.

In the blue-black of the evening sea air and in the flickering firelight, the children—Monique's Destiny, Garvin and GoGo's Princess, and Esther and Smitty's children—danced among the adults clustered in laughing groups. The guests, most of whom had been strangers, were now united in the celebration of the bride and groom.

Mary squeezed Naomi tightly. "Thank you. Thank you."

Naomi pointed at Ruthie, at Mona the baker, and at Bob the fisherman. "I had lots of help." She smiled. "It was all in divine order."

Mary looked at her husband: his arm encircled his grandmother as he stood talking to his two older groomsmen. "Look at him. He's glowing!"

"You're kind of shining yourself, sister girl."

Mary bumped her hip to Naomi's. "Hush, girl."

Naomi nodded toward the two old men. "So, how did you get the three wise men here? I thought they weren't going to be able to come."

Mary shrugged. "Moor loves them. Blue, Brighty, and Ali—they're his American family. I thought, why get him a present that will grow old. We turned in our first-class tickets and all of us flew coach." She smiled. "When he saw them, he cried like a baby. They all did."

Mary tilted her head toward the guitar player. "While you're looking at them, do you know the guy who's looking at you?"

Latrice wiggled her toes in the sand. She lifted her hands to smell the flowers she held.

Mary and Moor danced their wedding dance in the advancing moonlight while the others watched. Anthony, whose eyes kept drifting back to Naomi, played his guitar, a beautiful wedding song he had written.

Latrice's gaze moved to the two old men, Blue and Brighty, and their young friend Ali. The three wise men, as Moor called them, were laughing and nudging each other and were all smiles, as though the wedding were their own.

Moor had been so excited to see them. It had been worth it to sacrifice the first-class tickets.

Thelma's idea had been a sweet last-minute gift to Mary and Moor and had made it possible for the three wise men to make the trip from Baltimore to California: *"Why don't we trade in our tickets? We'll have to fly coach. But it will be enough for all six of us to fly."* Coach seats were good enough for them; there were going to be many more occasions for them to fly first-class.

Naomi took a big bite of the sheet cake. *"It's God providing, man."* Ruthie's words were sweet to her.

"Do I know you?"

Naomi turned. It was the guitar player.

"I keep thinking I've seen you somewhere before."

"No, I don't think so." She would have remembered him.

He held out his hand. "I'm Anthony." He reached and brushed a crumb from the side of her mouth. "I'm sure I've seen you. I remember your hair."

Naomi blushed. She shook her newly dyed, freshly weaved hair. It had been a long time since she had blushed. "I haven't been here that long, just a few months." She felt silly telling him. "I came out to play *Wheel of Fortune*... and I never left."

Anthony's smile broadened. "That's it. That's where I saw you—I was watching *Wheel of Fortune*." He grinned. "And don't feel bad. I've spent the last few months looking for Sly Stone."

As the light faded, Naomi walked with Anthony to join Mary, Moor, the bridesmaids, Meemaw, Moor's grandmother, and the groomsmen who stood gathered around the fire.

THIRTY-TWO

Baltimore, Maryland

T he restaurant where Latrice and Thelma sat was one of Latrice's new favorites. She had discovered it on one of her private dates. She'd looked in the Baltimore *Afro American Newspaper*, saw the ad, and tried it. It was that simple: no date, no pressure, just her.

She looked around the large open room. The ceiling and the walls of the restaurant were glass panels joined by metal into a shape that, to Latrice, looked like a large architectural igloo. At the center of the restaurant, the waiters moved in and out delivering orders to the chefs—who worked in an open kitchen at the restaurant's heart—and retrieving orders for customers. The circular counter that surrounded the chefs was a black circle, as were the tables and chairs. It all would have been too cold, except at the heart, in the cooking area, there was a constant flame.

Thelma's blue eyes kept darting to the area where the maitre d' stood. It was clear that she was excited about meeting the girls. She stirred her drink with her straw. "You know, for all the drama, the wedding turned out to be beautiful."

Latrice laughed and waved her hands. "Yeah, and the Lord must have heard you, sister, because you didn't have to wear a shiny, fluffy bridesmaid dress or any crazy shoes."

Thelma smiled. "Thanks for small favors. Because you know if it hadn't been night, if the fire hadn't been burning, those tie-dye get-ups we were wearing would have looked like the fool!"

Latrice could still see the wedding in her mind. She'd thought about it almost every day. "And I'm glad someone remembered to take pictures. Sister Puddin and Deacon Joe would have killed *somebody* if they didn't get photos delivered in their hands."

Thelma shook her head. "And I wouldn't have wanted to be the *somebody!* Puddin and Joe seemed to get a real kick out of the photos."

"It was amazing," Latrice agreed. "Naomi really came through."

"Yes. She did." Thelma nodded. "She really saved the day."

"And I don't think I've seen her look that happy in a long time. She looked . . . she looked at peace."

Thelma nodded her agreement. "She looked almost as happy as the bride."

"Speaking of the bride, you haven't heard from her, have you?"

Thelma smiled. "No, but I didn't think we would. Can you imagine? Honeymooning in Lesotho and South Africa! I don't guess we'll be hearing from Mary and Moor for a while."

Latrice could see the flames flickering as the wind blew. She imagined hearing the waves and smelling the fresh bay water. "And after all the time the sister waited, I don't blame her!"

Thelma looked around the restaurant and then back at Latrice. "So, I guess you'll be running off to get married

now?" Her face looked as though she were trying to be cheer-
ful.

"I hadn't even thought about it." It was true. Latrice was
enjoying Floyd's friendship. But even more, she was learning
to enjoy her own company.

Thelma thanked the waiter as he refreshed her water. She
looked from him to Latrice. "It wasn't that I was against
Mary marrying . . . or jealous of her because I wasn't . . .
because I'm not married."

Latrice placed her elbows on the table and locked her fingers to make a rest for her chin. "Girl, please. It's me, your
friend. 'Me thinks she doth protest too much.'"

Thelma lowered her eyes and smiled. "All right, Miss
Latrice. I *was*—just a little jealous, okay?" Her eyes widened.
"I just kept thinking, 'Lord, this is not how my story is sup-
posed to end, is it?'"

She sighed. "This is not how I imagined *our* story ending—the two of us sitting here alone. The man that's supposed to find me must have gotten lost. No one wants me to
be mad or upset about it, but I am . . . or I was. I was thinking that Mary and all the women that were chosen want me
to go away quietly and be satisfied. Would they have gone
away quiet if they remained unchosen?

"So, I tell myself, 'Get it together, Thelma. Get your
smile on, sister.' And just when I'm satisfied, just when I'm
content that it's just me and my little safe circle of single
friends—someone jumps ship." Thelma stirred her drink
again. "Suddenly there's a wedding and I'm back off kilter
again. Someone from the single side runs over to the married
side like thirty going ninety, like they can't wait to go.

"And what their running says is that they never wanted to
be single at all—it was all just an act. Then I have to think

about whether I'm kidding myself, about whether single was really my first choice, or whether I'm just settling for something I don't want because I'm afraid to hope for what I really want. Maybe I'm just acting too. Maybe the truth is that I'm tired of trying to make myself happy with food or travel or movies alone . . . or even you all, as much as I love you. Maybe I'm fooling myself. Maybe I'm tired of talking to neurotic, pre-menopausal women and calling it a happy time."

Latrice was silent. Thelma needed to vent. She understood.

Thelma shook her head and batted her blue eyes. "Hooray! Someone else got a man and I'm still alone! Someone bring out the candles and strike up the band!" she said sarcastically.

She shrugged. "Then I'm angry about having to go through thinking about it all again. I'm angry about my friends—who know how it feels—for asking me to stand up in front of them and everyone else while I pretend to be happy."

Latrice rubbed one of her hands across the white table cloth. It was the only sound between them until Thelma spoke again.

"I was praying and feeling angry. Maybe Mary's prayers got answered because she's perfect, because she was celibate. Then it came to me." The frown left Thelma's face. "Being married was never my dream. Instead of being mad or jealous, I needed to remember my own dreams." She looked back toward the restaurant's entrance. "The girls talking about the prodigal son's brother helped me understand that. I needed to stop worrying about how my Daddy was blessing my sister and keep my eye on the prize and how He's working in my life, you know?"

Latrice patted her hand on the table. "Yeah, girl. I know."

"What I also learned from Mary's wedding is that I can't stop change in other people's lives."

Latrice wanted to wave her hands in the air and shout Hallelujah!

"And that it's okay for me to like where I am and how I choose to live, even if everyone else does something different." Thelma looked past Latrice, as though she were seeing a picture in her mind. "And I learned that sometimes God makes room in our lives for other people, even though that rearranging can be scary." She looked back at Thelma. "Naomi and Ruth showed me that." She looked at the door, then back again. "I learned I have to focus on the love affair God is having with me. It's okay for my friends to evolve and change—they'll still be my friends. But Naomi and Ruthie taught me that I can risk loving more people—new people, that I have a capacity for loving other people that's more than I knew."

Latrice looked down at her nails, then back at Thelma.

"He made room in Naomi's life for Ruthie. He made room in Mary's life for Moor. And the Lord is making room in my life for Cat, and Pamela, and Agnes." Thelma continued. "You know, I've been in or taught school all my life. But I've learned it's okay to graduate and be something you never thought you'd be. I don't have to marry, or even adopt, to be a mother. It's okay to be happy being single." She smiled. "Though I'm still not convinced about the celibacy."

Latrice wagged a finger. "Be careful, girl. I said the same thing. And look at me now."

Thelma laughed. "Yeah, look at you."

Latrice nodded. "I had lessons to learn, too, Thelma. You know, as long as we've been friends—as much as Naomi and

I cut up together—I never knew about the abuse in her life. You know? You look at people and how they're acting, but you never know what's going on underneath. It's made me be grateful for who I am."

Thelma looked toward the entrance again. It was obvious that she was excited about seeing the girls. She looked back at Latrice. "That child—as strange as she looks to me—brought something out in Naomi."

"Yes. Yes, she has." Latrice used her nail to trace imaginary pictures on the tablecloth. "You know what you said about me running off to get married?"

Thelma nodded.

Latrice shook her head. "My path is not Mary's path. But Floyd—he treats me like a lady." She tilted her head. "I had forgotten about that. We used to be ladies. Men opened doors, they wouldn't curse around you, let alone at you." She smiled. "I'm learning that I'm old-school. And I miss the company of older gentlemen—I learned that when I went with Mary to talk to Moor's friends.

"But, like I said, Mary's path is not my path. I understand what Mary was saying now. For me being—I still can't bring myself to say the word—not sleeping with men has been like a drunk going off of alcohol . . . I think I'm seeing things a little more clearly. It doesn't make you better than anybody else, but it sure helps you see better." Latrice snapped her fingers. "I was making choices drunk, girl!" Latrice lifted her glass and then set it down again. "And I've been thinking about what Mary was saying about the sex books, images, and music we're feeding the kids. And it came to me: The people who are pushing the goods don't want us or our kids to get our heads clear. If we get sober, we might stop buying stuff—cars, clothes, people—we really don't want."

The two friends laughed together.

"And Mary's right—I can only think about today. Tomorrow, girl, I might be off the wagon!" Latrice waved her hands in the air. "But today, I'm enjoying me. I'm taking me out on dates."

"On dates?" Thelma's eyes sparkled as she giggled.

Latrice waved her hands dramatically. "Oh yes! I ask myself where I want to go and take myself there. I'm doing things I always wanted to do. It may not be forever, but I'm enjoying it right now."

Thelma shrugged and shook her head. "Well, I'm not there now. And I don't see it in my future. I love the Lord, but . . . if the Lord wants me to go there, He's just going to have to work on me."

"You keep saying it, sistah, and the Lord is going to get ahold of you!" Latrice smiled, staring into Thelma's blue eyes. "You like being single. You see it as the best possible place you can be. I guess Mary sees marriage as the best possible place for her. And truth be told, I thought being single and doing my own thing was the best place for me—my mountaintop." She toyed with her napkin. "Where I am now, I'm feeling my way. I don't think I want to be here forever." Latrice waved her hands and batted her eyes. "I mean, do I look like the flying nun to you?"

"Not quite, girlfriend." Thelma's blue eyes flashed as she laughed.

"I guess where I am now is in between, in my own personal valley. And I'm okay with that. I'm going to enjoy where I am while I'm here."

Thelma raised her glass. "Well, here's to you, my friend,

my sistah!" She set her glass back on the table. She looked once more toward the entrance.

Latrice's eyes followed. Cat, Agnes, and Pamela were standing at the door.

THIRTY-THREE

Vallejo, California

Anthony strummed his guitar while Pops—the old man had kind of adopted him—grilled thin steaks on a hibachi outside on the balcony off Pops' apartment—his pad.

Nothing had turned out like he planned. He thought he would spend his career as an executive in San Francisco's financial district, making money for corporations and for himself. Instead, he was playing in a band—a church band, but it was still a band. He had joined the church, been baptized, and now the Evangel was where he jammed. Anthony shook his head as he played. And on the side, he was now beginning to earn a living offering financial and investment advice to churches and their members.

Anthony had thought he would be living in his wildly expensive San Francisco townhouse. Instead, now, he lived in a modest ground-floor apartment not much bigger than Pops'. Anthony played a few chords, and then looked in the direction of the sliding glass doors that led to the balcony. And he thought he would have Desiree. Now, he was alone.

Pops—long-handled fork and towel in hand—slid the glass door open and came inside. "It is one beautiful day out there, man!"

Anthony nodded. "Yeah."

"You ain't feeling sorry for yourself, now, are you, man?"

"Nah. I was just thinking." Anthony picked a few notes of a melody that he was composing. "Thinking about how my life has changed."

Pops flopped down in the purple beanbag chair across from him. "Yeah, brother, it can take a while to adjust to all the change. I been up high, too, man." Pops gestured with the towel. "We think we're only doing good when we're riding high, when we're on top of the mountain where everybody can see us. We fight not to go into the valley, man."

Anthony nodded.

Pops nodded in affirmation. "We fight not to come down. But look around you, brother." Pops rose from his seat and walked to the glass door, slid it open, and beckoned to Anthony. "Come on out here, brother. Let me show you some truth."

Anthony laid his guitar on the table and moved to follow Pops.

The old man pointed at the view from his balcony.

Anthony looked as Pops directed. It was funny, but he had never paid much attention to the surroundings.

Beyond where he pointed, the sloping hills of the Napa Valley were covered with growing vineyards. There were workers tending the plants. On a more distant hill, there were cattle grazing. "Quiet as it's kept, things can be pretty sparse up on top of the mountain. Everything we need is going on in the valley—He even sends down rain, and water from waterfalls." Pops shrugged. "Maybe we're afraid God won't see us down here.

"But let me tell you something, brother man. You may have been fired, but God is still shining on you—nobody can stop that. Your dog might run away, money may run dry, woman might leave and take the wallpaper off the walls."

Anthony laughed. "And the telephone, so you can't make no calls!" Some old song lyrics came back to him.

"That's right, man. But ain't no valley so low that God ain't there, brother. His sun shines in the valley too. The bright light might be on the mountaintops, but God hovers over the valleys."

Anthony wasn't certain what heights Pops had fallen from—when he saw Pops singing with the band and wearing his star-shaped shades, he had his suspicions. But he knew the old man was right about the valley. "I've made peace with everything, I think." His face warmed. He laughed. "But seeing that wedding made me think, you know? I miss Desiree." He laughed, again. "No, not Desiree . . . but, I miss. . . ."

Pops slapped him on the back and joined him in laughter. "Ain't nothing wrong with love, man."

Anthony nodded. "That wedding made me think, I'd like to marry someday. But I'm not sure how that fits in with following God. Desiree I understood, but. . . ."

Pops laughed again. "Brother, that's a long story. If you want an honorable woman, you just got to get ready by learning how to be an honorable man. There's a whole lot of preparation before you ready to be a groom. But we got time." He pointed back toward the glass door. "Go in the house, get me a plate, and then pull yourself up a chair."

Anthony went inside, grabbed a plate from the cabinet, but before he picked up a chair, he stopped, pulled his hand-held computer from his guitar case, and sent Naomi a text message.

THIRTY-FOUR

Vallejo, California

Naomi snapped the latex gloves off her hands and dropped them into the waste can. "I'll see you in six months," she said to the little girl who hopped down from her dental chair—she reminded Naomi of her own children. The little girl's mother, waiting nearby, smiled gratefully.

The dental clinic was coming along; they had more patients than they could handle two days a week. They could only provide the basics—no pushing fancy doodads here. But the people were so thankful, and she was grateful for them.

Now that she had her car back, the commute from Bodega Bay to Vallejo wasn't unbearable. Once Ruthie graduated from dental assistant school, they would be able to at least double their clinic hours.

And thanks to Anthony's help in writing a grant, they had secured funding for the year. When they met at the wedding—he had recognized her from *Wheel of Fortune*—they had exchanged numbers. He wasn't just cute; the guy was a financial genius.

Naomi checked her watch. She was going to have to hurry. It was Wednesday night, prayer meeting night at Evangel where Anthony played in the band. It was funny, but he kept trying to convince her that one of the janitors—a fellow band member—was Sly Stone in disguise. Naomi shook her head. The man was too old to be Sly Stone—Anthony was dreaming.

Anthony had invited her to prayer meeting one Wednesday night, and it had become a regular thing. It reminded her of church in Baltimore. Now she had invited Ruthie, who was waiting in the entrance lobby.

The phone in Naomi's jacket pocket vibrated. It was a text message from Anthony.

How about dinner later?

Naomi smiled. She walked into her small office and pulled off her jacket. She looked at her image in the mirror and fluffed her freshly dyed and weaved blonde hair.

Is Anthony trying to date me?

He was not her usual type. She didn't know that much about him. How old was he?

Naomi took a deep breath to calm herself. No point in worrying. What she did know was that he seemed to be a decent, sincere man. He was saved! He was building a solid reputation as a financial advisor with churches in the area. He wasn't rushing her. And he could make his guitar wail!

But there was no point in worrying. *Hang loose.* There was a lot of preparation before she was ready to think about love.

Like the Bible said, *"Without warning your life can turn upside-down, and who knows how or when it will happen?"* The Word was right. There was no point in worrying.

This was not the place she thought she would be. She didn't have the relationship with her children that she wanted. Naomi sighed. But there was no need to fear. God's presence—His peace, His goodness, and His healing—were in the valley.

Naomi raised her phone to return Anthony's text message. She erased the letters and, instead, began to dial the number she knew by heart.

"Hello, Quincy? Can I speak to the kids?"

She could hear them picking up telephone extensions. As each one answered, it was hard not to let them hear her cry. When they had all answered, she began to speak. "I want you to know that Mama loves you guys." Her heart ached. It was so hard, she was so afraid that they would not forgive her. Naomi stopped fighting; she allowed herself to cry. "And I was thinking, I was hoping that you might like to come visit me in California. You can come to Bodega Bay. We can tour San Francisco. We can even take a day trip and visit Yosemite Park." She cleared her throat. "Mama's got some valleys she wants to show you."

There was no point in worrying. You just never know.

LETTER TO
THE READER

I am so grateful to God that I am able to write for you. Every email, every letter, every hug reminds me how blessed I am. I never imagined that faithful readers would search out my books, read them, and then invite others. Each book, though the development and preparation can be arduous, feels like a celebration—we get to visit again with old friends, new friends, good food, and what I hope is a good story.

Every time I write a book, it is a discovery for me. *Ain't No Valley* was an adventure that took me from memories of North Carolina to Baltimore, and from there to tranquil Bodega Bay, lively San Francisco, and the majestic mountains and waterfalls of Yosemite National Park in California.

My journey through *Ain't No Valley* taught me three important lessons.

The book drew me to Bodega Bay, a small town made famous by the Alfred Hitchcock movie, *The Birds*. Though I once lived in Vallejo and worked in San Francisco, I had never been to Bodega Bay. I researched the area, talked to people on the phone, but I could not rest until I went there.

There is no easy way to get to Bodega Bay. A few moments on the limo ride there from the Oakland Airport, I felt silly. A limo? Really? But the driver talked to us as we wound our way through the valley. Thanks to Rick of Dugway Enterprises. I spent two days there. The five days I spent, in total, in California were filled with valleys—Bodega Bay, Napa, Yosemite—and those valleys transformed my life.

My impression of valleys, before my trip, has always been that they are places to be avoided. Valleys are unfortunate places in between mountaintops. Valleys are places of waiting and delay, I always thought. They are places to be tolerated. That's what I have believed—dark, threatening places of death.

Many times, in my life, I have been afraid to change, to go to new places or try new things, because I was afraid I might slip into a valley. *What if I try writing and it doesn't work? What if I risk loving him and it doesn't work out? What if I move and things don't go well?* The valleys of my imagination taunt me, threatening me with darkness and despair. Those threats have often paralyzed me.

But God, through nature, spoke to me in the California valleys. They are places of sunshine. The valleys are fruitful and full of growth—trees, animals, fresh running water. Grapes and vines are found in the valleys, not on the mountaintops. God's love and goodness are on the mountaintops *and* in the valleys.

Ain't no valley where the sun don't shine!

Like King David, we have no reason to be afraid. As you read this book, may you find the courage to live the life you want to live. Instead of running *from* valleys, may you run *to* your valleys with laughter and hope. As you enter your valley, may you expect green grass, still waters, and every good and perfect gift from God above who loves you, from the One who delights in you!

As I wrote, I learned that love is like a wheel—like a wheel within a wheel. As I completed *Ain't No Valley*, it became clear to me that the three books—*Ain't No River*, *Ain't No Mountain*, and *Ain't No Valley*—are about different types of love.

In Greek, there are several definitions for love. There is *eros*, which is romantic and sexual love. Then there is *storge*, which is love of family. *Philial* is friendship. Then there is *agape* love, which is love of God. Agape is the highest form of love, it is love which works to benefit others. It is agape love that allows us to love our enemies.

I learned, as I wrote, that these forms of love do not stand alone. Instead, they work together like interlocking wheels— like a gyroscope—creating a symmetry, a precession, a steady-state that is mature love.

The image in my mind reminds me of the picture of the cherubs in the book of Ezekiel, wheels within wheels. When either of the wheels is missing or off-balance, it affects the others. They crash and fly off into space.

We've experienced, we've seen it—beautiful people who are experts in the ways of sexual love, but whose eyes are vacant and who spin out of orbit because they have no family, because their hearts are empty of the highest kind of love. We've seen it over and over, those who dedicate their lives to ministry, but who are sad when the church doors close because they have no friends, no family, no one to hold them. We've experienced people who love the world, who love God, but who are afraid to open their hearts to intimate love. We see it over and over: those who love God, but who cannot love people, and those who love people but cannot love God. We see it and we know intuitively that something is wrong—we know they are spinning out of control. We may have been that way ourselves.

This is a story about people whose wheels are spinning out of orbit, and about those who help them get back on track— people like Ruth, in the Bible's book of Ruth, who helped

Naomi find her way back home.

I learned that all these forms of love—agape, eros, philial, and storge—are linked. When we work to love in the area where we are weak—whether it's family love, agape love, romantic love, or friendship—strengthening the weak area strengthens the whole. It stabilizes us—one wheel of love turning around the other. It draws us closer to walking in true love, in the image of the One who made us.

As I finished the book, I sought help from others—like Bethany's Carol Johnson, my project editor Joyce Dinkins, my daughter Lanea, my son Chase, and my cousin LaJuana. I thank them because they helped make sense of the chapters in front of me. It became clear to me that the thread that held all the words together was the wedding.

I awoke one morning, after praying the night before for clarity, and was drawn to the wedding parables found in the Gospels. Those parables became the arc, the theme for the story.

In *Ain't No Valley*, and in God's kingdom, we are all invited to the wedding—great and small; Black, Brown, Red, Yellow, White; both genders; all nations and tongues! There is room for everyone—perfect and imperfect, sick and well! And when we receive our invitations, we are each commanded to invite someone else! What a celebration it's going to be!

As you read, I want you to know that you are invited to the wedding. Mary, Moor, Meemaw, Garvin, GoGo, and Mr. Green—they're all waiting for you to arrive! Not only are you invited to Mary and Moor's wedding, but if you have not been invited, please consider this your invitation to the greatest wedding of all time—the wedding of the Lamb! There is room enough, food enough, and the Lord will make certain the wine lasts until the celebration ends!

I learned, as I wrote, that this invitation, like the parables it is based on, comes with a warning. Each of us, if we choose to attend the wedding, must prepare ourselves. We must be ready for the Bridegroom's coming. Though we have been invited, we must be ready if we want to enter the wedding hall. We must throw off our dead men's clothes—the shame, the anger, the fear that has us bound—and we must learn to dress ourselves in love and kindness like the Master. Instead of being filled with hate and envy and jealousy, we must be filled with the light and the love of God.

I also learned that we must make this same preparation for our earthly marriages. We spend lots of time buying dresses and tuxedoes, renting wedding halls, selecting flowers and cakes, but we often ignore the most important preparations. We must be dressed in love and faith, and filled with hope, patience, and trust, before we are ready to wed. We may be experts at eros love, but we will never enter into true marriage until we are first prepared. We will not have true unions until our love is whole, each wheel turning—eros, storge, philial, agape—like a wheel within a wheel.

So, enjoy the story. You're invited to the wedding. If you are dressed in sin or wearing a crown, you're invited. If you've been rejected, or if you've rejected others, you're invited. If no one's invited you before, if you feel unworthy, you're invited. The door and my heart are open. There's a seat waiting for you. Kick off your shoes and sit down. This is your personal invitation, but remember to come dressed in love.

Blessings to you,
Sharon Ewell Foster
Sharonewelfoster@aol.com

READERS' DISCUSSION QUESTIONS

1. Like Naomi, have you been tempted to leave a situation that others viewed as ideal? Did you leave? Why or why not?

2. Like Anthony, have you ever—after having the world on a string—felt lost as you faced the unknown? How did you make it through?

3. Sometimes we're aided on our journeys by the strangest people—like Ruthie, Pops, or even Inez. Have you been lost in the valley and found yourself with a strange tour guide? Share the gory details!

4. Describe a time when, like Thelma, you were envious of a friend who seemed to be on a mountaintop while you were stuck in the valley.

5. Describe a time when friends might have been envious of you. How did you help each other?

6. Describe a time when you've felt left out or uninvited. How did you feel?

7. Describe a time when you've made others feel left out or uninvited. How did you feel? How do you think he, she, or they felt?

8. Sometimes when we're expecting disaster, we find love and joy in the valleys of our lives. Tell the story on my Web site *www.sharonewelfoster.com.*

9. It's wonderful to celebrate! It's part of who we are as people—part of who we are as spirits. Celebrations can be even more fun when they're shared. Share your celebration story—especially celebrations with people you normally wouldn't invite—at my Web site.